THE SECOND CH[A]
SWERVING LEFT AND RIGHT

Manning held the MP-5 A-3 rock steady, waiting for the other vehicle to swing across his line of fire. He loosed a burst and heard the rounds strike bodywork, but the car kept coming, relentless.

"Shoot the bloody radiator!" McCarter roared.

"Watch the bloody road!" Manning snapped, but he recognized a piece of good advice when it was offered.

The car swung back into his line of fire, and the big Canadian held down the trigger, unloading everything he had. The hood blew back and masked the windshield, smoke and steam erupting from the engine as he scored a fatal hit.

"That does it!" Manning shouted over the rushing wind, as the disabled chase car swung aside and hobbled to the curb.

"Not quite," McCarter warned him.

"Dammit!"

Coming up behind them, gaining speed, was another vehicle, gunners leaning from the windows, laying down a screen of automatic fire.

With so many guns against them, Phoenix Force was a heartbeat away from disaster.

DON PENDLETON'S

MACK BOLAN.

STONY MAN™

VORTEX

A GOLD EAGLE BOOK FROM

WORLDWIDE.

TORONTO • NEW YORK • LONDON
AMSTERDAM • PARIS • SYDNEY • HAMBURG
STOCKHOLM • ATHENS • TOKYO • MILAN
MADRID • WARSAW • BUDAPEST • AUCKLAND

First edition July 1995

ISBN 0-373-61901-4

Special thanks and acknowledgment to
Mike Newton for his contribution to this work.

VORTEX

Printed in U.S.A.

VORTEX

For the UN peacekeeping forces the world over.
Blessed are the peacekeepers,
for they shall catch hell from both sides.

PROLOGUE

Djibouti, East Africa

Before he set off toward the killing ground, Hassan Gourad already knew he was too late. In fact, it had been too late for the victims by the time he was informed of the event. The best he could do, all things considered, was to look around, take testimony from the survivors—if there *were* survivors—and report the facts to his superiors.

Another entry in the growing file that symbolized Hassan Gourad's frustration was his official impotence. It sickened him to think of what was waiting at his journey's end, but he had grown accustomed to the feeling.

It was nothing new.

The village, known as Juba, was a flyspeck on the map, perhaps 250 souls who scratched their living from the soil with tools their grandparents and great-grandparents had employed. There would be scrawny goats and cattle, maybe still alive. Gourad would have to kill them if his men found no survivors from the village. Hardened as he was to suffering these days, he wouldn't leave animals to starve or die of thirst.

The drive west from the capital consumed two hours, jolting over potholes on a road that had gone years without significant repairs. When they were halfway to their destination, less than thirty miles to go, the pavement vanished altogether. They would make it in the Jeep, with four-wheel drive, but it meant slowing down to let the truck keep up.

Gourad wasn't a fool. He didn't leave his home to search for evidence of an atrocity without supporting troops. It was a small contingent, to be sure—two dozen men, with rifles and a light machine gun—but he still felt better for their presence.

Once before, perhaps two years earlier, the enemy had staged another incident specifically to draw him out. Gourad had smelled the trap and come prepared, but it had been a near thing, even so. Eight soldiers killed on his side, and the enemy had slipped away, with only two dead left behind.

This time, however, he didn't believe it was a trap per se. At least, Gourad didn't believe *he* was the target. Greater forces were at work, for higher stakes. He simply had to view their handiwork and file the usual reports.

The vultures told him they were getting close. Gourad had never been to Juba, but he would have stopped the Jeep and walked there, homing on the airborne scavengers that circled high above the killing ground, like brittle leaves caught in a desert whirlwind.

The smell of death was unmistakable.

He estimated that the killings had occurred sometime between midnight and sunrise. The patrol had noticed vultures circling and responded shortly after 9:00 a.m., another twenty minutes wasted prior to making their report by radio. It would be 12:15 before he reached the village proper, meaning that the sun and scavengers had ample time to do their grisly work.

The wind was in his face the last few miles. Gourad removed an olive-drab bandanna from his pocket, folded it and knotted it behind his head, the fabric covering his mouth and nose. It helped a little.

The driver's eyes were watering as they approached their destination from the east. Gourad instructed him to park outside the village, where a dusty Jeep sat waiting. In the vehicle were two sweaty soldiers and a small boy with a bandage on his forehead.

A survivor.

He would keep. Gourad walked into Juba with a dozen of his soldiers forming a ragged skirmish line behind him. There was no need for a tidy drill formation here. The dead were seldom critical, and he would rather have his men spread out, prepared for trouble if it came.

Up close, the stench was almost overpowering. He heard one of his soldiers retching, followed swiftly by another, then a third. Gourad thought none the less of them for their reaction to the sights and smell around them. They were only human, after all, and young. When they had ten or fifteen years' experience at picking over bodies, it would hardly bother them at all.

The monstrous would become routine.

There was a camera in the Jeep, with several extra rolls of film, but he preferred to make a walking tour of the slaughter ground before he started snapping photographs. It helped him get a feeling for the place and picture what had happened there.

It had been a night attack, which meant the village had been sleeping. Some of those he passed were naked, others nearly so. These were invariably female, and it made him scowl to think of the indignities they must have suffered prior to death. A medical examiner could verify the signs, but it would never come to that. Wild dogs and vultures, working underneath a blazing sun, had managed to defile the evidence already. By the time an expert made the drive out from Djibouti, he wouldn't find much with which to work.

At that, it hardly mattered. Dead was dead. The killers had escaped, and there would be no extradition.

Not this time.

Not ever.

No one had been spared by the invaders. Age and gender meant no more to them than shoe size or a victim's favorite color. They were paid to kill and did their job efficiently. With automatic weapons, they could sweep a village clean in minutes, pausing only if they wanted to amuse themselves along the way.

These were professionals at work, and he had crossed their path before.

Spent brass was everywhere, some crushed where it had fallen underfoot, the rest still bright and shiny. It had not begun to tarnish yet. Gourad picked up a cartridge case, examined it and recognized the 5.45 mm round fired by AK-74 assault rifles and the companion RPK-74 light machine gun.

No surprises.

Several of the villagers, mostly women and children, had been stabbed or slashed with knives instead of being shot. There were no mutilations, in the normal sense, which told Gourad that this wasn't a tribal matter. When the tribes or various religious sects went at it, killing one another, they took pains to make examples of the dead—decapitation and dismemberment, the bodies disemboweled, sometimes emasculated with creative uses for the severed genitals.

Aside from the apparent rapes, which were routine, the Juba massacre had been a relatively tidy in-and-out operation. The villagers surprised in sleep and routed from their huts at gunpoint, men, boys and older women dispatched with point-blank bursts of automatic fire.

Gourad had seen enough for his report, but he kept going, forced himself to see it all. There might be no one else on earth who would remember these pathetic strangers as they were today.

No one except the boy.

When he had made a walking circuit of the village, seen it all, Gourad returned to speak with the surviving witness. He didn't expect much information. By the look of him, the boy was only nine or ten years old, with haunted eyes, a dazed expression on his face. But nine or ten was old enough to speak, describe what he had seen and heard in the dark hours before dawn, when the killers came calling.

The boy spoke Arabic, one of Djibouti's two official languages. Gourad addressed the soldiers first, absorbing their reactions to the grim discovery, allowing them to tell him how the boy had wandered in from nowhere, bleeding, while they searched the village for survivors.

There would be no more, he realized. Except for one small child, the killers had been perfectly efficient.

Turning to the boy, Gourad took care to keep his questions simple and direct, allowing the child to ramble and explain things his way. His name was Saadi, and he told the story of his family's demise, the swift destruction of his village, without breaking into tears. The raiders came by air in "noisy birds" that had to have been two military helicopters. Saadi didn't know what time it was when they arrived, but it was dark out, hours yet before the sunrise. He was sleeping when a stranger burst into his father's hut and started shouting in an unfamiliar language, herding them outside.

Some of the raiders had been African, but the majority were different. Saadi called them "white men, only darker." They had carried automatic weapons, speaking among themselves in the peculiar tongue he couldn't understand. The black invaders shouted orders in Amharic, which the villagers of Juba understood from living close to Ethiopia.

The shooting had been relatively brief. Efficient. Brutal. Afterward, the raiders had amused themselves with Saadi's mother, older sister, other women from the village. That had taken up the best part of an hour, Saadi playing dead among the tangled bodies of his elders, waiting for the nightmare to conclude.

At last, when they had finished with the women, silenced bitter sobbing with their knives and pistols, the invaders had retreated to their waiting "birds" and flown away. Their path was southeast, toward the Ethiopian frontier, no more than thirty miles away.

Long gone.

They would be safe at home in Dire Dawa now, or some encampment in the countryside. Gourad stood facing toward the east and thought about the "dark white men" and their unfamiliar language. It wasn't the first time he had heard a similar description. Twice within the past six weeks, in fact, he had been summoned to a killing ground like this one, counting bodies, photographing the remains. His gruesome snapshots gathered dust in army files.

But he could recognize the killers' work by now.

And while he couldn't prove it yet, Gourad believed he understood their game.

There was a world of difference, though, between mere understanding and a viable solution to the problem. Anyone could solve a riddle, given time enough; few could take the message and apply it to their daily lives with any great success.

He felt a new pang of frustration, wishing that he could lead his tiny force across the border and pursue the killers to their lair. It would be suicide, of course, and ruination for his government on top of wasted lives. In fact, the killers must be waiting, hoping for an opportunity like that to come within their grasp. It was the sort of "provocation" that would make their next move logical and justified before the court of world opinion.

Long enough to do the job, at least.

Plan B, another hopeless fantasy, involved a cunning trap—Gourad and his commandos waiting for the raiders with advance intelligence, prepared to strike them when they made their next incursion. Sadly that required a contact on the other side, and none had surfaced yet, despite sporadic efforts to recruit a willing spy.

Which left him with the usual: observe and photograph, report and wait for more developments, no matter that the next "development" would be another massacre, more wasted lives.

Frustration soured into bitterness as he retrieved his camera from the Jeep, stuffed extra rolls of film into his pockets. Twenty-four exposures to a roll, six rolls. He meant to use them all.

At least, he thought, they wouldn't have to shoot the animals. Someone had done it for them, herding goats and cattle to the far side of the village, dropping them with automatic fire. He wondered if the animals had died before the people, or if killing livestock warmed the raiders up for bigger things.

No matter.

They would take the boy back to Djibouti, place him with the agency in charge of foster care. If everything ran true to form, he would be living on the streets within six months—assuming he survived that long. The orphanage was overcrowded now, a sieve where children poured out through the cracks and made their own way, living hand-to-mouth by means of begging, petty theft or worse. If Saadi lived to see his fifteenth birthday, it would be a minor miracle.

Too bad they missed, Gourad was thinking when he caught himself, ashamed. If he allowed himself to think that way, the killers would have won, eroding his humanity. He couldn't bring himself to weep for Juba's murdered citizens—not here and now—but he would nurse the hunger for revenge.

Somehow, someday, Hassan Gourad would bring the executioners to reckoning. He couldn't see the path yet, but he knew it lay before him. All he had to do was mind his footsteps, keep his full attention focused on the goal.

Revenge or justice? Was there really any lasting difference in the world today?

None of those whose bodies he had seen and photographed in recent weeks had been a friend or relative, but they were all *his* people. Each and every death diminished him, to the extent that he did nothing to repay the acts of madness. When he got up in the morning, saw his own face in the mirror, he was looking at a failure.

Crossing to the far side of the village with his camera, he began to work his way back toward the military vehicles. It was a slow, grim process, framing shots, repeating some and making sure that he omitted nothing, changing film repeatedly and pocketing the rolls he had exposed.

He spent the best part of an hour breathing death, recording it on film. Before he finished with the work, Gourad had made up his mind to retain a set of photos for himself, when they were printed in Djibouti. He wasn't sure yet how he meant to use them, but he would think of something.

When he finished, it was time to raze the village. Digging graves would take all day and push his soldiers to the point of mutiny. The wild dogs would return as soon as they were gone, in any case, and dig the bodies up again to feed themselves. Since there was no one left to claim the village as his own, it made more sense to drag the corpses back inside their hovels, cart the livestock in behind them and apply the torch.

A different kind of stench, this time. Gourad was something of a connoisseur by now. He fancied he could guess a corpse's age, with nothing but his nostrils as a guide. As the bodies began to burn, he stood and watch the rising smoke blot out the sun.

So much for dreams, the sanctity of human life. The vultures settled at a distance, glowered at him, silently reproaching him for wasting precious meat. Instead of shooting them or chasing them away, he left them there to tend the fires.

It was a long drive back, and he had multiple reports to type and file, before he went off duty for the night. When that was done, and he was safe at home, he would begin to contemplate the fine points of revenge.

And pray that he was undisturbed by dreams.

CHAPTER ONE

Northern Somalia

The mountain pass ran north to south, a hundred miles southeast of Berbera. By 10:00 a.m., the sun was high enough and hot enough that Bolan could have fried an egg on any of the several large, flat stones that formed the shelf in front of him. His sniper's nest was sweltering, his desert camouflage fatigues already damp and dark with sweat. The short bill of his cap provided some amount of shade, but he was still compelled to squint against the glare.

The convoy was already late, and Bolan had begun to fear it wouldn't come at all. His field intelligence was marginal, at best, and his source wasn't responsible if the selected targets should postpone their journey. Anything could happen, from a breakdown in the motor pool to cancellation on a private whim.

Another quarter hour, give or take, and he would have to make a choice: remain in place and wait, or scrub the mission. Choose another target. Start from scratch.

At 10:08, the compact walkie-talkie on his belt hissed static for perhaps two seconds. No one spoke; they didn't have to. Bolan had devised the signal in advance to minimize their traffic on the air.

The convoy had been sighted.

Bolan's prey was rolling toward the trap.

Beside him, in the shade, his weapons were a trifle cooler than the man himself. The rocket launcher was a Russian RPG-7, one meter overall, approaching sixteen pounds in weight. Its armor-piercing rockets had been primed beforehand, all except removal of the safety pin, and Bolan slipped the first of three into the launcher's muzzle now.

His backup weapon was a folding-stock Kalashnikov, the famous AK-47 with its curved 30-round magazine. Replaced by newer models in the Russian army, it was still the most widely used assault rifle on earth, manufactured or mimicked by factories from Eastern Europe to the People's Republic of China.

Neither weapon, if discarded on the field, could be traced back to the United States.

The lead vehicle was a Ferret Mk4 light scout car, a British model from the 1960s, with a three-man crew and a 30 mm Browning machine gun mounted on the manually operated turret. Close behind the Ferret came an open staff car, four men visible, immediately followed by a pair of open trucks with twelve to fifteen soldiers each. Bringing up the rear was an Israeli RAM V-1 light armored reconnaissance vehicle, mounting a pair of 7.62 mm light machine guns for its three- or four-man crew.

It was a mixed bag, altogether, and entirely typical of rolling stock available to the Somalian warlords when they started shopping on the open market. Even with embargoes from the west, there was no shortage of matériel available for those with ready cash on hand. The troops, if such they could be called, were armed with everything from M-16s and FN FALs to Tommy guns and M-1 carbines. Any one of them would do the job, if they could score a hit, but Bolan didn't plan to offer them a sitting target.

As the Ferret Mk4 came in range, he primed the RPG by slipping out the rocket's safety pin before he raised the launcher to his shoulder. With the bulky armor-piercing round in place, the RPG weighed more than twenty pounds, but Bolan had no difficulty handling it. The tricky part, when he prepared to fire, would be the backflash, but his roost had been selected with security in mind, a deep notch in the stone behind him adequate to vent the retro blast.

The others were in place and waiting for his shot to open the hostilities. They wouldn't fire until his first round opened up the gates of hell. Directly opposite his sniper's nest, concealed inside a cave mouth, Jack Grimaldi manned a light machine gun, while the troops of Phoenix Force were situated at strategic points along the pass. It would have been a Phoenix Force warrior—probably McCarter, stationed farthest to the north—who spotted the approaching convoy first and signaled to the others with his radio.

It all came down to this, the briefings, travel, waiting. Bolan and his men had come halfway around the world to meet these strangers underneath the blazing sun of Africa and slaughter them on sight.

So be it.

Peering through the launcher's sights, he chose a point of impact just above the ferret's bug-eyed headlights, in between the banks of smoke-grenade launchers. The Ferret was a rear-engine vehicle, which meant his HEAT round would explode directly in the driver's face.

He let the Ferret come a little closer, clocking six or seven miles per hour through the pass, and squeezed the trigger when his target had approached within a range of eighty yards. He felt the backflash of the rocket as it hissed downrange toward impact, but the RPG's design eliminated any recoil, leaving Bolan free to watch the show.

A clap of smoky thunder brought the Ferret to a jolting stop. It shuddered, leaking smoke and flame, somebody screaming as the fire caught hold and spread. Along the pass, the Executioner's comrades opened up with everything they had on preselected targets, pouring automatic fire into the convoy from all sides.

The Ferret's gunner was alive, but he had no idea where Bolan's armor-piercing round had come from. Rather, through the drifting smoke, he somehow got a fix on Jack Grimaldi on the far side of the pass, and cranked his turret to the left, his heavy MG spitting 30 mm rounds. The bullets etched a zigzag path across the rock face, climbing, homing in on the Stony Man pilot's position, leaving deep scars in the stone.

Reloading swiftly, Bolan primed his second missile, drew a quick bead on the stationary turret and squeezed off. The RPG-7 HEAT round's impact was equivalent to hammering a paint can with a pickax. The conical hollow charge focused the blast into a high-speed jet that sliced through armor into the interior with catastrophic force. The hatch blew off and lofted like a Frisbee on a tongue of flame before it clattered back to earth. The 30 mm MG lost its voice.

One rocket left.

The remnants of the convoy were retreating, after a fashion, trying to run through the pass in reverse. Bolan fed the RPG its third rocket, shouldered the twenty-pound weapon and sighted downhill through a drifting pall of smoke.

SIYAD SALAMEH HAD BEEN twenty-one years old when civil war engulfed his homeland, in the early days of 1991. The flight of General Muhammad Barrah from Mogadishu left Somalia in a state of anarchy, officially proclaimed a nation without government in 1992. By that time, forty thousand persons had been killed in savage fighting, from the suburbs to the open countryside, and local warlords were the only hope for sanctuary in a land that seemed to be disintegrating.

Salameh took his chances with Mohammed el Itale, rising swiftly through the ranks as he displayed a talent for exterminating rivals, terrorizing hostile villagers, hijacking cargoes that included weapons, food and pharmaceuticals. At twenty-four, he was a captain in the second largest private army battling for supremacy in what was shaping up to be an all-out struggle to the death.

And loving every minute of it.

As a youth, Salameh never would have guessed that he possessed such martial skills and leadership ability, but he was learning more about himself each day. The thrill he got from killing, for example, watching bodies twitch and topple as the bullets hit them.

It was wonderful.

On top of sheer enjoyment, he had learned that there was profit to be made from war. Each time his soldiers seized a load of food or medical supplies, Salameh was entitled to a share of the disposal price. It averaged ten percent, and while he knew Mohammed el Itale kept the great bulk for himself, the young Somali didn't mind. He had more money now than all the other members of his family put together, going back three generations, and the end wasn't in sight. When they were finally triumphant, sweeping into Mogadishu and control of all Somalia, the spoils would be much greater. Salameh would be a wealthy man in one or two more years... if he survived that long.

This morning, riding in his staff car, eating dust behind the Ferret, he was bound to punish villagers outside Odweina for their flagrant lack of zeal in helping to support Mohammed el Itale's forces. Twice they had been ordered to surrender "taxes" in the form of cash or food, and twice they had refused. Such insolence couldn't be tolerated if the army hoped to keep respect among the peasants.

An example would have to be made, for all to see.

It was the kind of work Salameh loved.

He *hated* following the Ferret Mk4 scout car, but security demanded that an armored vehicle precede his own in case of ambush. Even here, on so-called friendly territory, they were still at risk from enemies. The narrow mountain pass was particularly dangerous, but he wasn't afraid.

Like most young men at arms, Salameh had a sneaking hunch that he would live forever, even as his friends and enemies were laid to rest. The feeling helped to build his confidence and keep him sharp, aggressive on the battlefield.

He was relaxing, thankful for the stony ground that kept the dust down at the higher elevations, riding with his eyes closed in the staff car's shotgun seat. Salameh wore a Browning semiautomatic on his web belt, but he had no other weapons with him. Thirty-seven soldiers gave him all the feeling of security that he required for such a mission, facing unarmed peasants in their miserable homes.

He might not even fire the pistol that he wore, unless the sight and smell of blood excited him, and he couldn't restrain himself. It happened that way, now and then, when he was on a roll.

The last thing Salameh expected, driving through the pass, was an explosion out of nowhere, drowning out the diesel engine noises. Black smoke poured from the Ferret Mk4 as his eyes snapped open, riveted. His ears were ringing from the shock wave as he started shouting orders to his driver, kicking at the floorboard of his staff car as if that would somehow help them out of their predicament.

An ambush!

Even as the staff car started to roll backward, inch by inch, the rock walls of the pass erupted in a storm of automatic-weapons fire. Behind him, manning the machine gun mounted on the rear deck of his staff car, Salameh's young bodyguard began to strafe the west wall of the canyon, hot brass falling everywhere.

The trucks and RAM V-1 behind him were retarding his escape. Salameh twisted in his seat to shake a fist at the nearest truck driver, cursing his family for nine generations, aware that his words went unheard in the racket of gunfire. They were *creeping* backward, inches at a time it seemed, while bullets whined around his head and rattled on the staff car's fenders, doors, took out a section of the dusty windshield.

Groping for his pistol, Salameh returned fire, aimlessly, without a clear-cut target. It was something, just to fire the weapon, feeling better for the buck and recoil in his fist. A wasted gesture, but at least the others wouldn't say that he had been a coward in the face of death.

The Ferret's crew was still alive—or one of them, at any rate. The 30 mm opened up to join the storm of gunfire, spewing tracers toward the left or east side of the gorge. Perhaps they had a chance.

Another rocket hurtled down from somewhere on the right. Salameh saw it from the corner of his eye and braced himself for the explosion, half expecting it to strike his vehicle and finish him in a consuming ball of fire. Instead, he saw the Ferret take a second hit, the turret this time, and the 30 mm's voice fell silent.

Grabbing up the two-way radio, he brought it to his lips and bellowed, "Get us out of here!"

The RAM V-1 was backing up at speed now, taking hits but still refusing to attempt the three-point turn that would be tantamount to suicide for all concerned. Escaping in reverse, at least they had a fighting chance. If one vehicle tried to turn and failed, the pass would be sealed off, transformed into a bloody slaughter pen.

The Browning's slide locked open on an empty chamber, and he ditched the magazine, replacing it with another from his belt pouch. He had spotted movement on the hillside, a man, no doubt about it, but his pistol wouldn't make the range. Salameh wasted two shots on the moving target anyway, in lieu of sitting still and watching for the bullet that would end his life.

Or would it be a rocket?

Number three was burning toward him, even as the question surfaced in his mind. Salameh ducked, his head between his knees, and he could have sworn he felt the missile pass above him, trailing fire. Behind his car, the leading troop truck's cab exploded, spewing twisted shrapnel, all in flames. The soldiers—those still capable of moving on their own—were bailing out and running for the rocks on either side. The truck, he saw, wouldn't be going anywhere.

And neither would the staff car.

Instinct told him it was time to move. He hit the hard ground running, dodging toward a nearby mass of boulders. If he could gain the cover of the rocks, conceal himself, he might escape detection. Safe from plunging sniper fire, at least, he could attempt to hide from any mop-up crews the enemy sent down when they were finished playing with his men. If only he was fast enough to reach—

The bullets struck him one-two-three, ripping through his shoulder, chest and abdomen. Salameh didn't register the pain, at first. There was a numbing shock, the stunning force of impact, and he stumbled, went down on his knees, sprawled facedown on the hot, unyielding ground.

It was incredible. Salameh knew that he was dying, but he felt no fear. Perhaps it bled out through his wounds and left him with the sense of icy calm that radiated through his body now. Instead of sweating on his bed of sunbaked stone, he found that he was shivering.

His religion taught that a soldier killed in battle was the luckiest of men, assured a place in paradise. Small consolation at the moment, as the pain kicked in, but Salameh derived what consolation he could from the idea.

His dreams of power and the lovely women, all that money, were wasted, bleeding out into the dust. Survival instinct told him he should try to crawl away, find someplace more secure to spend the final moments of his life, but he didn't have energy enough to try.

If death was coming for him, let it find him here.

The slim young captain who would never see another birthday closed his eyes and wished his pain away.

Sometime within the next few moments, lying there, his wish was granted.

JACK GRIMALDI COULDN'T quite decide if he was thankful for the cover of the smallish cave he had selected as a sniper's roost, or whether he should curse himself as seven kinds of idiot for choosing it. The shade was something, granted, with the temperature already simmering outside, but now he had the other problem.

Ricochets.

He had been ready, waiting with his Russian RPK machine gun, when the Ferret took its first hit from a rocket. Even so, the gunner in the turret wasn't finished outright. Maybe he was wounded, maybe not, but he was still entirely capable of raising hell with his 30 mm MG, raking the slopes of the pass in search of a target.

And he was starting with Grimaldi.

Those bullets, more than twice the size of .50-caliber machine gun slugs, were chewing up the rock face, climbing toward his cave, and there was nothing Grimaldi could do but duck for cover. When the Ferret's gunner found his cave, by accident or otherwise, there was a hellish racket, bullets rattling around inside the cave and whining off the stone above, behind, on either side of where Grimaldi lay. One hit could finish him, but he got lucky somehow, keeping low and riding out the storm.

It was a second round from Bolan's RPG that saved him, though, enveloping the scout car's turret in a swirling ball of fire. You had to feel a little sorry for the men inside, even if they were the enemy. If Grimaldi was given any kind of choice, he knew that he would rather die out in the open air than penned up in an armored coffin, smoked and fried.

He concentrated on the second vehicle in line, the staff car, as the convoy started to retreat. There were three men in the vehicle, including one to operate the .30-caliber machine gun mounted on the rear deck, set to fire above the driver's head. He didn't seem to have a target yet, but he was firing high and wild, along the west side of the pass, contending with a couple of the men from Phoenix Force.

Grimaldi's weapon was the LMG configuration of the AK-47—longer, slightly heavier and fitted with a 75-round drum in place of the usual 30- or 40-round box magazines. Otherwise, there was no difference to speak of. It chambered the same battle-proved 7.62 mm cartridge, spewing bullets at a cyclic rate of some 660 rounds per minute, theoretically. The need for changing drums or magazines reduced that rate in practical terms to somewhere between 80 and 150 rounds per minute, which was fine for Grimaldi's purposes this morning.

Sighting carefully, he drilled the staff car's gunner with a burst of six or seven rounds, the full-metal-jacketed projectiles ripping through his chest and torso, blowing him away. The dead man kept his grip on the machine gun long enough to fire a last burst toward the sky before he lost it, toppled over backward, rolling from the vehicle to wind up facedown in the dust.

The driver next. Grimaldi strafed him with a pair of short precision bursts, and watched the guy's contorted face explode.

Two down, and one to go.

The passenger was off and running for his life as the Stony Man pilot swung the RPK around to follow him. Grimaldi had no way of knowing who the runner was, but he would have to be some kind of officer—if you could rightly use that label with a private band of mercenary thieves and murderers.

Whatever, he was fair game now.

Grimaldi led his target by a yard or so, experience replacing any kind of fancy calculations in his head. His index finger curled around the light machine gun's trigger, taking up the slack, a dozen rounds unloading in about one second flat.

It was enough.

The runner seemed to stumble over something, twisting as he fell and went down on his face. A casual observer might have thought that he had tripped, been stunned or winded by the impact, but he didn't rise again.

Grimaldi calculated that half his first drum was gone, but he wasn't running short of targets yet. An RPK round had disabled one of the procession's flatbed trucks, and khaki-clad hardmen were unloading from the back in total chaos, scrambling frantically for cover that was difficult to find. The Stony Man pilot tracked a pair of runners who had cast their lot together, accidentally or by design, and chased them with a long burst from his machine gun.

The taller of the two went down in an awkward somersault, headfirst, his arms and legs tangled, while his weapon spun away. The second, shorter gunman glanced back at his friend without a break in stride, and was facing toward Grimaldi when the bullets hit him, spinning him like a demented dervish, crimson spouting from his wounds.

Grimaldi framed another runner in his sights and held down the machine gun's trigger.

CHAPTER TWO

The worst of it was waiting, with the enemy in sight and drawing closer by the moment. Crouching in the shadow of a rocky overhang, David McCarter was the first to see the convoy coming, and he flashed the signal to his comrades as agreed, two short taps on the button of his walkie-talkie.

He watched and waited as the minicaravan passed just below him, entering the gorge. McCarter tracked the flatbeds with his AK-47, close enough to strafe the grim Somalis where they sat with weapons braced between their knees. He kept his finger on the trigger, ready in a heartbeat when the signal came.

The RAM V-1 would be a tough nut for his rifle with the hatches closed, but they were open at the moment, crewmen taking full advantage of whatever ventilation they could manage in the broiling heat. The driver had to keep his seat, of course, but two more stood erect with heads and shoulders visible, their arms draped casually over pintle-mounted light machine guns. It was difficult to tell if they were cocky, self-assured or simply negligent.

No matter. In a sudden ambush, it would all come out the same.

McCarter had them covered going in, and he was ready when the RPG-7 HEAT round struck the Ferret Mk4 scout car. They had blood and thunder in an instant, but the armored car was still responding with sporadic fire from its machine gun, buying time for its companions to retreat.

The Briton stroked the trigger of his AK-47, squeezing off a 4-round burst that nailed the forward gunner on the RAM V-1. He saw the man jerk forward, dead before he even had a chance to fire, his body slipping out of sight, inside the armored cab.

It had to have spooked the driver, seeing his companion dead and leaking, for he almost stalled the engine. Saving it before he made that fatal error, he was able to reverse directions, backing up as automatic weapons drummed the caravan from both sides of the pass.

McCarter had the second gunner in his sights, the dark face glistening with perspiration as he swung around his assault rifle in search of solid targets. Phoenix Force was too well covered to present any easy mark, so the hardman cut loose at nothing in particular, a spray of wasted bullets rattling across the rock face, fanning empty air. Sun twinkled on the brass exploding from the weapon's ejector port, all wasted in a desperate fury to do something, anything, before it was too late.

Tough luck.

McCarter shot him in the head and chest from forty yards, the bullets from his AK-47 shredding flesh and fabric, smearing blood across the hot deck of the RAM V-1. It didn't stop the driver, though, and in another moment, someone dragged the dead man back inside the armored car.

That meant a four-man crew, and two of them still fit for duty. When an arm snaked out to close the hatch, McCarter strafed it with a 3-round burst. He missed, but gave the crewman something to consider as he ducked back out of range. Another burst went home inside the open hatch, a possibility of death by ricochet, but he was playing long shots now, frustration seething in his gut.

McCarter palmed a fragmentation grenade and yanked the pin, rose from cover far enough to make the pitch. He was exposed to several guns now, but the shooters either missed their chance or else were concerned with covering themselves from plunging automatic fire. In either case, the Briton failed to stop a bullet as he gauged his distance, wound up for the throw and let it fly.

A lucky pitch, all things considered, and he watched the frag grenade bounce once before it wobbled through the open forward hatch. The blast was muffled, but it sent twin puffs of smoke up through the hatches, followed by a warbling cry of pain. The RAM V-1 stopped dead, its driver killed or gravely wounded, blocking off the caravan's retreat.

When Bolan's final rocket nailed the middle truck and sent its riders scrambling for whatever sanctuary they could find, McCarter knew the battle was as good as over.

It was hardly even sporting, now—like shooting game fowl on a baited field—but "fair" was relative. A fair fight was the one you walked away from, more or less intact, while inflicting the maximum possible damage on your enemy.

Like now.

McCarter swallowed his revulsion, fleeting as it was, and went to work with the Kalashnikov.

THE AUTOMATIC FIRE was trailing off, sporadic single shots or 2- and 3-round bursts replacing the staccato symphony of full-scale combat. Bolan scanned the killing ground across his AK-47's sights and watched for movement, anything to help him fix a target in the drifting dust and smoke.

He guessed there had been thirty-five or forty soldiers in the convoy, to begin with. Counting bodies down below, he guessed that fewer than a dozen were alive and fit for action. A few more minutes, and it would be time to close the ring of steel, mop up the stray survivors and move on.

No prisoners from this batch. Bolan could have pulled his troops out now, allowed the stragglers to survive and spread the word of their defeat among Mohammed el Itale's troops, but there was no point taking chances. Dead men *could* tell tales, in certain circumstances, and the corpses scattered here would tell their comrades that a change was coming. They had ruled the roost in this vicinity for eighteen months or more, but now the tables had been turned.

It was a start.

He spied a gunner peering from the shadows of the burned-out Ferret scout car, switched to semiautomatic, aimed and dropped him with a single bullet through the forehead. Easy. Bolan had exhausted his supply of rockets for the RPG, but high explosives weren't required to root the few survivors out from under cover.

He waited, saw another slim Somali moving near the staff car, but Grimaldi cut him down before the Executioner could fix the human target in his sights. A tattered burst of firing on the convoy's starboard flank told him that Katz and Encizo had targets of their own.

He raised the walkie-talkie to his lips and keyed the button with his thumb. "I'm going in," he said, and slipped the radio back in its pouch without expecting a reply.

He rose and worked his way downhill, along a narrow, rocky trail that would have been ideal for mountain goats. He watched his footing and the vehicles below him, keeping the AK-47 leveled in the general direction of his enemies as he descended to the road.

No movement near the Ferret scout car, and he circled wide around it, moving in the opposite direction of the windblown smoke. A scrabbling sound from the direction of the staff car put him on alert, his rifle pivoting to find the source of noise. A dusty figure carrying an M-1 carbine lurched from cover, talking excitedly at Bolan, and he answered with a 3-round burst that punched the soldier onto his back.

Downrange, he caught a glimpse of Calvin James and Gary Manning moving toward him, from the general direction of the convoy's rear. They didn't fix their eyes on Bolan, rather searching in among the shadows, pausing now and then to fire a single shot or burst of automatic fire at someone cowering beyond his line of sight.

The cleanup.

It was a dirty job, but someone had to do it in a war where prisoners were worse than useless, fatal liabilities to a guerrilla force in motion. If you left a living enemy behind, the odds were he would shoot you in the back, or else alert his comrades to your movements and participate in your destruction when you met again. The facts of life in combat were more properly the facts of death.

He knew the game by heart from long experience. They hadn't christened him the Executioner in Vietnam for nothing, after all.

A ringing silence settled on the killing ground. Bolan kept up his guard as he moved to meet the Phoenix Force warriors, knowing he was covered by Grimaldi, Katz and Encizo from on high. If anybody moved around the stranded vehicles, one of them would inevitably see the danger coming and respond.

Teamwork.

"All done, I'd say." There was relief in James's voice, as well as resignation.

"Right."

"This ought to send a message back," Manning said.

Bolan nodded and surveyed the field. He drew no sense of pleasure from the massacre, but it was necessary. They had saved lives here today, as well as spilling blood.

"Let's wrap it up," he said.

Their vehicles were hidden to the south and west, behind the nearest stony ridge, concealed by tarps in desert camouflage. The risk of being spotted from the air was minimal, but you could never be completely sure.

He keyed the walkie-talkie one more time. "Stand down," he said, repeating it for emphasis. "Stand down."

Round one was over, but the fight was just beginning.

And Bolan knew it could still go either way.

CHAPTER THREE

Mogadishu, Somalia

There is a certain air about a city locked in private warfare with itself. Beirut and Belfast have the atmosphere, along with Sarajevo, certain neighborhoods of Bogotá and Medellín. The people have a wary look about them, checking more than traffic when they cross the street. A backfire sends them dodging for the nearest cover. Public buildings smolder in the unforgiving light of day or flaunt their wounds for all to see. Law has no meaning, in the normal sense, and order issues from the nearest gun.

Mack Bolan knew the feeling from Saigon. Another world, another life. He recognized the frank suspicion and distrust on faces that he passed along the sidewalk, knowing there was more to it than the anomaly of his white skin. American and European diplomats were still on duty in the Somalian capital, along with soldiers and negotiators sent by the United Nations. Even so, outsiders meant one thing in Mogadishu: trouble.

Moving west from city hall, he took his time, missing nothing as he scanned the busy streets, aswarm with bicycles, pedestrians, the shoppers drawn to open market stalls. The prime commodities were food and medicine, with prices jacked up through the stratosphere, black marketeers prepared to gouge for blood wherever possible. Repackaging prevented anyone from proving that the food and medicine were stolen from the latest Red Cross shipments, but it clearly didn't fall from heaven into waiting, greedy hands.

In spite of everything—the skirmishes and air strikes, sanctions and negotiations—private warlords controlled Somalia, for all intents and purposes. Four years of civil war and banditry, combined with widespread drought and famine, had reduced the nation of some 7.3 million souls to a feudalistic state, where local strongmen made up the rules as they went along, enforcing them through terror.

That much would be bad enough, if the Somalis had been left alone to kill one another, sink or swim with the supplies on hand. But such wasn't the case. Aside from UN and American involvement in the crisis, word had filtered out to Stony Man that Red Chinese "advisers" had been meddling in Somalia, buying friends with arms and ammunition, playing on the well-known Somali distrust of neighboring Ethiopia and the long-standing interest of both nations in capturing tiny Djibouti.

It was typical, Bolan thought, for Beijing to take advantage of a power vacuum. China had been planting outposts in the Third World, mostly Africa and Southeast Asia, since the 1950s, leaving Russia to contend with Europe and the Latin countries of the Western Hemisphere. The Chinese Reds had left their tracks from Vietnam and Indonesia to Mozambique, Sudan, Namibia, Zaire and Madagascar. In South Africa, Beijing had armed the African National Congress in its long war against apartheid. There was always hope of setting up a friendly puppet state, and if they failed... Well, that was life. The cold war might

have ended in the West—though some would dis-
agree—but in the Far East it was still alive and well.

According to the CIA, Mohammed el Itale had been
working with the Red Chinese for eighteen months or
more, stockpiling arms and sheltering advisers from
Beijing. It was unclear how much of their ''advice'' he
followed, but the latest rumbles of incursions in Djibouti meshed with earlier reports of Red Chinese objectives in East Africa.

The outcome of their morning skirmish with Mohammed el Itale's forces had been bounced by satellite to Stony Man, some thirty minutes after Bolan and
Phoenix Force disengaged. McCarter handled the
computer linkup with an eight-pound unit that included a collapsible dish antenna and transmitter
powered by krylon-cadmium fuel cells. The miniature equipment boasted 256K memory, redundant
circuitry and an electronic countermeasures device,
with housings hermetically sealed and shockproof. In
action, the minicomputer could lock on an orbiting
satellite from virtually any surface point on earth and
fire off a burst of scrambled data in microseconds. It
was also set up to receive transmissions from their Blue
Ridge Mountains hardsite, making radio and land-
lines absolute.

The word from Stony Man that morning had instructed Bolan to make contact with ''a friend'' in
Mogadishu. Even with the scrambler, with just one
chance in perhaps four million of a message being intercepted and decoded, there had been no name. The
agent would find Bolan, somewhere in the public
market near the British embassy. He would be wearing red and carrying a copy of the London *Times*. His

introduction would include specific comment on the weather.

Bolan found the market, made himself available and waited. On the street, a pair of UN soldiers in their sky-blue helmets watched the flow of traffic, automatic rifles slung but close at hand. He tried to place them, recognized their weapons as Galils and made them as Israelis. Somali natives glared and gave them room, foot traffic veering wide around the soldiers like the water of a stream that flows around a jutting stone.

Again, he knew the feeling. They were strangers in a strange land, sent to help people who, in many cases, didn't feel they needed help. And where assistance was requested, urgently desired, the foreign troops were always at a loss for adequate solutions. Playing cop and counselor, so far from home, they were denied the very tools and power that would let them do their job effectively, reduced to ducking bullets, standing by and watching while the natives starved to death or killed one another.

Bolan had no personal illusion that his mission in Somalia would "save" the country or upset the morbid status quo. He operated in pursuit of a specific goal, specific targets, and withdrew when he had done his job. Today, in Mogadishu, he was looking for intelligence that would promote his move against Mohammed el Itale. Anything beyond that would be gravy, and he wasn't counting on a bonus.

The warrior idled past the market stalls, examining the merchandise. There were no weapons on display, these days; the UN presence had achieved that much, at least. You had to shop around a bit for submachine guns, rifles, rocket launchers and grenades.

Unless, of course, you had connections to a private dealer or a personal militia.

He checked his watch and saw that it was time. If his connection stood him up, it might be no great loss, but he would never know for sure. And there would be the question of exposure, covers blown, new risks involved.

As if the game he played was not already fraught with danger.

Bolan wandered through the milling crowd and waited for the stranger who would put him on the scent of targets yet unknown.

For Siad Samatar, at twenty-one, the choice of masters had been no real choice at all. He was intelligent enough to see beyond the propaganda of the native warlords, understanding that despite their talk of unity and peace, they had a huge financial stake in chaos. It was the same in any war-torn land, he realized. Some called for peace while working quietly behind the scenes to help perpetuate the violence on their own behalf.

Once he had seen that much, Samatar couldn't join ranks with any of the private armies that were scourging the Somali countryside. It would have constituted treason to his homeland, a betrayal of himself. The Red Cross didn't need him for its handout program, and the UN peacekeepers were simply watchdogs, tethered at strategic points to try to minimize the public carnage. That left the Chinese or the Americans, and he knew the agents from Beijing were looking out for China's interest, first.

Of course, the same thing could be said for the Americans. They weren't altruists, by any means,

committed to expenditure of cash and time without
some positive result. Still, when he thought of the
Chinese, Samatar could see his homeland as an out-
post of the "people's revolution," with the emphasis
on revolution while his people sacrificed their lives.
With the Americans, at least, he had a sense that they
were interested in restoring peace and order. If their
motives had an element of selfishness, as in opposing
Chinese inroads on the continent, Samatar could live
with that.

In fact, it suited him just fine.

The one thing he despised about Somalia's civil war,
above all else, was the meddling of strangers, be they
yellow, black or white. The Russians, Ethiopians,
Chinese and more had joined in turning up the heat,
kept lethal action at a rolling boil since General Barrah fled in January 1991 with all the money he could
steal. If he could use one group of foreigners to drive
the other out, Samatar would play the game and take
his chances.

He was looking for a white man in the crowd, described as tall and dark. That had to mean his hair,
since no Caucasian would seem dark beside Somali
natives. Probably a soldier, but he wouldn't be in
uniform. Samatar hadn't been trusted with a name,
and that was fine. The stranger didn't know his, either. They were starting off on level ground.

The young Somali was wearing a short-sleeved shirt,
bright red, with khaki trousers and a faded baseball
cap to shade his eyes. He had a week-old copy of the
London *Times* tucked underneath one arm, and he
had memorized the password. They would speak in
English, which he managed fairly well, and thus reduce their odds of being overheard by passersby.

Spies were always a consideration when you lived in Mogadishu. Starving men and women saw no harm in taking money to repeat a conversation overheard in passing or to describe a neighbor's daily habits. If the spy was a militia member, ideology competed with the normal greed. You could feel good about betraying former friends when patriotic zeal and profit ran together in a blur.

Samatar approached the open marketplace, aware of UN soldiers on the street, ignoring them. He had a pistol in his belt, beneath the loose hem of his shirt, but the peacekeepers didn't make a practice of frisking Somalis on the street without due cause. It would have been a full-time job, in any case, and Samatar didn't intend to draw his gun unless his life was threatened.

Which, he realized, was still a distinct possibility.

He was playing a dangerous game, with his life on the line, but a man had to choose where he stood in the world, defend that choice to any cost. The young man had made his call, and he wasn't prepared to back out now, allowing fear to dominate his life.

It was a relatively simple matter, picking out his contact. There were five Caucasians in the marketplace; two UN soldiers, two apparent diplomats in carbon-copy suits and one tall loner, looking casual but ever so alert.

Samatar maneuvered through the crowd, taking his time on the approach, coming up on the tall man's blind side. Or, at least he thought so, but the man surprised him, turning to face him at the final instant. Blue eyes pinned Siad and held him fast, took in his crimson shirt, the paper folded underneath his arm.

The white man waited, silent.

"It is beastly hot today," Samatar remarked, as if the two men were old friends.

"I'm told it will be hotter still tomorrow," the stranger replied.

"Possibly, unless it rains."

Samatar couldn't suppress a smile as he completed reeling off the coded introduction. In his several months of working with the CIA, this was the first time he had been required to meet a Western spy in public. The potential danger had his nerves on edge, but there was something of a thrill, as well. Some time would have to pass before the novelty wore off.

"We should go somewhere else to talk," he told the white man, glancing briefly to his left and right. A relatively small percentage of his countrymen spoke English, but it took only one extra pair of ears to blow the game and lead to killing.

"Where?" the white man asked him, frowning slightly.

"Follow after me," Samatar replied, and turning away, he began to weave a path back through the crowd.

IT COULD TURN OUT to be a trap, Bolan thought, even with the password. If the opposition picked up his contact and sweated him a little, they would know about the shirt, the paper, all of it. He wouldn't know unless he played along and took the chance, and why else was he there?

He gave the young Somali time to put some space between them, nothing obvious as he began to follow through the crush of shoppers. If the man in red was covered, it would make no difference either way; the

Executioner was burned already, and the best that he could hope for was to find a way out of the trap when it was sprung. If they hadn't been shadowed, though, he had a chance.

He had considered using Calvin James for backup, one more black face in the crowd, but James spoke no Somali, and his Arabic left much to be desired. Potential difficulties scrubbed the plan, and Bolan went in on his own, preferring solitary action to a move that jeopardized the team.

If anything went wrong, this way, they had a chance to carry on without him, salvage something on the play. If nothing else, they had a shot at running down Mohammed el Itale, leveling the score. It wouldn't solve the larger problem they were sent to tackle, but it soothed the warrior's mind a bit to know that he wouldn't go unavenged.

They left the marketplace behind and traveled north, past shops and a dilapidated school, with children playing on a scruffy field. Another block, and Bolan's contact veered into a park. Aside from half a dozen UN soldiers lounging on a grassy knoll, some sixty yards away, they had it to themselves.

The young Somali sat underneath a spindly shade tree. Bolan hesitated, then took his place beside the stranger. His Beretta, under the baggy cotton shirt he wore, was inches from his hand. If anything went wrong, the young man with the red shirt and the London *Times* would be the first to die.

The stranger introduced himself as Siad Samatar. It could have been a code name; Bolan didn't know or care. His own ID was made out in the name of Mike Belasko, covering his bets.

"We're open here," Bolan said, watching the pedestrians who passed no more than fifty feet from where he sat.

"No worries," his contact replied. "I have taken care to see we were not followed."

Bolan had been taking care on that account himself, but it was difficult to say for sure, in strange surroundings. Crowded streets made tracking easy, but they complicated an attempt to spot the tail. For all he knew, there could be half a dozen shooters watching him right now.

He wasted no time getting down to business. "I was told that you could help me find Mohammed el Itale and his friends."

"Of course. You want Chinese."

"That's part of it. I also need a handle on his leading rival. What's the name again?"

"That would be Jouad ben Ganane. Very strong in Mogadishu. Very dangerous."

"I'm counting on it."

"They are deadly enemies, Mohammed and Jouad. They try to kill each other many times, no luck."

"That's better yet."

The young man thought about it for a moment, frowning. "Ah," he said at last. "You want to start a war."

"We've got the war. I just might stir things up a little."

"There is much black-market business here in Mogadishu. Both Mohammed and Jouad sell food and medicine, loan money, tax the merchants for protection from one another. They don't fight so much these days, with the United Nations here. Their homes are elsewhere. Jouad ben Ganane lives near Afgo, to the west. Mohammed el Itale may be found in Buran, with his Chinese friends."

"They must have operations here in town," Bolan said. "Something like an office or command post?"

"In here," Samatar plied, and placed his folded paper on the ground between them. "The financial section."

"Seems appropriate."

"You will destroy the men who bring my country grief?" the young man asked him, frowning.

"That's the plan, but I don't work miracles. You've got a world of problems here."

"It will be a beginning, even so. Too many men have put themselves before the people. We are dying so a few can live in palaces and drive in shiny cars."

The Executioner was starting to relax a little with his contact. It could be an act, of course, but Bolan was a decent judge of character. He thought the young man was sincere.

"One thing you need to understand," he said. "A deal like this, count on it getting worse before you notice any real improvement. I don't see the bad boys giving up without a fight."

"My people have no fear of fighting if they think that it will lead to something better. The United Nations tell us eighty thousand casualties since General Barrah fled from Mogadishu, but they gave up counting those who die from hunger and disease. It has to stop."

"Let's see what we can do. What happens if I need to get in touch again?"

"I have a telephone," Samatar informed him proudly. "Usually it works. You'll find my number by the editorial on economic aid for Africa."

"Okay. I'm going now. Take care."

"I have survived this long. It is no small accomplishment."

And that, the Executioner reflected, was an understatement. Life was never easy in a state of siege, but it grew doubly complicated when a young man with a mission started playing off his luck against the odds.

As Bolan left the park, passed by the UN soldiers, he didn't glance backward toward the Somali. He was inclined to trust the man, at least until he found a reason not to, but he couldn't be responsible for keeping him safe and sound. The man knew what he was doing, recognized the consequences if his various potential enemies found out and set the wheels of retribution turning.

Bolan, meanwhile, had a war to fight. The men of Phoenix Force were on a mission of their own, three hundred miles from Mogadishu, and they would be out of touch for several hours. Jack Grimaldi was in charge of airborne transportation for the strike.

Which left the Executioner to manage on his own.

No problem.

He had wheels, equipment, ready cash on hand—and now he had a list of targets. Jouad ben Ganane and Mohammed el Itale, plus the Red Chinese. It was enough to keep him busy through the afternoon and evening, right. Before he kept his rendezvous with Phoenix Force, there would be ample time for him to raise some hell in Mogadishu and environs, stirring up the local heavies.

It would be a start, at least. And where it ended up was anybody's guess.

He was a world away from Stony Man Farm in Virginia, but he knew the team was thinking of him even now, their thoughts and energy devoted to the progress of his mission. There was nothing they could do to help him in the instant when a life-or-death decision was required, but the advance intelligence relayed from Stony Man's computers via satellite had brought him this far, and with periodic updates, it should be enough to see him through.

Successful military operations were a lot like cooking from a recipe. You needed various ingredients, in the correct proportions, if you wanted something palatable as the end result. Intelligence and planning, proper hardware, nerve, audacity... and luck. Miscalculation anywhere along the line could spell disaster, Bolan knew from grim experience, and it was all the more precarious on unfamiliar ground, when time was of the essence and the odds were all in favor of the house.

No matter. He was rolling now, and wouldn't allow himself to be diverted by uncertainty or doubts. The Executioner had played against uneven odds before and come out on the winning side. This time, with Phoenix Force and Stony Man behind him, you could even say he had a strong edge on his enemies.

The storm was coming, but it hadn't broken yet. Before it passed, there would be striking changes in the local status quo, for good or ill. Whichever way it played, Mack Bolan prepared to see the struggle through.

The Executioner was shifting into battle mode.

CHAPTER FOUR

Eastern Ethiopia

Eleven thousand miles above Earth's surface, NAV-STAR waited for the next incoming signal to arrive. At five feet wide and seventeen feet long, the satellite was roughly equal in size to the average sedan, but it relied on solar panels for its power, in the place of crude combustion engines. One of eighteen global-positioning satellites that ringed the planet, it had a life expectancy of 7.5 years.

Not bad, all things considered, when you had to spend your life in outer space.

Once Jack Grimaldi registered coordinates, the navigation was a snap. He beamed the latitude and longitude to NAVSTAR, where the satellite's computer automatically calculated time, location and the airspeed of his UH-60 Black Hawk. From the orbiting receptor, the accumulated information was relayed to Stony Man, nine thousand miles away, across the broad Atlantic and the bulk of Africa. At Stony Man, computers crunched the data into map form and relayed it back through space to a receiver mounted on the Black Hawk's instrument panel. The visual display was crystal-clear: detailed topography, along with human data—settlements and such—that was updated on a daily basis from intelligence reports. NAVSTAR's receiving unit served as well in ships and surface vehicles as in the air; one version, tailored for the infantry, wasn't much larger than a cordless telephone. Its accuracy was amazing: the recipient's location was determined within fifteen feet, his speed within a range of one-half mile per hour, and the local time within a millionth of a second.

If only it could cook and clean, Grimaldi would have said he was in love.

"Six minutes," he informed his passengers. No answer, but he knew they would be double-checking weapons and equipment, getting ready for the drop. The twin T700 turboshaft engines gave the Black Hawk a maximum cruising speed of 167 miles per hour, but Grimaldi was holding it closer to 140 mph, flying low to frustrate radar. They were less than fifteen feet above the deck in places, and Grimaldi saw the desert simmer, heat waves rising from the sand.

He had to drop his passengers a mile out from their target, sit and wait while they went in on foot, then pick them up when he received the signal they were finished. Waiting on the ground would be a bitch, but there was no alternative. He couldn't waste the fuel required to cruise aimlessly around the desert while Katzenelenbogen's warriors hiked a mile and carried out their strike. No way.

At least, Grimaldi told himself, the enemy was likely to be grounded. They were mostly limited to helicopters in the eastern sector, with their vintage European fighters concentrated farther inland, guarding Addis Ababa. He could be wrong, of course, but gambling was a part of war. It kept things interesting.

If anything went wrong, and he was spotted by an enemy patrol, Grimaldi was prepared to fly and fight. The Black Hawk carried Stingers, Hellfires and a

20 mm Gatling mounted underneath its stubby wings, prepared to meet an airborne challenge or to strike at targets on the ground.

"We're getting there."

The landing zone was a small oasis, chosen for location and the cover it would give Grimaldi while he waited for a summons to the killing ground. He set the Black Hawk down, killed the engines and swiveled in his seat to watch the men of Phoenix Force unload.

"We'll be in touch," Katz told him, pausing in the open door.

"Hell, I can hardly wait."

ONE MILE HAD BEEN selected as the optimum insertion distance from their target. It was far enough away that no one in the compound ought to see or hear the chopper, and close enough for Katzenelenbogen's men to make the hike in twenty minutes, give or take, without collapsing in the desert heat.

Once they arrived, of course, the heat would be a different story, most of it man-made.

The target, strictly speaking, wasn't Ethiopian, although it lay within that nation's boundaries and was protected—more or less, sporadically—by forces of the shaky coalition government in Addis Ababa. The on-site occupants, however, were predominantly Cuban, soldiers "loaned" by Castro in a last-ditch bid to shore up his declining status in the world.

Fidel had few supporters in the Western Hemisphere—no heads of state, since the collapse of the Ortega government in Nicaragua—and Soviet disintegration under Gorbachev and Yeltsin left Havana isolated from the world at large, committed to an ideology and course of action that was generally discred-

ited. In search of allies, Castro had been forced to cast
his net in Africa—Angola, Ethiopia and any other
trouble spot where would-be revolutionary leaders
needed men and guns to back their play. In Ethiopia,
the Cubans had assisted native troops in their long-
running conflict with Somalia. More recently, it was
believed, despite disclaimers of aggressive plans by the
authorities in Addis Ababa and Mogadishu, elements
in both countries had renewed their interest in annex-
ing tiny Djibouti. If the Cubans managed to provoke
an incident through midnight border raids, they would
be called upon to "pacify" Djibouti as a form of
"self-defense." For militant Somalis and their Chinese brain trust, likewise, turmoil on the border with
Djibouti was a golden opportunity.

This compound, if the Stony Man field intelligence
was accurate, had been the launching pad for several
recent strikes across the border, in Djibouti. Nailing
down the opposition here would send a message back
to Addis Ababa and serve as the opening gun in the
Phoenix Force campaign to suppress border raiding.

They were in position twenty-seven minutes after
Jack Grimaldi dropped them off at the oasis, five grim
men in desert camouflage, all armed with weapons
manufactured by the Russians or their onetime allies
in the former Eastern Bloc. If anything went wrong
and any of the gear was left behind, examination
would result in fingers pointing all the wrong directions.

Yakov Katzenelenbogen hated bullies. He had seen
the photographs of victims from the recent border
raids, and he was looking forward to this opportunity
to pay back a measure of the violence meted out to
helpless villagers.

His men were all in place, at intervals around the compound, waiting. Katz surveyed the camp—the tents and Quonset huts that showed up bright and clear on photos taken from surveillance satellites, three helicopters standing on the west side of the compound, under guard. Analysis of photos, infrared included, placed the head count for the Cuban garrison at sixty soldiers, give or take a dozen. They were long odds, granted, but surprise went far toward leveling the odds.

His watch showed it was time, and Katzenelenbogen focused on the grounded choppers with his RPG. He had four rockets with him: three to blitz the whirlybirds, and one to set the motor pool on fire, if there was time and opportunity.

He chose the middle chopper, hoping he could bag two airships for the price of one. He took a breath and held it, squeezed the trigger slowly and saw the rocket blaze downrange.

Show time.

CALVIN JAMES WAS READY at the southwest corner of the compound, when the RPG-7 round came in on target, taking out the middle chopper in a clap of smoky thunder, severed rotors and a storm of shrapnel ripping through the birds on either side of Katzenelenbogen's target.

There was instant chaos in the camp, with soldiers running every which way, charging out of tents and huts with their uniforms in disarray, all clutching weapons. One guy burst from the latrine, a pistol in his right hand, trousers hoisted in his left.

James would have laughed, if it were not such deadly business. Lying prone behind his RPK machine gun, thirty yards outside the compound's fence, he wished the hobbling runner well and slammed a short burst through his chest. The Cuban went down kicking, rumpled trousers snagged around his knees.

A second rocket finished off the choppers, spreading hungry flames from ruptured fuel tanks. James had swiveled toward the CP hut by that time, spotting two more soldiers as they blundered into daylight. Something glittered on the older Cuban's collar, the insignia of rank.

James stroked the trigger of his RPK and dropped them squirming in the sand. A second short burst finished it.

Despite the broiling desert heat, there was a definite advantage to the daylight strike. Their enemies were clearly visible, while James and the other Phoenix Force warriors wouldn't be revealed by muzzleflashes in the darkness.

Still, he could have used some shade.

James strafed the communications hut, a long burst punching through the corrugated metal walls. He might not tag the operator, but with any luck he could destroy the radio or keep the duty officer so busy scrambling that he had no time to send an SOS. The others would be closing in before much longer, nailing down loose ends.

Scratch that. He caught a glimpse of Rafael Encizo, sixty yards away, racing for the wire, his AK-47 blazing from the hip. A frag grenade cleared passage through the fence, and James was following another clutch of moving targets with his RPK when more explosions rocked the camp's perimeter—first on his right, McCarter, then directly opposite, as Gary Manning made his move.

They needed cover, though, and everybody couldn't rush the wire at once. James held his ground and milked the RPK for short, precision bursts that knocked his human targets down and left them sprawling in the dust. The Cuban troops were fighting back sporadically, still dazzled by the rapid-fire explosions, dodging streams of automatic fire that came from beyond the fence. Confused and disoriented, most of them had no idea exactly what was going on, but they were fighting for their lives.

And losing.

The former Navy SEAL picked out another pair of moving targets, hosed them with his RPK and grimaced as they went down thrashing.

He was batting cleanup now, while his companions did the grunt work, and he didn't envy them at all.

IT WAS IRONIC, Rafael Encizo thought, that he had come halfway around the world to fight his fellow countrymen in the defense of Africans, but he felt no affinity for Castro's troops, no matter where they pitched their tents. Fidel had scourged his family, destroyed their dreams, and Encizo's whole life had been devoted to revenge.

Not random, mindless acts of violence, but a systematic whittling at the roots of Cuban communism, waiting for the day when it would topple like the Kremlin and his people would be free again. Fidel wasn't immortal, after all, and when his cult of personality was crushed...

He scrambled through the gap his frag grenade had opened in the compound's chain-link fence. A trailing strand of razor wire tugged at his cheek, drew blood, but Encizo ignored it, seeking targets for his AK-47 as he made his way inside the camp.

The first two came at the Phoenix Force commando from the direction of the motor pool, young men approximating Encizo's complexion and his stature, likewise armed with folding-stock Kalashnikovs. Their uniforms were different, though, plain khaki in the place of desert camouflage, and there was no mistaking their intent as they confronted Encizo from twenty feet away.

It was their shock that saved him, gave him time to pivot on one heel and swing the AK-47 toward his targets, with his trigger finger taking up the slack. There was no time for aiming, and he didn't need to, rattling off a burst that punched the two young privates over backward, crimson spouting from their chests as they went down.

A bullet whispered past his face, immediately followed by another. Closer. Encizo dodged to his right, in the direction of the bullet-punctured commo hut, slugs kicking up a trail of dust behind him. Sliding into cover, he unclipped a frag grenade, released the safety pin and lobbed the bomb with his right around the corner, back in the direction he had come from.

Startled shouts erupted, as someone saw it coming and attempted to withdraw. Too late, the blast eclipsing panicked voices. Encizo came back around the corner with his AK-47, mopping up, a mercy round here and there for soldiers writhing on the ground.

He heard the rocket coming, saw it streak across the compound to his left and detonate inside the covered motor pool. A flatbed truck absorbed the brunt of the explosion, rearing on its back wheels like a living thing, flames boiling out from underneath the hood.

A heartbeat later, flaming gasoline was everywhere, the other Jeeps and trucks already catching.

A Cuban soldier burst from the inferno, running for his life and trailing flames behind him like a grounded comet. Someone else was screaming in the motor pool, unable to escape the fire, but Encizo ignored it, tracked the human torch and dropped him with a 3-round mercy burst.

Encizo had the CP spotted, closing rapidly, oblivious to bullets snapping past him as he ran. Two men, one of them wearing captain's bars, lay tangled near the front door of the hut, and the Phoenix Force warrior leaped over them, advancing on the camp's command post. He reached the door and hit it with a flying kick, bursting in to find it empty.

Damn!

Well, he could still prevent the Reds from coming back when he was gone, destroy whatever documents they might have stashed inside the filing cabinets on his left. He palmed a thermite can and yanked the pin, retreating from the CP as he pitched it underhand, across the commandant's desk.

Fight fire with fire, and then some. The Fidelistas were welcome to anything they could salvage from the ashes, when the ruins cooled. Meanwhile, Encizo's task was to reduce their numbers and eliminate as many of the opposition as he could.

He left the CP firing, caught three privates moving in to corner him and took them by surprise. The dazed expressions on their faces as they went down might have been comical under other circumstances, if the stakes had been any less than life and death.

Encizo had a quick glimpse of McCarter, dodging bullets on the far side of the camp, but didn't move to join him. Each man of the Phoenix Force had his specific orders and objectives; none had been detailed to baby-sit the others.

He reloaded on the run and made his way in the direction of the mess tent. Grim death was on the menu, and his "brother" Cubans were in for a feast.

As a ONETIME MEMBER of the SAS, David McCarter didn't favor set-piece battles, but he sometimes had no choice. The enemy was where you found him, and there were occasional advantages to playing off against the odds. If you survived it, any members of the opposition who did likewise would lose something in the way of confidence. And next time, when the two sides came together, the advantage might have shifted.

Strategy aside, he played the cards as they were dealt, and that meant crouching in the shadow of the Cuban mess tent with an AK-47 balanced on his knee, selecting targets.

He had dropped two soldiers coming in, and three more in the mess tent proper. They were sprawled to his left, one draped across a wooden table, two more huddled on the ground. One of the three had fired a short burst from his own Kalashnikov, for all the good it did him, high and hopeless as McCarter's bullets cut him down.

The motor pool, and the base command post were burning. To McCarter's left, perhaps a hundred yards away, the tangled ruins of the helicopters smoked and smoldered. Stripped of vehicles and radio communication, the surviving Cubans weren't going anywhere—but they could still fight back.

As if to emphasize that point, a rifle bullet sizzled close above the Briton's head. He ducked, an automatic reflex action, knowing it was useless by the time he heard the bullet. There was no way to decide if someone had him sighted or the round was just a stray, except to hold his ground and wait.

Three Cubans suddenly erupted from the nearest Quonset hut, pounding toward the mess tent. By the time they spotted McCarter, sighting down the barrel of his AK-47, there was nothing they could do to save themselves. The Briton stitched them with a level burst from left to right and dropped them in their tracks, two pitching over backward, while the third man toppled forward on his face.

How many left inside the hut? There was no way to be sure.

McCarter primed a frag grenade and held it in his left hand, moving with the AK-47 in his right. It was a relatively short sprint to the south end of the dome-like barracks, to crouch in the shade that seemed to make no impact on the heat. It was a bit more awkward, getting to the door, but he would settle for a window, and found one standing open just around the corner from his hiding place.

Unlike the pyrotechnics spawned by Hollywood, McCarter knew that his grenade wouldn't destroy the hut, or even guarantee a shrapnel hit on occupants beyond a given radius. Still, he was hoping that the blast would flush survivors from the structure into the open, giving him a chance to deal with them in proper style.

He broke from cover, lobbed his deadly egg in through the window and retreated as the clock ran down. He hugged the sand and made himself as small as possible, aware that flying shrapnel had a fifty-fifty chance of punching through the corrugated metal walls and tearing flesh outside.

The blast was muffled, almost minuscule, compared to Katz's RPG-7 rounds. Still, it was adequate, immediately followed by the ragged sound of screams and scrambling feet. The Cubans were unloading, and McCarter made an educated guess that several of their mates were being left behind.

He had the entrance covered when they started spilling out, five men, and two of those displaying minor shrapnel wounds. The Briton raked them with his AK-47, dropping one, two, three before they knew exactly what was happening. The last two had him spotted, firing wild and breaking in a search for cover, but they couldn't run and also watch their backs. McCarter used the last rounds in his magazine to cut them down, reloading even as their bodies settled in the dust.

That left the wounded in the Quonset hut, still waiting for him.

"Heads up, lads," the Phoenix Force commando said, advancing on the open door. "We're almost done."

THERE WAS A POINT in any battle, Gary Manning thought, when you could definitely say the tide had turned, for good or ill. He felt it in the compound, as return fire from the Cubans faltered, started dying off in first one sector, then another.

It was time for mopping up.

The tall Canadian was crouched behind a silent Quonset hut with his Kalashnikov, alert for any target he could find. Beside him lay the body of a Cuban corporal who had closed with Manning, hand to hand, and come off second best.

So much for stealth.

He spotted Rafael Encizo moving from the CP hut in the direction of the gutted motor pool. Behind him, breaking from the general direction of the camp's latrine, two Cubans fell in step behind him, closing fast. How long before they opened fire on Rafael?

It would have been a waste of time to shout a warning, in the circumstances. Too much background noise, including angry voices, automatic weapons fire and the occasional explosion. Manning brought the AK-47 to his shoulder, tracking on the forward target, squeezing off a short burst at a range of fifty yards.

The Cuban staggered, reeling as the bullets stitched a line of holes across his chest. He went down on one knee, resisting gravity for just a heartbeat longer, finally slumping over on his side.

By that time, his companion knew that there was something wrong. It was too late to save himself, but he was trying. Torn between the target he could see and the elusive sniper who had nailed this comrade, Number Two backpedaled, turning toward the nearest barracks tent for cover.

It was close, but no cigar.

The second burst from Manning's AK-47 caught the hardman on the run and punched him forward several feet. He hit the sand facedown and slid with arms outstretched, like an exhausted baseball player bodysurfing toward home plate.

Encizo hesitated, glancing backward, then caught sight of Manning. He raised an open hand in thanks before he cleared the fire lane, dodging under cover near the motor pool.

A handful of surviving Cubans had been driven into hiding in a Quonset hut some thirty yards due east of Manning's vantage point. It was impossible to guess their number, but they kept up an active fire through the windows, squeezing off short bursts and ducking back before the men of Phoenix Force could take them down.

They could pull out now, withdraw and leave the Cubans penned up in their hut until they figured out the coast was clear, or they could finish it.

As if in answer to his thoughts, another RPG-7 round streaked into camp from Katzenelenbogen's perch. It struck the northwest corner of the hut, sheared through corrugated steel and detonated with a crash on the inside. Smoke started pouring from the open windows, Manning ready with his AK-47 as the cornered Cubans started shouting back and forth in Spanish, setting up their final break.

It was a desperation move, but there appeared to be no options. Spilling through the doorway, wrapped in wisps of smoke and gagging on the cordite stench, they came out firing wildly, breaking left and right without apparent forethought. Manning heard his comrades open up as he began to fire short bursts from thirty yards, the human targets reeling, twitching, going down.

And it was over, just like that.

The walkie-talkie on his belt gave out a burst of static, followed by the tinny sound of Yakov Katzenelenbogen's voice, addressing Jack Grimaldi. Manning rose and walked into the middle of the compound, joining his associates and waiting for the chopper. It would be no trick for Jack to find them, following the pall of drifting smoke.

It wasn't every day you found a signpost pointing straight to hell.

CHAPTER FIVE

Mogadishu, Somalia

A mile north of the ruined presidential palace, Bolan parked his drab sedan behind a small, run-down hotel. The alley he had chosen was a narrow strip of dirt and gravel, piled with trash on either side. There were no trash receptacles, per se, and it was obvious that organized collection of discarded rubbish was a lost art in this neighborhood of the Somali capital, but vehicles or foot traffic had kept a lane clear down the middle of the alley.

Bolan killed the engine, checked his rearview mirror, waiting for a moment to be sure that no one from the street had followed him. Aside from posted lookouts, there was a substantial risk of thievery, whenever private vehicles stood unattended for any length of time in the urban battle zone. It wouldn't do for the Executioner to complete his strike and find the car stripped or disabled, leaving him on foot.

When he was reasonably satisfied, the warrior unzipped his duffel bag and lifted out an MP-5 K submachine gun, less than thirteen inches long. Its magazine held thirty rounds of 9 mm Parabellum ammunition, which the little stuttergun could empty out in 2.25 seconds flat. Five extra magazines went into Bolan's pockets, backing up the sleek Beretta in his shoulder rig. The final touch consisted of two Dutch

V-40 "minigrenades," the smallest fragmentation bombs available.

The Man from Bad was dressed to kill.

He locked the driver's door behind him, opting for a measure of security, and pocketed the keys. If there were gunners on his tail when he emerged, it would be Bolan's job to dust them off or slow them down before he reached the car. Three seconds to unlock the door would cost him less than coming out to find the car had been hot-wired and stolen in his absence, when he needed it the most.

The old hotel had been considered swank at one point in its history, but that was long ago. Its paying guests had long since vanished, and the building had been marked for demolition when the Mogadishu government collapsed in ruins. These days, it was occupied by soldiers in the private army of Mohammed el Itale, serving as the warlord's private "embassy" in north Mogadishu.

Bolan hadn't been invited to drop in, but he was coming anyway, with a surprise for all concerned.

He tried the back door, found it locked and took a chance with his stiletto. Fifteen seconds put him in a murky, urine-reeking corridor with service stairs immediately on his left, a kind of spacious pantry on the right. There were no guns to stop him, and he wondered at the negligence of "soldiers" who would leave their backs unguarded in that way.

So much the better for his mission.

The warrior spent a moment scouting out the ground floor, spotting two young gunners planted in the lobby. They were armed with submachine guns, Swedish Model 45s, prepared—at least in theory—to confront invaders as they came in from the street. In fact, they were consumed with idle conversation, totally oblivious to the man sliding up behind them, aiming down the barrel of a silencer-equipped Beretta Model 92.

Two shots at something close to point-blank range, and Bolan kept the pistol in his left hand, submachine gun in his right, as he retreated toward the stairs. If someone wandered in and found the sentries dead, alarms would certainly be raised, but he was on the clock now, making haste.

The place was relatively small, six floors, but that meant twelve flights up, with every step at risk. A chance encounter with the enemy was probable, his short reaction time and the Beretta's silencer his only edge against a full-scale blowout that would warn the others.

But he made it, somehow.

Up on six, he had a choice of left or right along the dingy hallway. Rooms lined both sides, most of them with the doors removed or standing open, dark and silent. Only two spilled light and noise, away to Bolan's left. He moved in that direction, leading with the submachine gun now, his side arm tucked away and out of sight.

The time for silence was behind him.

In the first room, two young men were arguing about their laundry. Bolan didn't understand a word they said, but dirty clothes were piled up on the floor between them, and they took turns wagging stiff, accusatory fingers as they bickered.

Bolan whistled softly, catching their attention. He was ready as they turned to face him, taking in their startled faces, squeezing off a burst that dropped the two of them together, with the laundry sopping crimson from their mortal wounds.

Next door, he heard a scramble as the occupants responded to the sound of gunfire. The Executioner beat them to the doorway, barging in without an invitation, firing from the hip. Again, it was a duo, slightly more hygienic than their comrades, listening to music on an old transistor radio.

His bullets made them dance.

Back to the stairs and down. The fifth floor was deathly still, perhaps deserted. Bolan spent a moment on the landing, ticking off the doomsday numbers in his head, and gave it up when no one challenged him. Below, a dozen voices clamored for attention—cursing, questioning, demanding explanations, barking orders.

Bolan went to join them, palming one of the V-40 minibombs and yanking out the safety pin. A face came in view below him, on the fourth-floor landing, bleating out a wordless cry of fear or anger at the sight of a Caucasian on the stairs.

He dropped the frag grenade and saw the face duck out of sight. No matter. Gravity and physics did the rest, a drop-bounce-wobble-roll scenario that sent his deadly present hopping down the stairs. When it exploded seconds later, there were shrieks of pain and high-pitched wailing in the stairwell, telling Bolan he had scored.

He came down firing and reloaded on the move, bypassing targets that were down and out with shrapnel wounds. He had no time to spare on overkill, when others of the garrison were firing back at him or running for their lives.

He might not get them all, of course. It was illogical to think that he could make a clean sweep each and every time. Survivors weren't a problem, though. In fact, they could be useful, carrying the word of panic to their fellow soldiers, confusion amplified by fear and anger, sowing chaos in the ranks.

So much the better.

Bolan left the runners to their own devices, falling upon their braver comrades like the judgment of the damned.

FROM WHERE HE SAT, Bulo Moyale had a clear view of the U.S. diplomatic compound, looking south. It was a quarter mile away, but there were no tall buildings in between the compound and Moyale's rooftop perch. Distracted by a fantasy, he raised his heavy M-14 and practiced aiming at the huddled buildings where the Americans lived under guard.

It would be easy, if he had the proper weapon. Like a Stinger, maybe, or the larger British Blowpipe missile.

Easy.

There would be reprisals, though, if they found out where he had fired from. If he taxed his brain, Moyale could remember air raids launched by the Americans, with Cobra gunships and the big, slow-flying Spectre airplanes, with their rapid-firing cannons—20 mm, 40 mm and the giant 105 mm. A number of Moyale's friends had died in those engagements, running for their lives, and he had no desire to join them in the ground. Much less in pieces, torn to shreds by flying steel and high explosives.

Still, a man could always dream.

If he could drive the white men out of Mogadishu, Moyale thought he would be a hero to his people. They would carry him around the city on their shoulders, give him money, food and women—anything he wanted. It would be like heaven, for a little while at least.

Moyale had no faith in lasting happiness. Experience had taught him that the good times always ended, giving way to bad. The tables always turned, but any man would be a fool to shun good luck when it came knocking on his door. It might not last, but it was better to enjoy oneself for several days or weeks than never to have lived at all.

Just now, however, there was sentry duty.

He was sitting on the rooftop of a onetime office building, waiting for the enemy to come so he could use his M-14. The several floors below him had been occupied primarily by firms in business with the government, and when the government effectively collapsed in 1991, two-thirds of those who rented space beneath that roof had seen that it was time to leave Somalia. Several other firms had tried to carry on, but it was hopeless in the climate of a nation feeding on itself, and soon they, too, were gone. The vacant building still survived, though, and it had been irresistible when Jouad ben Ganane came in search of a command post for his drive to capture Mogadishu for himself.

Three years ago, that was, and if they hadn't actually seized the capital, at least Ganane and his men had made a decent living for themselves. A show of strength was really all it took, and merchants fell in line, coughed up their weekly tribute. There were always customers for hijacked clothing, food or medicine.

If he could truly realize his dream and drive the white men out, Moyale knew, things would be different in Somalia. He wasn't convinced, though, that all the changes would be beneficial. First of all, without the Red Cross and United Nations, there would be no food or medicine to steal and sell on the black market. They would also have a hard time with Mohammed el Itale, who commanded larger forces in the countryside.

Ironically the white men helped Ganane's private army stay in business, even as they tried to bring him down. Moyale smiled at the peculiar thought, amused at the bizarre turns life could take from time to time. An enemy became a friend, and yet—

The building trembled underneath him. Nothing major, like an earthquake, but he felt the tremor in his legs and buttocks, sitting on his folding metal chair. The muffled sound that followed obviously came from an explosion. He had seen enough grenades and satchel charges going off, during the past three years, to know that sound by heart.

Moyale bolted from his chair and double-timed in the direction of the stairwell, thumbing off the safety on his M-14. No sooner had he opened the door than he heard gunfire echoing below him. Two, three floors, the way it sounded, but he couldn't tell for sure.

He hit the staircase running, taking two and three steps at a time. He kept his finger on the outside of his rifle's trigger guard, afraid of tripping on the stairs and wasting ammunition, maybe even injuring himself. It would have been the ultimate indignity to shoot himself while running to defend his comrades from an enemy attack.

It could be nothing else, Moyale realized, perhaps Mohammed el Itale's men, or soldiers from the UN garrison attempting to disarm the "outlaw elements" once more. Perhaps some other, smaller warlord, hoping to enhance his reputation with a raid against the second-largest force in Mogadishu.

It made no difference in the end. Moyale had been trained to kill his leader's enemies, and he was anxious for the opportunity to do his job. He had a young man's courage, bolstered by testosterone and pride.

The sound of automatic weapons picked up volume on the fourth-floor landing. It was closer now, perhaps one floor below him. Moyale heard his comrades shouting, angry words and curses, but it told him nothing of his unseen enemy.

On three, he found the first two bodies, crumpled where they fell when bullets cut them down. A lake of blood had spread around the corpses, squelching underneath his shoes with every step, and he took care to keep from falling as he moved around them. Glancing at the faces, the Somali saw that they weren't close friends, but he had known them both, of course, and that was bad enough.

More firing, from the floor below, and he descended toward the sounds of battle, leading with his M-14. Another body was stretched out on the stairs, head down, with crimson soaking through the khaki shirt where exit wounds had churned the flesh to bloody pulp. Moyale didn't bother to identify the latest corpse, his full attention focused on the problem of survival in a combat zone.

A hand grenade exploded somewhere close enough for shrapnel to come flying up the stairwell, etching abstract patterns in the dirty plaster walls. He ducked but kept going down the stairs, intent on helping out his comrades if he could.

The second-story landing was a slaughter pen. Four bodies—no, he saw a fifth—were huddled there, in awkward attitudes of death. Moyale had to step on bodies, no clear way around them, and he swallowed rising bile, his finger curled around the trigger of his M-14, prepared to fire.

He caught the sound of running footsteps on the stairs and set off in hot pursuit, catching a glimpse of someone turning at the bottom of the next-to-last flight down. Moyale fired a burst on automatic, ripping plaster, chewing up the banister. He didn't recognize his target, but the gunner was a white man, dressed in civilian clothes.

Moyale didn't know if one man could be capable of all the damage he had witnessed, but he had this pale-skinned killer on the run. It gave him courage, made him hurry, charging down the stairs.

One flight to go.

The Somali came around the corner, starting down the final flight of stairs, and found his adversary waiting for him at the bottom, with a submachine gun in his hands. Too late, Moyale tried to save himself, reverse directions, but he lost his footing and almost fell. The price of staying upright was a sacrifice of aim. His M-14 was spewing bullets high and wide, Moyale clutching with his free hand at the banister, to keep himself from going down.

The white man fired a burst that slammed Moyale backward, whipped the automatic rifle from his hands and cut his legs from under him. Moyale knew that he was falling but couldn't help himself. He closed his eyes and tried to raise one arm above his head to break the impact.

Hopeless.

Sprawling at the bottom of the stairs, he found the white man standing over him, a curious expression on his face. He didn't seem enraged, or even agitated, by the proximity of so much death. Instead, he studied the Somali as a bug collector might examine yet another specimen, with passing interest but no real emotion.

There was something in Moyale's eyes, a blur of crimson. When he tried to wipe them clean, he found his arms immobilized. In place of pain, a creeping numbness made him feel as if his body had been sculpted from a block of lead.

So this is how it felt to die, he thought.

A moment later, just before the crimson turned to midnight black, he saw the white man turn and walk away.

THE BASIC PLAN was simple: shake and bake, divide and conquer.

Half a dozen major warlords had been raising hell around Somalia for the past four years, but two had lately risen to the top of their bizarre profession. One—Mohammed el Itale—was believed by Stony Man and agents of the CIA to be a favored subject of Beijing. His leading rival, doing fairly well so far without a foreign sponsor, was Jouad ben Ganane. Between them, their militias easily outnumbered all the other competition put together. Dropping one would simply put the other in the catbird seat.

But dropping both, well, that would put a new spin on the ball.

With Phoenix Force behind him, Bolan could have theoretically attempted to destroy both private armies on his own, but it was risky to the max, and he preferred to let his adversaries make a contribution to their own demise whenever possible. To that end, he had opted for a course that would—with any luck—encourage Itale and Ganane to suspect each other in the latest series of attacks. A sweet fringe benefit of Bolan's plan, if it succeeded, would be disappointment or destruction of the Red Chinese contingent operating in Somalia.

Keeping up incessant pressure was the key, and Bolan was prepared for anything as he proceeded toward the next point on his hit list.

A quarter mile due east of Mogadishu's international airport, Mohammed el Itale kept his home away from home. The neighborhood had been attacked by AC-130 Spectre aircraft early in the UN occupation, but a desultory follow-up allowed Itale to return, rebuild and set up housekeeping again a few months later. While his year-round home was near Buran, far to the north, Itale's economic ties to Mogadishu kept him anchored in the capital, as well.

The Executioner was off to make a phone call.

It was well past sunset when he reached the warlord's neighborhood, a circumstance that helped him with his plan. A white man on these streets was more than obvious; he might become a target simply by the virtue of his race. More to the point, Bolan wanted to perpetuate confusion when Itale heard about the raid.

Before he left the car, he pulled on a ski mask and spent a moment darkening the skin around his eyes with battlefield cosmetics. Lightweight leather gloves completed the disguise, and while it was a superficial effort—useless if his adversaries caught a break and bagged him at the scene—it should be adequate for hit and run in the confusion of a firefight.

Bolan chose his weapons and locked the car behind him, walking half a block to reach the eight-foot wall encircling Itale's second home. The wall was easy, up and over. He hesitated at the top to use his silent whistle, dropping into shadow on the other side when he was satisfied the warlord had no dogs on night patrol.

The human sentries were on duty, though, and Bolan dealt with two of them before he reached the house.

The house was brightly lit, with moving figures visible inside. Itale wasn't home this evening, Bolan knew that going in, nor had he hoped to meet the warlord on his first round of attacks in Mogadishu. There was such a thing as rushing matters, and he knew that taking out a leader prematurely, when the structure of his fighting force was still intact, might not succeed in crippling the larger group.

So, he was beginning with a move designed to shake Itale's confidence, perhaps convince him that a visit to the capital was needed, start the warlord thinking, turn his mind in the direction of familiar enemies.

The C-4 plastique had been measured in advance and fitted with timers. Bolan normally preferred a radio-remote detonator, but he had opted for discretion in an area where bodyguards would almost certainly be packing walkie-talkies, and patrols with two-way radios would make life doubly dangerous for any bomber using too-sophisticated gear.

He placed the charges thirty feet apart, waist-high against the outer wall. Eight fist-size blocks of plastique ticked down to doomsday as he set them and withdrew across the darkened yard—and met the young man with the submachine gun halfway to the outer wall.

He never knew exactly where the youngster came from, had no time to think about it as he saw the sentry start to shout a warning, grappling with the weapon he had slung across one shoulder. Bolan hit him with a forearm to the throat that left him gagging, following with a sharp jab to the head that stretched the guy out on the ground unconscious.

The plastique blew as Bolan reached his car, and he was rolling out of there before the neighborhood responded in a rush. He checked the rearview mirror, spotted flames obscured by trees and drifting smoke, Somalis streaming out into the street to find out who had died, and how.

He didn't know or care how many of Itale's men had been inside the house. For now, it was enough to score a hit against the warlord on his private turf, an insult to his dignity that would demand some physical response.

The war was heating up, and Bolan still had miles to go before he put the second phase in motion.

There was no such thing as too much heat, when you were rattling a larger force. And it was time for him to stoke the fire.

CHAPTER SIX

Buran, Somalia

Mohammed el Itale was a man accustomed to the shifting tides of war. When he was eighteen years of age, his father had been killed in battle with the Cubans, fighting over Ogaden, in eastern Ethiopia. He had been twenty-nine when shaky peace terms closed the book on that dispute, however temporarily. At thirty-two, he had seen the government in Mogadishu close its doors, while civil war erupted in the land. Today, at thirty-six, he was among the strongest, most feared men in all Somalia.

It seemed a miracle of sorts, if you believed in matters spiritual. Unlike so many of his fellow Sunni Muslims, though, Itale recognized that God showed a preference for helping those who helped themselves. And for the past ten years or so, Itale had energetically helped himself to anything and everything within his reach.

Statistics were notoriously unreliable, but his militia had at least six thousand young men under arms. Their number might seem insignificant in a nation of 7.3 million souls—less than one-tenth of one percent—but with their training, modern weapons and Itale's brain behind them, they comprised the single largest native fighting force within Somalia. If the UN forces were removed, it should be relatively simple for

Itale to defeat his enemies and elevate himself to a position of sincere respect.

Of course, his enemies weren't about to take it lying down. They had been fighting, off and on, since early 1991. Itale hadn't been the strongest of his nation's warlords when he started out, but courage and intelligence had served him well. It also didn't hurt that he was absolutely ruthless with his enemies, waging war without quarter, and generous to his friends—or subordinates—in sharing the spoils of victory.

Itale was a man of the people, but he also recognized that charity began at home.

Accustomed as he was to violence, there had been troubling news this day. First, the destruction of his convoy to the west, above Odweina, had been absolutely unexpected. He was stunned to hear that thirty-eight of his soldiers and five expensive vehicles had been destroyed, wiped out, with no apparent clues as to the men responsible.

While he was picking up the pieces and trying to construct a puzzle picture from the shattered fragments, there was more news from the south. His field command post and his private residence had both been raided in the very heart of Mogadishu. Twenty-one were dead when the smoke cleared, and the UN "peacekeepers" were making noise about renewed assaults on his militia if the raids continued.

At the moment, though, Itale was more concerned about learning the identity of his latest assailant. He had the usual list of suspects, beginning with Jouad ben Ganane, but pursuing the obvious could sometimes lead a man far from the truth. He wondered if a faction of the UN occupation force could be involved, attempting to provoke an all-out showdown that would help them sweep Itale and the other war-lords out of Mogadishu, crush them in the country-side.

It wouldn't be that easy when the shooting started, but he put no treachery beyond the Europeans. When the day came—*if* it came—Mohammed el Itale counted on his countrymen to rise and help him fight the blue-eyed devils, crush them underfoot and drive them back into the sea from whence they came. Somalia could become another Vietnam, if the Americans and Europeans weren't very cautious, circumspect in every move they made.

On second thought, he doubted whether any of the officers commanding UN troops in Mogadishu had the courage or initiative to launch a new, covert offensive on their own. Their function was distinctly limited, and they were under constant scrutiny from various reporters—British, French, American, Chinese and Russian.

Thinking of his Chinese allies brought a tired frown to the warlord's face. They wouldn't be amused by recent setbacks, but he didn't think they would abandon him. There had been too much time, material and cash invested in his army for Beijing to pull out on a whim. Their strategy, from Mogadishu to Djibouti, hinged upon Itale and his private army.

No, it wasn't time to panic yet, but he was properly concerned. Whatever happened next, his troops had to be on full alert, prepared for anything.

And he would have to take swift steps to shift himself from a defensive posture to the offense, take control and punish those who dared to challenge his authority.

As soon as he could find out who they were.

If necessary, he would take his list of enemies and kill them all.

Afgo, Somalia

A FEW MILES WEST of Mogadishu, in his rural villa on the Shabell River, Jouad ben Ganane listened carefully while one of his lieutenants filled him in on all the latest news. Eleven dead, so far, and it didn't improve his humor when they told him that Mohammed el Itale's troops had suffered even greater losses in a series of attacks by unknown enemies.

The last thing Ganane wanted, at the moment, was a mystery to solve.

He liked to keep things simple, when he could—and "simple," to Ganane, meant that everything he wanted fell into his hands with minimal effort. No snags or obstacles of any kind to slow him down in his pursuit of wealth and glory.

For a child of peasants, he had come a long way from his village roots, but there was far to go. Ganane wondered sometimes if there could be such a thing as total satisfaction, even when he finally ruled Somalia with a fist of steel. When he was well established in the presidential palace, would he long for new frontiers, new enemies to conquer?

First things first.

Right now, he had eleven soldiers dead in Mogadishu, no idea of who had killed them, and his instinct told him that the worst was yet to come. There had been something close to peace, or its facsimile, in recent weeks, but that was over now.

In normal circumstances, he would blame Itale for the raid and act accordingly, retaliate in force against the rival warlord's men or property. This time, however, someone else was striking at Itale even as Ganane's men were killed. The same assailant, or another? Was it possible for more than one conspiracy to bear fruit overnight?

He knew the answer to that question would be yes. These days, in Mogadishu, no one could be trusted. Guns were everywhere, despite the UN efforts to disarm Somalia's population, and a private quarrel could easily result in bloodshed. On a wider scale, it only took a handful of young toughs to organize a local army and declare war on their neighbors. The example set by men of power like Itale and Ganane served as inspiration for the peasants to reach out and seize a little bit of power for themselves.

It would be foolish, granted, for a peasant band to challenge Ganane, with four thousand troops behind him, but there were fools born every day, and desperation—be it sprung from poverty or any other cause—drove men to foolish risks.

When he thought about it further, though, Ganane wondered if his enemy, Mohammed el Itale, might be responsible for his misfortune after all. It would be relatively simple for Itale to present himself as victim in a string of incidents that he, himself, had set in motion. Sacrifice a few of his subordinates, if necessary, and exaggerate their number in reports to the authorities. Meanwhile, his strikes against Ganane would be blamed on someone else, and the United Nations soldiers would refrain from punishing Itale for his crimes.

It all made sense.

There was a certain risk in jumping to conclusions, but Ganane had been waging war against his fellow countrymen for years now, and he knew the tricks of which his enemies were capable. Some men would sacrifice their families and loved ones in pursuit of profit, gladly, never giving their betrayal so much as a second thought. Ganane drew the line at selling out his relatives, though he had once been forced to execute a cousin for the crime of rape, committed while the cousin was employed on business for Ganane in the southern provinces.

But that was business, and his family had supported the decision. Some acts placed a man beyond the pale...at least, if he was caught. Without a witness, it was something else entirely.

Safe within his rural fortress, Ganane had no fear of an immediate assault upon his person. If the UN wished to reach him, they could always send their aircraft, but Itale had no planes or helicopters that Ganane knew of. He was grounded, and Ganane's spies were stationed on the various approaches to his home at Afgo. Theoretically it was impossible to take him by surprise and trap him in the compound.

Knowing that, and hoping it was true, he turned his thoughts to hitting back. The loss of men and property was one thing, but it paled to nothing in comparison with the potential loss of standing he would suffer should the recent strike go unavenged. If Ganane let himself be publicly insulted, it would be an open invitation to his enemies to trample him and strip him of his hard-earned privileges.

He had some thoughts about the subject of revenge, but he would have to gather more intelligence before he put the hasty plan in action. It was critical for him to learn Itale's whereabouts, make sure he had the target in his sights before he risked a killing shot.

To try and fail would make Ganane look more foolish than he did already. Worse, it would provoke his adversary to a new round of attacks and justify the violence as a kind of self-defense.

All things to those who wait, Ganane told himself. As long as he wasn't required to wait too long.

Jijiga, Ethiopia

IT MIGHT NOT BE the worst day of his life, Fikre Mariam decided, but it would be close. It was well after dark now, and his office still felt like a baker's oven, even with assistance from the ceiling fan. His khaki uniform was dark with perspiration, and he knew that only part of it was traceable directly to the desert heat.

Across the cluttered desk, Raul Rodriguez glared at Mariam with eyes so dark they might be black, if anyone got close enough to see for sure. The Cuban officer was furious, and rightly so, enraged by the destruction of his secret camp and loss of several dozen men. That much was bad enough, but now he came to Mariam, expecting answers and solutions.

They conversed in English, since the Ethiopian lieutenant colonel spoke no Spanish, and Rodriguez couldn't manage Amheric or Tigre. Under other circumstances, Mariam might well have chuckled at the irony of stalwart revolutionary warriors forced to speak a language both of them despised, but this wasn't a time for levity.

"You do not seem to understand the situation," Rodriguez said, leaning forward with his elbows on the desk top, his dark eyes boring into Mariam's. "My forward base has been wiped out! A handful of sur-

vivors, mostly wounded. The equipment and facili-
ties, all gone."

"And the survivors told you nothing?"

They had covered all this ground before, but Mariam could think of nothing else to say.

"They speak of soldiers, white men," Rodriguez
replied. "Not Somalis."

Mariam was puzzled more by the description of the
raiders than by the raid itself. Considering their recent border probes, it came as no surprise that someone from Somalia or Djibouti might retaliate against
the Cuban force in Ethiopia, but white men?

They could rule out the United Nations, for a start.
That august body moved with glacial speed and followed certain rules, preceding every concrete action
with a drawn-out period of hearings, arguments, fact-
finding tours, ballots cast by the assembly. When the
UN moved at all, it normally sent referees to stand
between belligerents and threaten force, reserving
bloodshed as the last resort. A sudden, lethal strike
without the weeks of warning, economic sanctions and
debate would be unheard of.

"Mercenaries?" Mariam was somewhat startled
when he spoke the word aloud. He had been thinking
to himself, the only logical solution to the mystery.

"Perhaps."

Rodriguez didn't sound convinced, but mercenaries—mostly European, with a few Americans thrown
in—had worked the battle zones of Africa for generations. From Algeria, down through the Congo to
Angola and Zimbabwe, paramilitary forces had been
used to topple shaky governments or keep rebellious
blacks in line while their Caucasian masters made a
fortune out of gold and diamonds. Raul Rodriguez

and his Cubans were a variation on the theme, imported from the far side of the world to lend their guns and muscle in a deadly power play. They might not ask for money on the spot, but Mariam had no doubt whatsoever that Havana would present a bill for services when all was said and done.

"It is a logical conclusion," Mariam continued. "Someone in Djibouti, or perhaps in Mogadishu, has decided that the border raids must stop. They hire a band of mercenaries, give them map coordinates and here we are."

"My men are trained professionals," Rodriguez said.

"And so, apparently, were their opponents. It would seem your men were taken by surprise. How many raiders were described?"

Rodriguez shrugged and slumped back in his chair. "The statements are confused. One man believes he saw two strangers, but there were converging lines of fire. They used Kalashnikovs, the old 7.62 mm model. At least one of them had an RPG."

"Russian weapons."

"Yes, for what it's worth."

Both men were well aware that weapons manufactured by the former Soviet Union and its Warsaw Pact allies had been sold throughout the world, sometimes given away free of charge by the KGB in its drive to promote wars of "national liberation." There were millions of Kalashnikov rifles, RPG rocket launchers and other Russian-made weapons in circulation, from Havana to Ho Chi Minh City and all points in between. The hardware was untraceable, reliable in battlefield conditions, and the ammunition was available around the globe.

Which told them nothing.

"If I had to guess," Mariam said, "my strong suspicions fall on the Somalis. It is not beyond their capability to strike a bargain with Djibouti. In the circumstances, forging ties with Mogadishu may appear to be the lesser of two evils."

Glowering across the desk, Rodriguez thought about it and finally shook his head. "I smell Americans," he said at last.

"You Cubans blame America for everything. You're like Iran, that way. The crops fail or it doesn't rain, blame Washington."

"This is no laughing matter!"

"Absolutely not." It was important that he not provoke the Cuban officer unnecessarily, for both their sakes. "I understand the seriousness of the problem, certainly. But I believe we must be logical in our approach to the solution and avoid rash judgments."

"The attack demands a swift response," Rodriguez said.

"An *accurate* response, above all else. It would be worse than useless to strike the wrong target."

"Who, then?" Rodriguez demanded.

Mariam produced a cautious smile. "I have a few ideas on that," he said.

Stony Man Farm, Virginia

EIGHT THOUSAND MILES due west, among the Blue Ridge Mountains of Virginia, anxious eyes and ears were focused on the killing grounds of eastern Africa. Aaron Kurtzman had been monitoring the computer feed that came in via satellite, along with sporadic landline communications from Washington and Langley. They were fairly up to date, as far as he could tell, but it was never good enough for Kurtzman. Anything could happen on the firing line, and "watching" from so great a distance made him feel helpless.

The door whispered behind him, and he half turned, watching Barbara Price as she approached his station. Any stranger would have said she was relaxed, at ease, but Kurtzman knew the truth. She was adept at covering anxiety and getting on with business, but the calm facade didn't suggest a cavalier attitude toward the lives entrusted to her care.

"What's happening?" she asked him, pulling up a chair.

"We've got reports from Mogadishu of a 'serious disturbance' in the suburbs. That's Mohammed el Itale's place. Long story short, somebody blew it up with plastic charges. Only bagged the small-fry, but it sent a message."

"What about the Cubans?"

"Phoenix made it out okay, reporting a successful penetration. We're a trifle short on sources with the Ethiopians, you understand, but it's a safe bet that our buddies from Havana aren't amused."

"Still functional?"

"Oh, sure. We don't have any kind of solid head count on their force in Ethiopia, but one camp won't derail their effort. It's not even close."

"At least our guys are still intact."

"So far."

Regretting it the moment that he spoke, Kurtzman hastened to make amends. "We're cooking, though, if you think about it. Striker has the hard guys out of

Mogadishu wondering about each other, picking sides. Mohammed el Itale won't sit still for somebody remodeling his home away from home. My guess would be, we'll see some fireworks pretty quick."

"What are we getting from the Company?"

"Their man touched base with Striker, handed off a list of targets. We assume he's working off that list right now. They've got a way to keep in touch, if Striker needs him."

"That's a risky business, ratting on the warlords."

Kurtzman nodded. "He's been at it for a while, I understand. There's some concern about exposure, but Grimaldi's taking care of it for Striker. They've got Calvin on the standby, just in case."

"So, what about Djibouti?" Price asked.

"It's coming up. You know our friendly contact there, Hassan Gourad?"

"The army officer. He blew the whistle on this deal, to start with."

"Right. Phoenix Force is dropping in to say hello and find out what he needs, specifically."

"He needs a change of scene," Price stated, sounding grim. "They've got him in a sandwich, any way you slice it. If the Ethiopians don't squeeze him, the Somalis will."

"That's politics."

"That's bullshit. Get the Cubans and the Chinese out of there, and these people might start working on a way to get along."

"Or they might keep on killing one another," Kurtzman pointed out.

"It's their choice, either way. The UN crowd can handle it from there. I hate these power games, Havana and Beijing pretending that they own the world.

Somebody ought to tell them that the cold war's over."

"Is it?"

"Geez, I thought so, anyway."

"I look around," Kurtzman said, "and I see more countries on the map, with different names, but they're still fighting one another, maybe worse than ever. Same old same old, is the way it looks to me."

"Did anybody ever tell you you're a party pooper?"

"I believe it's come up once or twice."

"Well, there you go."

"I'm working on it."

"Sure. You've filled Hal in?"

"It's been about an hour. Nothing worth another phone call in the meantime."

"Sorry. Guess I'm just on edge."

"That makes you human, Barb."

"Don't let it get around."

He smiled at that. "Your secret's safe with me."

"I've got some paperwork to finish, then I'm turning in. You'll buzz me if we get a flash?"

"First thing."

"Okay. I'll see you."

"Bright and early."

"Early, anyway."

The door hissed shut behind her, leaving him alone. He didn't mind the solitary shift; in fact, it gave him time to think. Too much time, maybe, but he liked to look at every problem from a multitude of angles, try to put himself inside an adversary's mind and peer out through the hostile eyes.

It always helped to know a man, before you tried to kill him.

He turned to face the huge map on the wall, eyes focusing on eastern Africa, where seven of his closest friends were facing sudden death in the defense of total strangers, using space-age hardware, fighting for a cause as old as man.

"Stay frosty, guys," he whispered, turning back to the computer.

It was easy, letting down one's guard, but it could be the last mistake a soldier ever made. A few more hours, Kurtzman told himself. Another check, to make sure everything was going well, according to their plan.

There would be time enough for sleep another day.

CHAPTER SEVEN

Djibouti, Djibouti

Hassan Gourad was thankful that his day was coming to an end. No fan of paperwork at any time, he was particularly troubled by the grim, futile routine of logging field reports that proved—at least, in his view—that his country and its people had been violated once again.

The latest incident had been recorded from a border settlement so small it didn't even have a name. Perhaps a dozen families had colonized the patch of desert land, no more than forty miles from the frontier with Ethiopia. On Sunday night, the tiny village had been razed by "unknown persons," forty-seven men, women and children shot or hacked to death in the familiar pattern Hassan Gourad had come to recognize so well.

As usual, there were no tracks to indicate the killers had arrived in motor vehicles, and while Gourad had no surviving witness to describe the helicopters this time, it was obvious to him that he was dealing with the same group of assassins. They flew in from Ethiopia, performed their bloody task, then flew out again.

Simplicity itself.

Almost three weeks had passed since the attack on Juba, and Gourad had given up on hearing from his contact at the U.S. Embassy. They called the man a "cultural attaché," but it was an open secret in Djibouti that he drew his paycheck from the CIA. Small countries were a bit like small towns in that way, with secrets difficult—if not impossible—to keep.

With no response from the Americans, Gourad supposed that he would have to act alone. There was a limit to his capabilities, of course. He had superiors to think of, some preferring to ignore the border raids as long as possible, postponing the inevitable conflict. Others recognized the problem and were all for self-defense—provided that their action didn't lead to open war with Ethiopia.

And then again, there was the problem of Somalia to consider.

Almost from the day of its creation as a sovereign state, Djibouti had been under pressure from its neighbors. Both sides wanted to absorb the tiny nation, either through a referendum or by force, if there appeared to be no other way. Djibouti's army was proportionate to the country it served, and there would be no contest if invaders crossed the border from Somalia or Ethiopia—much less from both at once.

Renunciation of territorial claims was one thing, words on flimsy paper circulated to the media, but Gourad looked first to actions when he judged a man—or country—on its merits. If the pressure from outside hadn't been bad enough, Djibouti also suffered from the sometimes violent rivalry between Afars and Issas, natives who were ethnically related to the Ethiopians and the Somalis, respectively.

Djibouti had its quislings, even now, and that was one more problem for Gourad to deal with as he tried to save his native land from being overrun by enemies. Each time he spoke, Gourad was forced to weigh his words and judge his audience, aware that in a world where life was cheap, the first mistake could be his last.

The first attempt upon his life, in fact, had already been made. Within a few days of the Juba massacre, while he was working on the final draft of his report, Gourad had come home to discover prowlers in his house. One of the men immediately fled; the other turned on him with a dagger, forcing Gourad to use the pistol he had never fired in anger. When he searched the body afterward, there had been money in the prowler's pocket, but he carried no ID. His name was still unknown and doubtless would remain so, but his mission was apparent: with his helper, he had rifled Gourad's private papers, attempting to open a small fireproof safe in his den.

In search of what?

Gourad was certain his assailants had been looking for whatever documents or evidence he had collected that would demonstrate aggressive plans by either of Djibouti's neighbors. Failing to discover and destroy that evidence, if it existed, they would settle for destruction of the man himself.

Hassan Gourad was, therefore, on his guard as he departed from his office in the dark of night. It was a short walk to his car, a military policeman guarding the small parking lot against intruders. Even so, he kept a firm hand on his holstered pistol as he checked his vehicle—back seat, the floor—before he slid behind the wheel. He could have checked for bombs, as well, but it seemed unlikely that intruders would have had the time to plant a charge and slip away unseen.

In fact, the car didn't explode when he turned the key. He left the parking lot, turned right and made his way through narrow streets toward home. The headlights in his rearview mirror caused him no alarm until the second left-hand turn, when they were still behind him, hanging back, but definitely following.

Should he turn back and seek the safety of his office, or lead the bastards home and face them there?

Before he could decide, his adversaries made the choice on his behalf. A second car pulled out in front of him, exploding from an alley on his left, and tried to block the intersection up ahead. Instead of braking, though, Gourad stamped down on the accelerator, swung the wheel hard left, swerved around the plug car, bounced across the curb and swung back onto pavement when his adversaries were behind him.

Now, the only trick would be escaping with his life.

"WHERE IN BLOODY HELL did *they* come from?" McCarter blurted, reaching for the gearshift as a car came out of nowhere, heading off Hassan Gourad.

"It's an ambush!" Gary Manning drew his 9 mm Browning BDM semiauto pistol as he spoke, leaned forward in the shotgun seat and cranked down his window.

"He's running!"

"Quick, don't lose him!"

"Call it in."

The driver of the plug car made a swift recovery, and he was closer to their quarry than McCarter. Surging forward in a tight left turn, the plug became a hot pursuit, McCarter bringing up the rear. He saw a muzzle-flash and heard the first report of gunfire, tattered on the rushing wind.

Beside him, Manning had the walkie-talkie in his hand, a flash to Katz and Encizo, who were waiting for Gourad at home. The plan had been to follow him, make sure he got home safely, introduce themselves and have a little chat, but it was suddenly unraveling. The shooters had a different plan in mind, and if they scored a lucky hit at this speed, Phoenix Force wouldn't be making any small talk with Gourad.

The terse report took all of six or seven seconds. By that time, McCarter had reduced his adversary's lead by half, accelerating in pursuit. He left his side arm in its holster for the moment, concentrating on the road, the vehicles in front of him.

Another burst was fired at Gourad, then the driver of the chase car noticed that he had a tail. It all went down at once, Gourad's car screeching through a right-hand turn at speed, the gunners following, while one of them reacted to the driver's warning and unleashed a burst at Manning and McCarter.

"Shit!"

The bullets missed, except for one that scored his starboard fender, and McCarter made the turn on smoking tires. A muttered curse from Manning was immediately followed by a shot, as the Canadian responded to their enemies.

"We'll have the local gendarmes on our ass in no time," McCarter said.

"One problem at a time," Manning snapped, squeezing off another shot.

In front of them, the chase car swerved, responding to the impact of the bullet on the trunk.

"You might try aiming higher," McCarter suggested.

"Thanks for that. Who taught you how to drive?"

"We're still behind them, aren't we?"

"Too damned far behind them, if you ask me."

"Right!"

McCarter stood on the accelerator, closing the gap. With less than thirty feet between his own front bumper and the chase car, he could make out several gunmen in the vehicle, their silhouettes etched by his headlights.

Manning tried a third shot, drilling a dime-size hole in the rear window of their adversaries' car. The driver swerved again, but kept on going. When he straightened out his course, McCarter had a glimpse of shooters leaning out on both sides of the car, their submachine guns angling to the rear.

"Hang on!"

He swerved before they opened fire, a hard jog to the left that put the starboard gunner out of line and made him waste his bullets. As for their assailant on the left, he tried to compensate, scoring several hits on Manning's side, but nothing critical. The tall Canadian returned fire, three rounds snapping from his BDM so rapidly they seemed to merge as one. McCarter saw the gunman jerk and drop his weapon, limp arms dangling from the window for a bit before his comrades dragged him back inside.

"Scratch one," Manning said.

"Better."

McCarter swung the car back into line behind their enemies. Up front, Gourad squealed through another turn and almost lost it, drifting toward the right-hand curb before he fought the wheel under control. His car had taken several hits, but he was in control—so far.

Another backward blast of automatic fire exploded from the chase car, two rounds scoring hits on metal as McCarter swerved aside.

"We need to wrap this up," Manning said.

"Tell me something I don't know."

"Try running up the driver's side."

"Okay, your call."

McCarter made the move without a second thought, accelerating, swinging wide around the chase car. It could blow up in their faces, granted, but he trusted Manning's instinct, and they needed to prevent the enemy from scoring on Gourad, if possible.

It might not be the best plan, but it was the only chance they had.

Mogadishu, Somalia

AMRITA SHEBELE DISLIKED working late, but she had grown accustomed to long hours in the two years since her husband's death. She made a point of stopping to correct herself: the two years since his murder. He had been a casualty of the chaotic situation in Somalia, gunned down on the street one night as he was coming home from work, and so Amrita had been left alone to make her way or starve.

It wasn't quite that bad, of course. Not yet. She had her brother's help, and Siad had been generous, although it troubled her from time to time, not knowing where his money came from. When she asked, he simply smiled and spoke in general terms, this job or that, but it was always vague and difficult to follow.

She suspected he was stealing, possibly involved in some black-market business, but Amrita couldn't fault him as she might have done in days gone by. Her husband's murder had awakened her to the realities of life and death in Mogadishu, more than anything that she had witnessed since the onset of the civil war.

There had been other deaths, of course, a friend or two among the victims, but she always managed to pretend that things were getting back to normal. When the UN came, Amrita told herself that it would all be fine, her nation's problems taken care of by the Europeans and Americans.

But she was wrong.

Amrita couldn't say that things had actually gotten worse in Mogadishu since the UN troops arrived, but it felt that way sometimes, watching the most powerful nations on earth chase their tails in pursuit of peasant warlords. It struck her as incredible that the United States and Britain, with their satellite technology and "smart" bombs, couldn't seem to locate men who posed in public for photographers and broadcast weekly interviews on CNN. With so much hardware and so many troops, they couldn't even save her husband's life.

It should have been a relatively simple thing, she told herself: protect one man who never harmed a living soul. His great transgression had been balking at demands from the extortionists who served Mohammed el Itale, looting cash from local businesses. Her husband had refused to share his meager earnings with the warlord, even when the windows of his shop were broken and he was assaulted on the street. A stubborn man, and proud, he stood his ground—until the afternoon when he was cut down in a hail of bullets, wounded thirteen times.

Amrita kept the small shop open, thankful for the first time that they had no children. When Mohammed el Itale sent his men to ask for money, she paid up. It left her short each week, but that was where Siad came in, assisting her with "loans" Amrita knew that she wouldn't be able to repay.

And life went on, the Mogadishu way.

Of late, her brother had been acting strange. He dropped a cryptic hint from time to time, suggesting he had found "a mission" that would soon resolve the bloody chaos in their native land. Big talk had always been a trademark of Siad's, and when she heard him babbling on, Amrita took it with a grain of salt. Still, there was decent money coming in from somewhere, and she had begun to worry that Siad had joined one of the warlords, seeking his place in the long civil war.

He might be killed, and while it worried her no end, Amrita knew she couldn't tell him how to live his life—or how to waste it.

Amrita felt no danger for herself, in terms of being targeted for violence. She knew that every resident of Mogadishu was potentially a victim, but she didn't dwell on danger as a fact of life. Sometimes, she thought that death would be a blessing, but she always caught herself before the train of morbid logic went too far. It would have grieved her husband to observe her in that mood, and she felt guilty for dishonoring his memory. It was bad enough that she paid off his killers to leave her alone, without Amrita negating his sacrifice entirely, throwing her own life away.

She was a short two blocks from home, the house she shared with brother Siad, when she heard the car behind her. It wasn't unusual, of course, to find a car on Mogadishu's streets, though the majority of residents couldn't afford such transport. Amrita wasn't startled by the presence of a car, per se, but rather by the way it seemed to come from nowhere, creeping up behind her.

Running without lights.

She glanced back, saw one of the doors just opening, a stranger climbing out. It was enough. She bolted, running for the house, whatever small degree of safety it might offer, but the driver was too quick. He pulled ahead of her and swung in to block her path with one wheel on the curb.

Amrita stopped, heard footsteps coming up behind her, turned and ran across the street. She had no destination in mind, no clear idea of who would dare to help her, but she had to get away. Whoever these men were, they clearly meant her harm. She had no choice but to escape, if that were possible.

No street lamp here to light her way.

The darkness swallowed her alive.

IT WAS A WAITING GAME, like so much else, and Calvin James was trying to relax. The residential neighborhood was fairly quiet, children pulled in off the streets at nightfall, parents busy with their evening meals and getting ready for the next day's work. Unlike the States, there was a limited amount of public entertainment, mostly priced beyond the budget of the average working man or woman. Homes along the street were small, but relatively clean and well maintained.

His job was waiting, staking out the house until his contact—Siad Samatar—came home. James didn't have a clue on where to find the young man, otherwise, and Katz had been specific with his order: wait it out. When Samatar showed up, James had some questions for him, matters that had come up since his meet with Striker earlier that day.

James knew the guy spoke English, but he had been brushing up on Arabic and some selected phrases of Somali, just in case. You never knew when someone would come up and ask you for the time or want to know why you were loitering around their neighborhood all night.

In fact, he tried to make himself as inconspicuous as possible. He was dressed like a native, more or less, and hung out in the shadows, waiting for Samatar to show his face. For all James knew, the guy could be out getting laid, might never make it home at all, but he would have to take the chance. If anything went wrong...

James wore a Browning automatic underneath his left arm, covered by a lightweight jacket, with an Uzi submachine gun on his right, in swivel leather. If he needed more than that, the former Navy SEAL decided, it would damn well be a hopeless case.

A sound of footsteps brought his mind to full attention. James saw a woman coming down the street, in his direction, moving with determined strides, no special hurry. In the darkness, he couldn't have said if she was young or old, with any certainty, although her stride and bearing spoke to him of youth. Mature enough to be out on her own at night, with no male escort. That was curious, but it was still a normal Mogadishu street scene, more or less.

Until the car came into view.

A dark sedan, no lights, was obviously following the woman, keeping pace. As James watched, from two blocks distant, the woman appeared to notice for the first time that she had observers on her tail. The car stopped short, a man stepped out, and the Phoenix Force warrior saw the woman break into a run, proceeding in his general direction.

Instantly the dark sedan surged forward and swung across her path to cut the woman off. Another man hopped out, but she was faster, veering left across the street, and running for her life.

James had a choice to make. He was supposed to wait for Siad Samatar, but he couldn't stand by and see a woman kidnapped while he took no action. One choice jeopardized his mission, but the other wouldn't let him sleep at night.

"Well, shit!"

The car was moving by the time James broke from cover. Running like an athlete, the young woman had already put some ground between herself and her pursuers, racing up a narrow side street. Two men followed her on foot, and James spotted two more in the car, a four-man team dispatched to grab one woman off the sidewalk.

In his hometown of Chicago, James would have guessed that he was looking at a would-be gang rape. On the streets of Mogadishu, where the average criminal wouldn't have access to a car, he had to reconsider.

Who had vehicles and made a business out of violence?

The warlords.

James drew the Browning autoloader as he ran. The Uzi slapped against his ribs, reminding him that he had extra firepower available, but it could wait. He didn't want to turn the quiet neighborhood into a shooting gallery if there was any other way to help the woman out. Her adversaries hadn't fired a shot, so far, and James was content to let it stay that way.

Four men against one SEAL.

He calculated that the odds were on his side.

The car was something else, though. No man living had the speed or the tenacity on foot to match a motor vehicle. The slender woman didn't stand a chance of shaking her pursuers by speed alone, and James didn't have a prayer of overtaking the sedan unless the driver slowed it.

As if in answer to his silent thoughts, the woman changed her course again, dodged down a narrow alley on her right. The car stopped short, its driver trying to negotiate the turn, but there was insufficient clearance for his vehicle to pass.

James smiled, imagining the furious reaction as the driver sped away and took the next street on his right, a race around the block to head off his quarry. The runners, meanwhile, disappeared into the alley, smelling victory, a chance to catch their prey in darkness, free of witnesses.

They still hadn't observed James approaching from behind, closing fast. He reached the alley almost on their heels, stood poised outside the entrance for a moment, listening. One of them shouted something to the woman, probably a warning or command to halt. James wasn't sure, nor did he care to waste time on translations at the moment.

Moving in a combat crouch, he slipped into the shadows, homing on the sound of voices while he waited for his vision to adapt. The woman was at bay now, cornered. The impact of an open palm on flesh reverberated in the alley like a crack of pistol fire.

James cocked his Browning as he went to join the party.

It was time to play.

CHAPTER EIGHT

Djibouti

The second chase car was a rude surprise. McCarter had the hammer down, and Manning had his Browning steady on the hostile driver's profile, when their vehicle was jolted by a sudden impact from behind. Too late to stop his finger taking up the trigger slack, and Manning lost it, saw his bullet drill the chase car's wind wing and take out a fist-size portion of the windshield.

"God damn!"

The new arrival came in running dark, perhaps responding to a radio alarm from someone in the first car following Gourad. Now Manning and McCarter were the filling in a deadly sandwich, ducking as a burst of automatic fire ripped through their trunk and fenders.

"Bloody hell!"

"Keep going!" the Canadian demanded. "I can take him!"

Short of giving up the chase and veering off to fight the second team of gunners while Gourad was sacrificed, McCarter had no choice. He stood on the accelerator, making up the ground that he had lost.

"Make sure you get it right this time," the Briton snapped.

"I've got it covered."

Manning understood the risk that he was taking, but he saw no ready options. They could get killed doing nothing, in the present situation, and for no result. At least this way they had a fighting chance.

He waited for the final instant, sitting with his shoulders hunched, until they pulled even with the leading chase car. Any second . . .

Now!

The move owed more to instinct than to conscious strategy. His arm snaked out, the Browning drawn to target acquisition, like a piece of steel responding to a magnet's pull. He barely glimpsed the driver's profile in his sights before he squeezed off three quick rounds and saw the lean, dark face explode in splashing crimson.

"Bump him!"

Manning yanked his arm back as McCarter swung hard right and rammed the chase car. Driverless, it was a captive of momentum, veering out of line and plowing across the curb in the direction of a small green house. Dismissing it at once from his consideration, Manning turned and made the awkward scramble from his own seat to the rear, prepared to bring the second carload of their adversaries under fire.

"You'll need more than the pistol," McCarter commented.

"Way ahead of you."

He bent and rummaged in the duffel bag behind the driver's seat, producing an H & K MP-5 A-3 submachine gun that featured a metal folding stock. Its magazine held thirty rounds of 9 mm Parabellum ammunition, which would last about two seconds at the little buzzgun's cyclic rate of some 800 rounds per minute. With a skillful touch, a gunner could improve on that and make the ammo last a little longer, but the duffel also held a stash of extra magazines.

If Manning couldn't stop the second chase car with the instruments at hand, they would be well and truly in an untenable position.

Another blast of automatic fire erupted from the dark sedan behind them, and the headlights suddenly blazed on, their high beams forcing the Canadian to squint. He heard the bodywork around him taking hits, and pebbled safety glass from the imploded window felt like gravel underneath his knees, as he prepared to answer the incoming fire.

He muffed the first burst, even so, a little high and wide. Instead of cursing bitter luck or railing at McCarter for his driving, Manning braced himself and tried again. His next rounds blew the starboard headlight, gouging divots on the hood, and cracked the windshield in between the driver and his shotgun rider.

Better.

Manning saw the chase car falter, swerving left and right to spoil his aim. He let the driver play a little, knowing the evasive tactics would do more to keep their enemies from firing than it did to hamper Manning. Even now, one of the gunners tried a burst and lost it on the tracking, wasted bullets screaming off into the night.

For his part, Manning held the MP-5 A-3 rock steady, waiting for the other vehicle to swing across his line of fire. He had the timing down, could see it coming like a cyclops with its one great, slowing eye. Make sure to lead, so there were bullets swarming in on target when the vehicle arrived, instead of chasing after it as it pulled away. He heard them strike, saw sparks on impact, but the car kept coming, boring in, relentless.

"Shoot the bloody radiator!"

"Watch the bloody road!" Manning snapped, but he recognized a piece of good advice when it was offered.

Rising slightly in his seat, he dropped his sights a bit and waited, counting down. The magazine was almost empty, had to be, but if he had enough rounds left...

The car swung back into his line of fire, and Manning held down the trigger, unloading everything he had. The hood blew back and masked the windshield, smoke or steam erupting from the engine as he scored a fatal hit.

"That does it!" Manning shouted over rushing wind, as the disabled chase car swung aside and hobbled to the curb.

"Not quite," McCarter warned him.

"Damnit!"

Coming up behind them, gaining speed, was another vehicle, gunners leaning from the windows, laying down a screen of automatic fire. How many guns? At least two, but he couldn't say for sure.

The one thing Manning knew, beyond a shadow of a doubt, was that the enemy had more tricks up his sleeve than Phoenix Force had bargained for. If they weren't extremely careful in the next few moments, it could be enough to win the game.

And that would mean disaster, since their lives were riding on the line.

Mogadishu, Somalia

IT WAS AS BLACK as pitch inside the alley, but James's eyes adjusted swiftly from the somewhat "lighter" darkness of the street, as he proceeded toward his target, huddled figures thirty yards from where he entered. He had to take it easy, dodging cans and bottles, any other bits of refuse that would make a telltale noise if he went blundering along. It seemed to take forever, and he heard another slap, the woman's cry of pain, when he was still too far away to intervene.

James didn't have a clue what they were saying, but he knew that it was nothing from the simple phrase book he had studied for emergencies. This was an interrogation, more or less, and he had closed the gap to thirty feet before the sound of ripping cloth told him the situation might be getting out of hand.

His mind flashed back to its original impression of a random crime in progress. Rape? He grimaced, knowing that it didn't matter. He wouldn't permit a woman to be beaten and abused while he stood by and watched—or listened—like a voyeur at a keyhole. If he missed his contact as a consequence of going on a mercy mission, he would simply have to make it up somehow.

Another ripping sound. The woman sobbed, struck out at one of her attackers, but the men were laughing as they dodged her futile blows. One of them punched her, snapping out a name James recognized.

Siad.

He couldn't risk a shot, despite the closing distance, with the goons so close he was afraid of taking down the woman by mistake. A few more yards was all he needed, edging in, his opposition still oblivious to a fourth party on the scene.

James had the Browning's hammer down, prepared to fire on double-action when the time came, but now he found a new use for the pistol, coming up behind the larger of his targets. The Phoenix Force warrior put his weight behind the swing, his side arm slamming home behind the goon's right ear with force enough to stagger him and drop him to all fours. He wasn't out, exactly, but he had a killer headache coming ... if he lived.

The second goon smelled trouble and released the woman, backing off to face his unknown adversary. James let him see the pistol, aiming at his face, and used one of the phrases in Somali he had memorized.

"Hands up!"

Their conversation would be strictly limited from that point on, but James had no intent of launching a debate. They needed time to slip away, and after that, he would be playing it by ear.

The woman spoiled it for him, bolting toward the far end of the alley, past her captor. Headlights flared in that direction, telling James the chase car had arrived, but he didn't have time to think about it at the moment.

As the woman passed the second goon, a scrabbling noise on James's left alerted him to danger. Target number one was struggling to his feet and coming back for more, as if he thought he were invincible.

It all came down to choices, knowing that the wait for Siad Samatar was blown, whatever happened, but he still might have a chance to save it with the woman, if she didn't vanish in the night or get herself shot down emerging from the alley. In the meantime, he was out of time and out of patience with the two Somali sluggers.

James hesitated for perhaps a second and a half before he shot the goon who had his hands up. It was a quick one-two to the shoulder and leg, effectively taking him out of the play.

Then he turned to meet the second goon before he closed the gap, his Browning in the big guy's face. His adversary had a knife now, long and sharp, but he was having second thoughts about the pistol, glancing at his prostrate friend and making up his mind.

Too late.

James shot him in the forehead, watched him topple over backward in a pile of garbage.

A blast of automatic weapons' fire ripped through the alley, and James dropped prone on instinct, cursing as he understood what it had to mean. The woman, dammit! He had messed around too long and lost her. She was dead now, and his last best hope of finding Samatar had gone down with her.

Wait.

If she was dead, then who was running toward him, sobbing breathlessly and ducking bullets as the submachine gun spoke again? James saw her coming and snaked a hand out. He caught her by the ankle and brought her down beside him, hissing in Somali, ''Quiet! I'm a friend.''

At least he hoped that he was saying what he meant to say, no time for checking out the phrase book, which was in the glove compartment of his car. Right now, survival was the top priority, and that meant clearing out before the gunner found his range.

''Come on!'' James snapped, already moving as he dragged the woman to her feet and pulled her close behind him, running back in the direction he had come from.

Running for his life.

Djibouti

IT WAS THE FIRST CAR, coming back for more. McCarter recognized the shattered, blood-smeared windshield in his rearview mirror, reckoning that they had shoved the lifeless driver out and given someone else the wheel. There were at least two soldiers still alive in the sedan, one driving, while his partner leaned out on the other side and chased them with short bursts of submachine-gun fire.

Up ahead of them Gourad was losing steam. His left rear tire was wallowing, perhaps a slow leak from a bullet hit or pure bad luck. It slowed him, but he still had a chance to run, with Manning and McCarter blocking for him, holding back the chase car.

It was all the more surprising, therefore, when he stopped dead in the middle of the street.

McCarter slammed on his brakes, spoiling Manning's aim. Their bullet-punctured vehicle slid sideways, rubber smoking, rocking to a halt some twenty feet from where Gourad's sedan had stalled. There was no sign of their intended target in the darkness, and McCarter couldn't tell if he had fled, or if his panic had him hunched down in the car, waiting to see what happened next.

The chase car's driver saved it with a skid that laid down thirty feet of rubber on the pavement, swerving toward the left-hand curb. His shooter fired another burst before they both unloaded on the driver's side. A moment later, the wheelman had his pistol working, pegging shots across the hood at Manning and McCarter.

Sliding out of the sedan on hands and knees, the Briton reached back for the duffel bag as Manning bailed out with his subgun. McCarter didn't mind the odds, considered them no worse than even, but he had two problems preying on his mind.

The first was time, and the awareness that they might not have much left before the UN troops or someone else arrived to intervene. It helped a bit that most Somalis didn't own a telephone, but gunfire blazing in the streets was all the general alarm required, a fair direction finder for the cavalry when it came riding in.

The second problem was Hassan Gourad himself. For all McCarter knew, they had already lost him, vanished in the general confusion of the past few moments. On the other hand, he could be wounded, even dying, which would readily explain his sudden stop. In either case, they would have sacrificed a vital contact in Djibouti—possibly their only contact, if the truth were told.

"We need to wrap this up," the Briton told his partner.

"I'm with you. Grenade?"

"Grenade."

McCarter reached inside the duffel and came out with a pair of frag grenades. He handed one to Manning, kept the other for himself and pulled the safety pin. Five seconds, more or less, once he released the spoon and let it fly.

"On three."

"Right."

Manning had his arm cocked, ready for the pitch, McCarter counting down the doomsday numbers. When he got to "three," they both rose and tossed their lethal eggs in the direction of the chase car, bracketing their enemies.

McCarter's grenade struck the roof of the sedan and broke to the left, rolling across the trunk and dropping out of sight a heartbeat before Manning's bomb struck the hood. They blew together, not a blink between them, smothering a ragged scream.

One down and out, and number two erupted from cover as if he were shot from a cannon, slamming into pavement in an awkward shoulder roll. He kept a firm grip on his submachine gun, somehow, and he came up firing. His aim was off, disoriented by the shock wave that had pitched him twenty feet beyond ground zero.

Manning hit him with a short burst to the chest that punched the gunner backward, down and out. His heels drummed on the pavement for an instant, thrashing in his death throes, but it passed, and he lay still. They kept the chase car covered for another moment, just in case, but there was no more opposition from that quarter.

Turning toward Gourad's sedan, they were advancing when a voice called out to them. A warning, by the sound of it, although McCarter didn't speak the language. Answering in English was the best that he could do.

"We're friends," he said, and hoped it sounded like he meant it.

There was hesitation on Gourad's part, waiting for a moment to collect his thoughts before he shouted back, "How do I know that?"

"Take a look around," McCarter said. "We saved your bacon. If we meant to harm you, these blokes would have done all right without our help."

Another fifteen seconds ticked away before Gourad stood, a pistol in his hands. He came to meet them, moving cautiously. "You followed me," he said, a note of accusation in his voice.

"That's right, and it's a bloody good thing that we did," McCarter told him. "You'd be dead right now, if we were bashful types."

Gourad considered that and tucked his pistol out of sight. "What now?" he asked.

"First thing," Manning said, "I suggest we get the hell away from here. It won't be long before we have unwelcome company."

Mogadishu

RUNNING with his shoulders hunched, in preparation for the bullet that would knock him sprawling, James pulled the woman after him. He ran a zigzag pattern in the narrow alley, breathing rancid odors when his feet sank into piles of rotting garbage, almost slipping several times. Momentum kept him upright, that and knowing what would happen to them if he lost it.

It was incredible that they hadn't been tagged already, in the circumstances. Granted that the gunner couldn't see them clearly, if at all, but they were running down the middle of a narrow shooting gallery, as much at risk from ricochets as any well-aimed bullets.

James heard running footsteps on the alley's gravel pavement. From the sound of it, at least one gunner was pursuing them and trying to improve his odds.

With all this shooting, it was obvious they no longer cared about the woman as a hostage.

He had no good reason to believe the woman spoke or understood his language, but he had to take the chance. If he didn't do something quickly, they were dead.

"Get down!" he ordered, stopping short and suiting words to action as he pulled her down beside him. For a heartbeat, he was worried that she might jump up and try to run, but she made no attempt to flee. Her new cooperation gave him time to whip the Uzi from underneath his jacket, flick off the safety and find his target racing toward them in the dark.

One man, apparently reloading as he came.

James hit him with a rising burst that stitched a line of holes between his crotch and collarbone. Explosive impact swept the gunner off his feet and dumped him on his backside, writhing for a moment in the scattered rubbish, finally going limp.

"Come on!"

As it had worked the first time, so it worked again. James couldn't tell if his reluctant partner understood him, or if she was simply mimicking his actions, but it made no difference at the moment. Breaking for the alley's nearest exit, James and the lady almost reached the street before the chase car cut them off.

James shoved the woman to his left and sidestepped in the opposite direction, flattening against the grimy wall as muzzle-flashes started winking from the car in rapid fire. From where he stood, James couldn't tell if he was dealing with the solitary driver or a group of men, but he assumed the worst and came out fighting.

At the moment, any other course of action seemed like suicide.

Nine or ten rounds had been fired from the Uzi's magazine, which left him twenty, plus another fourteen in the Browning BDM, before he had to step back and reload. The car was less than thirty feet away, a relatively easy shot, except when you were under fire.

Consider it a challenge.

Firing from the shoulder, James made his break directly toward the chase car, knowing it was perilous, still hoping he could pull it off. There was a natural reaction, when an automatic weapon went off almost in your face, to cringe. With any luck at all, it just might spoil the driver's aim and buy some vital time.

Two men, he saw that now, but it was too late for rethinking on his plan. The Phoenix Force commando held the trigger down and gave them everything he had, the gunner's head exploding, spewing crimson. The driver tried to cut and run but stalled his engine instead.

That blunder cost him everything.

The last four rounds from the Uzi nailed the driver in his seat and canceled any threat from that direction. Checking out the car, James verified that it was empty, turning back to face the alley and the woman, half expecting to find that she had fled.

But she was standing there and watching James, wide-eyed, as he pulled the empty magazine, replaced it, and tucked the Uzi out of sight beneath his jacket. They were absolutely out of time, but he would have to find some method of communicating with her, and he had to do it now.

She solved the problem for him, stepping forward as she spoke to him in English.

"Who are you?" she asked. "Why have you saved my life?"

CHAPTER NINE

Mogadishu

At their safehouse in the suburbs, Bolan sipped a cup of strong black coffee, facing Jack Grimaldi across the table, a pair of maps spread out between them. One depicted Mogadishu, while the other was a topographical depiction of Somalia.

"Nothing yet," Grimaldi said, "but what the hell, it's early."

"Getting later all the time."

Thus far, there had been no reaction to his raids from rival warlords in the capital. It didn't mean his efforts had been wasted, but he gave them points for self-control. Some more heat might be needed to produce desired results, but he was looking in a new direction at the moment, shifting gears.

"You want to make a few more stops before we go?" Grimaldi sounded dubious.

The Executioner considered it and shook his head. "Not now. Let's think about Serenli."

"Right." Grimaldi placed a finger on the topographic map. "Two hundred miles due west, on the Giuba River, opposite Bardera. That's the west bank. Say another hundred miles to Kenya, on the west. About one-fifty north along the river, you're in Ethiopia."

"Strategic," Bolan said.

"And then some. Good for border raids *and* hasty getaways."

"It's nowhere near Djibouti, though."

"So much the better," Grimaldi responded, playing straight man. "They can drill out in the boonies, night and day, then go north for some action when they feel the need. If anybody in Djibouti felt like hitting back, they couldn't make the stretch."

"It wouldn't be that far from Ethiopia," Bolan said.

"But the Ethiopians would have to risk a major incident with Mogadishu if they played that way. Anyway, it stands to reason that our marks have spotters out. A decent warning, they can slip across the border into Kenya just like that. Hang out until the heat dies down, or find themselves another playground."

"I wish we had a head count," Bolan said.

"The best thing we could do," Grimaldi answered, "is to wait for Phoenix, get some backup."

Bolan shook his head. "They're busy. I don't want to put it off."

"Your call."

"How long have these guys been in country?" the Executioner asked.

"Best estimate from Stony Man is going on two years. That's the command staff, now. Beijing restricts their team to ten or fifteen, assigned for training and support. The rest will be Somalis."

"Fair enough."

The CIA had filed reports on the Serenli training camp, with satellite photography and an evaluation that included Chinese officers on staff. The photos showed a fairly standard installation: firing ranges, hand-to-hand instruction, an elaborate course of obstacles. The graduates would have specific martial skills drummed into them, but that was only part of what it took to make a soldier.

There was also heart, and Bolan was prepared to test that element among his enemies.

In Vietnam and afterward, the Executioner had known some soldiers—and some cops—who had the training, skills and nerve to stand out in their chosen specialties, but some of them lacked heart, and it made all the difference in the world. Without that extra *something,* they were cold and brutal, looking out for number one to the exclusion of their comrades, the civilians they were sworn to protect. They ran amok, sometimes, but they were rarely brave, by any common definition of the word. When things went wrong, the would-be warriors mostly broke and ran...or else, they died.

Of course, there were exceptions to the rules, and one would be enough to trash his plans for good. A coward could get lucky, for that matter, when the heat was on and everyone was firing like a maniac at nothing in particular.

You couldn't count on luck, but it was something else to weigh the odds by means of preparation, toss in the advantage of surprise. Sometimes a soldier made his own luck as he went along.

"When do you want to leave?" Grimaldi asked.

"How's midnight sound?"

"Suits me."

Their chopper was secure in the U.S. diplomatic compound, under military guard. The watchmen didn't know who it belonged to, and they didn't care. A part of putting on the uniform was taking orders and performing on command. The bottom line: it was the only place in Mogadishu where the helicopter would be safe from tampering or confiscation by the UN forces or their enemies.

Three hours yet, before departure time.

"I think I'll catch a nap," Bolan said, wondering if sleep was even possible. "I'm setting the alarm, but you can call me at a quarter past eleven, if I'm not already up."

"Will do."

The tiny bedroom could have used an airing, but the sheets were clean, and Bolan didn't even mind the sagging mattress. If he had to choose, it still beat sleeping on the ground.

Fatigue surprised him, carried him away within a few short moments after he lay down, but it wasn't a restful sleep. Dark, bloody visions waited for him on the other side...and ghosts. Some were familiar to him at a glance, while others had no faces yet.

Still dreaming, Bolan shared his twilight hours with the dead of missions past and missions yet to be.

SAMATAR SMELLED TROUBLE when he turned the corner, moving toward his house. It wasn't an impression or a feeling, but a literal aroma: gunsmoke hanging in the air like incense offered to the god of battle. Someone had been firing in the street, or somewhere close at hand. They left an odor that reminded him of fireworks in the old days, when the city still had something left to celebrate.

He hesitated on the corner, saw his neighbors watching soldiers do their work—a UN team, with automatic weapons, sky-blue helmets. They had floodlights mounted on their armored vehicles, most of them focused on a car parked two blocks past his house. They had the car surrounded, soldiers bending down to peer inside, while others came and went from the adjacent alley.

Trouble.

Death.

It had been several hours since soldiers visited the neighborhood, and that had been a simple drive-through, nothing special. Every now and then, they felt required to make a show of force, but this was different. Something had gone seriously wrong.

He crossed the street and walked directly to his house. No one approached him, and the soldiers were too far away to notice, standing by their vehicles and covering the neighborhood at large. The house was dark, the front door locked. He used his key and went inside, calling to Amrita as he went from room to room.

No answer.

On his second pass, Samatar checked every room in turn for signs of physical disturbance. He was no detective, but it didn't seem that anyone had broken in while he was gone. There were no signs of struggle, nothing to suggest Amrita had been taken out by force. Still, she was gone, and it was well past closing for the shop that she had managed since her husband's death. She always came straight home, a short ten-minute walk, no detours or stops along the way.

Where was she?

Back outside, he scanned the groups of neighbors, looking for his sister. She was nowhere to be seen, and he felt the apprehension building in his chest, a physical sensation, as if his heart and lungs were on the verge of bursting. He was conscious of the pistol, heavy in his belt, but it was useless at the moment, more deadweight to slow him down.

The soldiers were removing bodies from the car now, dead men stretched out on the pavement. It seemed foolish to believe their presence and the disappearance of his sister were coincidental happenings, but how could he relate the two? If someone had discovered his betrayal of the warlords, if they came for him and found Amrita, how would that explain the shooting? She didn't possess a gun, much less the skill to use one. It was laughable to think that she would get the better of a trained assassin, much less two.

More soldiers were emerging from the alley now, and Samatar saw that they were carrying another body. By the time they finished, four dead men were lined up in the street beside the car. He couldn't see their faces, but it made no difference. There had never been a shortage of prospective soldiers for the several private armies haunting Mogadishu, and he had no good reason to believe that he would recognize these gunmen if he stared at them all night.

He had to find Amrita now, but where should he begin?

A lifetime spent in Mogadishu had conditioned Samatar to think of it as home, but now the city seemed immense and alien, a place where he could lose himself and everything he cared for in the time it took to walk around the block. Amrita could be any-where—or nowhere. If one of the warlords had abducted her, and she was still alive, Samatar knew that she might have been delivered to some point outside the city.

Where?

He didn't have a clue.

If evil had befallen her—and he could find no other ready explanation in his heart—the Somali knew it would be his fault. He should have kept his mouth shut, steered clear of the CIA, instead of acting like a cloak-and-dagger hero. There was every chance that bullets meant for him had found his sister, and the only hope he had, ironically, lay in the fact that she wasn't sprawled out in the house or on the street.

Suppose the gunners had come looking for him and found Amrita in his place. What then? Somebody else had found *them,* dealt with them as they were used to handling others, swift and sure. A rival warlord? Someone else?

There had to be people he could ask, his contacts on the street, but every move was perilous from this point on. If he was already suspected as a traitor to the warlords, every question, any move beyond the ordinary would be seen as confirmation of his guilt. Samatar would never find Amrita, couldn't hope to save her if he wound up dead. Still, if he took no action, how could he pretend to be a man?

It hit him then: there was at least one person he could ask for help.

The tall American who called himself Belasko.

Djibouti

"WHO ARE YOU?" Hassan Gourad asked.

"You asked for help," Yakov Katzenelenbogen replied. "Here we are. The names don't matter."

"You are not American," Gourad observed. His attitude was skeptical.

"We come from varied backgrounds, but we have a common goal," Katz told him. "If you're waiting for the First Marines, they won't be coming."

"I am not ungrateful for your help," Gourad addressed himself to Manning and McCarter, then turned back to Katz, "but there is much to do. Four men..."

"We're way ahead of you," Katz stated, fishing in his pocket for an envelope of Polaroid photos. Gourad accepted them and frowned as he examined each in turn.

"What's this?"

"A Cuban base camp, eighty miles across your western border. Used to be, I should say. They've been closed for renovations."

"You did this?" He glanced from one man to another, wonder playing tag with disbelief behind his eyes.

McCarter scowled. "Let's just say we were in the neighborhood."

The five of them were seated in Gourad's small living room, with Katz and Manning on the sofa, while McCarter, Encizo and their shaken host took the remaining chairs.

"How did you know that I would be attacked tonight?"

"Now, that was luck," Katz told him honestly. "We planned to meet you here, and sent a car to follow you from work in case you wound up going somewhere else. We didn't see the ambush coming, any more than you did."

"Any thoughts on who might want you dead?" McCarter asked.

The question earned a chuckle from Gourad. "I'll
have to make a list. The Ethiopians, of course, and
their 'advisers.' Then, we have the warlords in Somalia and their Chinese sponsors. Take your pick."

"You don't have any friends," Katz said.

"A few, but they are cautious men. They see our
country cut off and surrounded, and they don't know
where to turn."

"You mean to say they've given up?" McCarter
asked.

"Oh, no. They'll fight if we're invaded, but they live
in fear of provocation. If some villagers get killed in
border raiding, they prefer to look the other way, instead of calling someone to account. We do not have
the troops or the equipment necessary to defend ourselves against a larger army, much less two."

"That didn't stop you reaching out for help," Katz
said.

"I took a chance," Gourad replied. "It might have
come to nothing, but I had to try. Some things are
worse than death, I think. To be a slave, for instance."

"What kind of intelligence have you collected on
these raiders?" Katzenelenbogen asked.

"It has been difficult, but I have eyes in Ethiopia.
The soldiers from Havana are involved, beyond all
doubt. Where the Somalis are concerned, the troops
that kill our people have been natives, but their weapons, for the most part, are Chinese."

"You're sure of that," Encizo asked.

"We have collected cartridge casings and a rifle lost
when one of them was wounded. There is no mistake."

"And protests have been filed?" Katz asked.

"Of course. We hear denials out of Addis Ababa. In Mogadishu, there is no one to respond. The lawful government is... How would you say, history?"

"That's how we say it," Manning told him, frowning.

"No one in authority, no one to punish if the laws are broken. The United Nations forces say they are attempting to control the warlords in Somalia, but they seem to have no luck. Each day, I read that they have searched in vain for men who flaunt themselves around the capital like star rocks."

"You mean rock stars," McCarter corrected.

"Ah. In any case, my government has little confidence in outside help, and we have problems of our own. The Issa and Afar still fight among themselves, demanding union with Somalia and Ethiopia. Another protest demonstration has been scheduled for tomorrow, and I will be very much surprised if there is not a riot."

"You tell fortunes?" Manning asked him.

"I rely upon experience. Wherever half a dozen Issa and Afar are brought together, there is violence. Some of it, I think, is fostered by the propaganda from their ethnic homelands. We permit them freedom of the press, and so they fan the flames of hatred. If and when our country is invaded, it will feel like civil war."

"You're not much of an optimist," Katz said.

"A realist," Gourad replied. "If there is something you can do to help, I welcome your assistance. But I fear you are outnumbered and outgunned."

"That sounds familiar," Manning said.

"Let's take a crack and see what happens," McCarter added.

"What about this demonstration?" Katz asked. "Are there specific organizers?"

"Certainly. I have a list."

"Connected to the groups that cross your borders?"

"I would bet my life on it."

"It's good you put it that way," the Israeli said, "because you might have done exactly that."

Mogadishu

"YOU WERE WAITING for my brother?"

Calvin James was concentrating on his driving, trying not to stare at the young woman seated next to him. She was a beauty, any way you judged the contest, and he needed the distraction like a bullet in the head.

"That's right," he told her, "if your brother's Siad Samatar."

"Who were those men who tried to kill us?"

James shrugged. "I thought you might have some idea. They spotted you right off, the minute you showed up."

"I could not see their faces clearly, but I don't believe I know them." Hesitating, she corrected that. "*Knew* them."

Past tense for dead men, right.

James didn't know where he was going at the moment, but he wouldn't feel secure until he put more ground between himself and the location of the shooting. They would have to stop soon, maybe at the safehouse, and he wondered whether Striker would be there.

"You don't know where your brother is right now?" he asked her, killing time.

Amrita shook her head. "He works at different jobs. I never know from one day to the next where he will be, what hours he will keep."

She sounded skeptical about the job scenario, and with good reason. James didn't think it was his place to inform her that her brother was a spy, but it appeared that she was getting close without suggestions from the sidelines.

"Am I now your prisoner?" she asked.

James shot a quick glance toward her, found that she was almost smiling. Almost.

"I'm not taking any prisoners," he said, regretting how it sounded even as the words got past his lips. "I mean to say, you're not. My prisoner, that is."

"Then can you help me find my brother?"

"That's the plan," James said, "but if *you* don't know where he is, I guess we're out of luck."

"You've met him?" Amrita asked.

"No. A friend of mine touched base this morning. I was hoping for—"

He left it dangling, still uncertain what to say. Amrita took the cue and started prodding him.

"More what?" she asked. "Is Siad dealing contraband? Does he trade weapons? Medicine?"

"It's not that bad."

"You must need information then."

"I really can't say any more."

"You've said enough," Amrita told him. "I was curious before, about the source of all this money. Now I know."

"You really need to ask Siad about his business," James said. "Another time."

"I hope I have the chance."

"Does Siad have a place he goes, some evenings, when he's not at home?"

Amrita shook her head. "He always comes home."

"What about tonight?"

"I did not say he comes home *early*."

James hesitated, but he had to ask the question. "What about a woman? Would you know if he was..."

"Yes," she said. "I think so. He is not a monk, of course, but Siad would have mentioned someone special."

"I'd like to get in touch with him before he goes back home."

"You think someone might still be waiting for him there?" she asked.

James shrugged. "It's doubtful, but you never know. Until we figure out who's looking for him, it's impossible to say how smart or rational they are."

He checked his watch. The night was getting on, and traffic on the streets was thinning out. Another hour, give or take, and they would be fair game for questioning by members of the UN task force. James started thinking of alternatives to aimless driving, somewhere they could stop and rest, consider options.

Striker.

"Someplace we can try," he told her, reaching underneath the driver's seat and fishing out his compact two-way radio. The frequency was set, and all he had to do was key the button for transmission.

"Phoenix Three to Striker. Do you read me, over?"

Seconds later, the reply came. "Affirmative. What's shaking, over?"

It was Jack Grimaldi's voice. So far, so good.

"I had some competition at the meet," James said. "No sign of Striker's contact, but I've got another passenger. We need a place to crash right now. Is that a problem, over?"

"Who's the pickup, over?"

James frowned, imagining Grimaldi's first reaction when he heard the news. "The contact's sister, a civilian. She had people waiting for her at the house. I had to take them, over."

Momentary silence hung in the air before Grimaldi spoke again. "You'd better bring her in. We had a call-in from the brother just before you came on, over."

"He's all right, then, over?" James could see Amrita from the corner of his eye, beaming.

"Seems fine. Concerned about your passenger, I'd say, but that's about it, over."

"Right. We're coming in. Ten minutes ETA. Over and out."

"Siad is safe," she said, as if it helped to speak the words aloud.

"I don't know if I'd go that far," James told her, worried that she might expect too much. "He's cool right now, but he's got someone looking for him, too. I don't call Mogadishu safe for anybody, as it is."

"We've been through worse," Amrita told him. "This will pass."

"Storms always do," James said, "but while they're blowing, you should learn to keep your head down, all the same."

She frowned at that, considered it. "A life in hiding," she informed him, "is no life at all."

"If you want to see no life at all," he countered, "go back home and take a look at those guys in the alley."

"I've seen death before," she said, and let it go at that.

"Okay. Let's see if we can pass the night without you seeing any more."

CHAPTER TEN

Southwestern Somalia

Crossing the Giuba River south of Serenli, Jack Grimaldi kept his chopper well below the sweep of radar—if, in fact, there was a unit functioning in that part of the country. One advantage of a breakdown in the civil government, Grimaldi found, was the reduction in defensive capabilities of major targets. When the army scattered and the mob took over, vital gear was either trashed or else went unattended, lacking personnel with the experience and training needed for its use. It made things easier.

Sometimes.

Grimaldi had exchanged the Black Hawk for a lighter, faster Cobra gunship. Seating two, the smaller whirlybird had a maximum cruising speed of 207 miles per hour, and it packed a killer punch. A turret underneath the nose was fitted with a 7.62 mm M-28 minigun and an M-129 40 mm grenade launcher. Stubby wings on either side supported additional armament, including an M-35 20 mm Gatling gun, an M-230 30 mm chain gun and two M-20/19 rocket pods with nineteen 2.75-inch rockets each.

Grimaldi could have blitzed the camp himself, but he was flying backup. Bolan recognized his friend's misgivings, but he also knew the pilot would perform his duty as instructed, covering the action on the ground.

For his part, Bolan was dressed in black, his face and hands darkened with combat cosmetics. His weapon of choice for the raid was an M-16 A-2 assault rifle fitted with the M-203 grenade launcher attachment, exchanging potential deniability for guaranteed firepower. In the worst scenario, if Bolan lost the weapon somehow, it would fit in well enough with the confused selection carried by Mohammed el Itale's private army. One more M-16 amid the ruins of the camp would make no difference, either way. The bandoleers of extra magazines and 40 mm rounds that crossed his chest would keep him rocking, with a backup complement of frag grenades and the Beretta Model 92 worn underneath his arm.

"Two minutes," Grimaldi said, sounding small and distant in the headset Bolan wore. It would be going with him, to preserve communication with the Cobra once he launched his probe.

As planned, the gunship would be touching down some distance from the camp, with the Executioner closing in on foot. He wanted time inside the compound to evaluate his enemies and see what they were made of, test the skills they had acquired from their Chinese instructors.

He didn't expect the leaders of the Beijing delegation to be present in the compound. That would be too much to hope for, and from Bolan's point of view, a hit on their commander at the moment would be premature. Far better, he had already decided, to increase the pressure one step at a time, allow the shock waves time to spread. He would prefer to have his enemies locked in combat, one against the other, making Bolan's effort that much easier.

"We're going down."

The warrior had his safety harness loosened by the time the Cobra went to ground, its runners settling on the desert hardpan. Bailing out, he ducked below the rotors, which were slowing, coming gradually to a halt. Grimaldi would avoid the waste of fuel required to keep the chopper running while he waited for a summons from the camp, thereby ensuring they could make it safely back to Mogadishu when the job was done.

Except that nothing could be guaranteed with any certainty from this point on.

"Stay frosty," Bolan told the pilot, then he put the whirlybird behind him, moving through the darkness.

"You the same," Grimaldi answered.

They had fixed the camp with NAVSTAR, using aerial surveillance photos as a point of reference, and the mobile unit Bolan carried led him from the Cobra's landing site directly to the compound over arid, broken ground. The camp was mostly dark at 12:15, except for dim lights showing from a structure that he took to be the CP hut.

They might have sensors posted, but he didn't think so. This part of Somalia was Mohammed el Itale's territory, his backyard, as safe from interdiction by his enemies as any plot of ground the warlord held. There would be sentries posted, surely, but he counted on them being somewhat lax in the performance of their duties, this far from the shooting gallery of Mogadishu.

Double-timing for the final hundred yards, he came in from the north side of the compound. They were five miles from the river and three times that distance from Serenli, far enough removed to carry out the strike without a fear of reinforcements rolling in. There were no UN soldiers in Serenli at the moment, but Itale would have people there, protecting his investments. Bolan's key to pulling off the strike would be to go in hard and fast, reduce the compound's capabilities of talking to the outside world and go from there.

When he had seen enough, learned all he could about the enemy, it would be time to summon Grimaldi.

But he would start the probe with silent slaughter from the shadows.

Beginning now.

FOR CAPTAIN Chiang Li Sen, the duty in Somalia was a daily trial. The heat and flies were terrible, hygiene pathetic, and the people he'd been sent to train had no apparent sense of order in their lives, no discipline to speak of. From the day of his arrival, it had been an uphill battle, for his "students" had a limited interest in military art and strategy.

They wanted weapons and the skill to use them, anything that had to do with killing and didn't require much physical exertion. But they balked at calisthenics, bungled drilling and rushed through maintenance on their equipment. None of them would last an hour in the People's Army, but he had to keep the project in perspective. He wasn't expected to produce a revolutionary fighting cadre. Rather, his assignment was directed toward the propagation and perpetuation of disorder in a land where Beijing had a vested interest. Captain Sen's superiors were interested in helping the Somalis—some of them, at any rate—expand their influence at the expense of neighbors. When the smoke cleared, China would have bought herself a grateful client state.

And if the project failed, at least they had the satisfaction of distracting the United Nations for a time, preventing closer scrutiny of human rights' abuses in Tibet and China, border skirmishes with Vietnam and Burma, the trade in heroin from Yunan Province through Cambodia to the United States and Europe.

Smoke and mirrors.

Victory was sweet, of course, but even failure could be beneficial, if you played your cards correctly.

Chiang Li Sen was seated at his desk and sipping cold beer from his small refrigerator when the world exploded. That was an exaggeration, certainly, but not by much. The shock wave rattled walls and windows, brought him to his feet, and by the time he reached the doorway, leaping flames lit up the camp as if the time were half-past noon instead of midnight.

As he feared, it was the gasoline tank. They kept a large supply of gasoline on hand to fuel the vehicles, and it was burning now, a sea of flame and boiling smoke clouds on the compound's easternmost perimeter. Someone was screaming from the general direction of the fire, and Sen saw several native soldiers moving hesitantly toward the blaze.

An accident?

He couldn't rule out negligence—one of his "students" smoking near the tank, for instance—but the sound of the explosion had been different somehow, painfully familiar.

Like the vicious crack of plastique charges going off.

It was a short trip back to reach his desk, exchange the bottle for his pistol belt, perhaps ten seconds, with the time it took for him to slide the belt around his waist and buckle it, adjust the holster on his hip. But it was enough time for another blast, this one from the direction of the motor pool. Emerging from his CP hut, Sen was quick enough to catch the secondary detonations, fuel tanks going up as flames spread rapidly from one vehicle to the next.

No accident.

A burst of automatic weapons' fire erupted from barracks on his right, beyond the motor pool. If he had needed any further proof of an attack in progress, there it was. A 5.56 mm weapon by its sound, which might be one of his men or the enemy... until he heard the muffled cough of what could only be a 40 mm grenade launcher. There were no such weapons in camp, at least on his side of the fight. As the captain moved toward the sound, the high-explosive round went off like heavy metal thunder, flattening the commo hut.

He started shouting orders, casting desperately around him in the firelight for another officer—Chinese, if possible, but someone with authority, in any case. If they didn't control the situation in short order, it would quickly slip beyond their grasp. Without a clue to the identity or number of his enemies, Sen would have to start with basics, forming a defensive line to hold what ground remained and push their attackers back.

He spotted a lieutenant, Chou Yat Zung, approaching at a run. The officer had nearly reached him when a bullet struck him in the chest and staggered him, his legs collapsing. In a heartbeat, he was on his knees, and Sen watched him topple over sideways in the dust, limbs twitching in a spastic dance of death.

He spun in the direction of the gunshot, reaching for his pistol, knowing it would be a fruitless contest. What he saw was chaos, native soldiers running aimlessly, without apparent goals or strategy, their shadows lengthened and distorted by the hungry flames.

He drew the pistol anyway, deriving comfort from its presence in his hand, and started moving toward the smoking ruin of the motor pool. Sen would do the best he could to salvage something from the wreckage. If his best wasn't enough, then he would die in the attempt.

It was the revolutionary soldier's way.

GRIMALDI HEARD the summons loud and clear. He fired the Cobra's Avco Lycoming engine, waiting for a moment while the rotors picked up speed. When he was airborne, skimming toward his target with the NAVSTAR screen to guide him, there was time to run a last check on his weapons systems.

Barely.

He could have found the compound on his own, without the satellite-projected map. The place was burning, bright flames lighting up the desert for a hundred yards around. The people looked like ants at first, but they became more human as he closed the distance, homing in on the attack.

"I need your twenty, Striker, over."

"Moving," Bolan told him. "Start off with the north side of the compound, over."

"Roger that."

It gave him several acres, reasonably sure that Bolan wouldn't be on the receiving end of any bullets or explosive charges emanating from the Cobra. Fair precision work was possible on vehicles and buildings, with the gunship's weapons systems. He could also target moving personnel and make it count, but picking out a given soldier in the midst of combat, with the dappled firelight, would require some kind of psychic.

He would have to keep his fingers crossed and hope that Bolan didn't charge into his line of fire.

The barracks structures were a standard Quonset-hut design, made out of corrugated steel and painted in a desert camouflage pattern. They would be hell to live in, baking ovens in the desert heat, but there was worse in store for these commandos now that darkness had arrived.

He raked the huts with the weapons mounted in his turret, first. The minigun, a variation of the Gatling principle, laid down 6,000 rounds per minute, armor-piercing slugs that made the metal huts resemble giant colanders with firelight bleeding through the holes. The 40 mm M-129 kicked in with high-explosive rounds and finished it, the huts disintegrating in a string of rapid-fire explosions, twisted sheets of metal flying off in all directions, interspersed with mangled body parts.

Grimaldi spied a group of native soldiers racing for the cover of the mess tent. Circling around to follow them, the Stony Man pilot opened up from eighty yards with the M-35 20 mm cannon, another Gatling spinoff with a rate of fire that matched the smaller minigun's. It fired a mix of armor-piercing, tracer and explosive rounds that churned flesh into pulp and whipped the desert floor into a minor sandstorm as he strafed the ragtag enemy.

All down in seconds flat, and none of them was moving when Grimaldi made his second pass. He hit the mess tent proper with a pair of 2.75-inch rockets, and the warheads found a hot spot, probably a propane tank that served the stove and ovens. When it blew, the spacious tent went up in flames, reminding the pilot of old-time photos he had seen from a disaster that engulfed some stateside circus in the 1930s.

Hell on earth, and then some.

From his bird's-eye view, Grimaldi saw a runner leave the tent, his uniform on fire and trailing sparks. He brought the Cobra into target acquisition, triggered off a short burst from the minigun and watched the human torch disintegrate.

There was a lookout tower at the northwest corner of the compound, with a light machine gun mounted on the platform. It was spitting at him now, the gunner too unnerved to score a hit, but he was trying. Rather than allow him any practice time, Grimaldi swung around and framed the tower in his sights, unleashed another rocket, following its bright trail toward the mark.

There was a flash, a puff of smoke, then he saw the lookout tower start to wobble, listing, going down in flames. The gunner never felt it, having been consumed in the initial blast, and that was fine. The structure came apart like kindling when it hit the ground, a dust cloud smothering the fire.

Grimaldi sent another pair of rockets into the latrine, insurance, just in case some of the enemy had gone to ground there. Once again, he marked the flash and smoke of detonation, saw the lean-to structures fly apart.

Swinging toward the western fence, he strafed a group of sentries who were running for their lives. A couple of them stopped and turned their rifles on the chopper, showing better nerve than common sense. A storm of 20 mm bullets cut them down and chased their laboring companions to a dusty, thrashing death.

The ammo counter on his guns showed he was running low, but the pilot was still well up on 40 mm rounds and rockets, ready for the worst his opposition had to offer.

"Running out of targets here," he said into the mouthpiece, hoping Bolan was alive to hear his words.

"Let's wrap it up," the deep, familiar voice came back.

Grimaldi smiled.

"We aim to please," he said.

THE M-203 LAUNCHER belched another high-explosive round, and Bolan watched it detonate downrange, three runners vaulting through the air in crazy somersaults that left them limp and broken on the ground. He instantly dismissed them from his mind, uncaring whether one or more were still alive, as long as they had no fight left.

It had been touch and go before Grimaldi started plastering the compound with his guns and rockets, chewing up the terrified defenders. Half a dozen soldiers had the Executioner pinned down before the Cobra made its first appearance, scattered now and seeking cover that was hard to find.

It had become a slaughter pen inside the compound, bodies scattered everywhere. He gave up counting, settled for an estimate that told him the facility was geared toward serving eighty or a hundred men at once. There didn't seem to be that many present—Bolan estimated forty-five or fifty, tops—but it was still enough to challenge one lone warrior and defeat him if he didn't watch his step.

Grimaldi was insurance, something extra to reduce the odds and make a permanent impression on survivors. Bolan didn't fool himself into believing he would take out every soldier in the camp: while it was not impossible, a sweep of such proportions would require more time and energy than he was ready to expend on mopping up. For now, it was enough to scourge the lion's share and leave the rest to propagate their tales of terror in the ranks.

There were occasions when a frightened soldier who survived did more to undermine his own cause than a hundred kills.

A bullet whispered past his head, and Bolan ducked back under cover of the only standing Quonset hut. He had already cleared it with a frag grenade and automatic fire, five soldiers dead inside, but it was useful as a place from which to scan the compound, watch the shifting action with a fair degree of personal security.

Until the snipers had you spotted.

He heard the bullets drumming corrugated metal, but he couldn't see his enemies, and that was bad. They could advance, improve their own position, while they kept his head down with a steady fire. If Bolan showed his face right now, he stood an eighty-twenty chance of getting tagged.

Unless...

He keyed the headset microphone to reach Grimaldi. "Can you blow the Quonset, southeast corner, over?"

"That's affirmative," the pilot told him. "What's your twenty?"

"Hauling ass for somewhere else," he said. "Let's do it. Out!"

He took the long way, breaking to his right and sprinting down the full length of the hut, to emerge— if he was quick enough—around the northeast corner. Bolan's adversaries would be looking for him at the other end, if they expected him at all, with Jack Grimaldi's light show coming up.

He heard the Cobra closing, rotors beating at the air, and he had nearly reached his destination when the rockets sizzled from their launchers, streaking in on target—one, two, three. The hut came apart like something made of cardboard with a giant cherry bomb inside. The shock wave lifted Bolan of his feet and shoved him forward, finishing the race like Superman, boots churning empty air before they hit the ground.

He tumbled through a shoulder roll, heard shrapnel pattering around him as he got up on his knees. The flames were close enough to singe his eyebrows, baking one side of his face until it felt as if he had a sunburn. Tracking with the M-16, he swept the field in search of enemies, the soldiers who had pinned him down.

He found them gaping at the ruin of the hut, their weapons dangling uselessly from flaccid arms. Four would-be soldiers clad in dust and khaki, grinning at the destruction of their enemy, prepared to cut and run before the gunship swung around to bring them under fire.

They never made it.

Bolan had his rifle shouldered, sighting quickly from a range of forty feet as he began to milk the M-16 for short, precision bursts. He dropped the nearest gunner first, a string of 5.56 mm tumblers ripping through his heart and lungs, dead before he toppled forward on his face.

The second guy in line was spattered by his comrade's blood, glanced over at the crumpling body, gaping at it with a dazed expression on his face. He tried to cope with what was happening, but he was out of time, the bullets plowing into him a heartbeat later, snuffing out his life.

Two down, and two remaining.

Number three was quick enough to bolt, and Bolan let him run, the muzzle of his weapon tracking swiftly onto number four. He was the tallest of the lot, prepared to stand and fight, though the Executioner couldn't tell if it was courage, or if he was rooted to the spot by fear.

He shot the gunner where he stood and swung away before the body melted backward in a boneless sprawl.

And that left one.

The runner had some speed, you had to give him that, but trying to outrun a bullet was a hopeless task. The range was forty yards when Bolan stroked the rifle's trigger one last time and gave his enemy a shove between the shoulder blades. Momentum kept the dead man on his feet for two or three more strides, then he stumbled, going down in an untidy heap.

A kind of silence had descended on the killing ground. Not perfect silence, certainly—crackling flames, and an occasional soft moan here and there—but in comparison to the cacophony of battle, it was deathly still.

Enough.

He keyed the mike again and told his wings, "I'm out of here. Look for me sixty yards beyond the wire, southeasterly."

"Affirmative."

He put the slaughter behind him, thankful for a respite, but he knew the war was far from over.

If the truth were known, in fact, he guessed that they were only getting started.

The worst was yet to come.

CHAPTER ELEVEN

Djibouti

Tribes were gathering by 10:30 a.m. In place of native dress, the men were clad in short-sleeved shirts and baggy trousers, some in faded blue jeans, while what the women wore ran toward classic Sunni Muslim dress, their heads and faces covered. Many of the men on both sides carried heavy sticks, some camouflaged with cardboard signs, and others looked as if they were suffering from glandular infections, pockets fat with stones handpicked for throwing when the proper moment came.

They were the Issa and the Afar, tribesmen with ethnic roots in Somalia and Ethiopia, respectively, and their rivalry—extending into politics and blood revenge—had rocked Djibouti since the tiny state was organized. A period of relative quiescence in the later 1980s had been broken with a vengeance in the present decade, when hostilities resumed along the borders shared between Djibouti and her neighbors.

Simply stated, Issa tribesmen wished to see Djibouti annexed by Somalia, while the Afar longed for an Ethiopian merger. Neither group regarded themselves as citizens of Djibouti first, and their common religion—with ninety-four percent of Djibouti residents reported as Sunni Muslims—seemed to make no difference in the conflict.

It had been a long night, waiting for the demonstration to begin, and Yakov Katzenelenbogen still had sneaking doubts about the job he had accepted on Hassan Gourad's behalf. It had potential, granted, but it could as easily go wrong, blow up in Katz's face and jeopardize his men.

Still, they were in the middle of it now, and backing out would only mean that they had wasted precious time.

In essence, they were gunning for the leaders of the demonstration. Not the public spokesmen, but select provocateurs from Addis Ababa and Mogadishu who moved among the native populations, sowing seeds of hatred and rebellion, standing by to fan the flames whenever the opposing sides were close enough to strike a spark between them.

Like today.

The Phoenix Force warriors had examined photographs and knew whom they were looking for, two agents in particular, with their attendance at the demonstration all but guaranteed. The trick, with four Caucasians hunting, would be getting close enough to make the tag and still escape without a lynching.

It was totally impossible, of course, which left the flip side. The long-distance option. Reaching out to touch someone.

It would be risky, even operating from their chosen vantage points, but Katz had faith in Manning and McCarter. Encizo had a doorway staked out on the far side of the square, prepared to move if anything went wrong, but Katz was hoping he wouldn't be needed. Any move conducted at ground level, in the middle of a crowd scene, would be tantamount to suicide.

Conversely, if they pulled it off, the impact on their enemies would be as great—or nearly so—as any damage they had earlier inflicted. Skillful spies and saboteurs weren't a dime a dozen, like the Cuban troops in Ethiopia or native "soldiers" used by the Somali warlords. They were trained and seasoned, sometimes highly paid, and skilled at what they did. Removing two or three such men at once could have the same effect as taking out a company of border-raiding grunts.

Assuming they could pull it off.

The Issa and Afar were lined up on the east and west sides of the square, respectively, as if in deference to the general direction of their ethnic homelands. They began by shaking fists and signs at one another, shouting epithets, and challenging the thin rank of police who stood between them looking worried.

Katz was posted on a balcony, one floor above the street, where he could scan the crowd with his binoculars and try to spot their targets. Manning and McCarter were above him, rooftop level, doing much the same through sniper scopes, but it would take them longer to peruse the square, restricted as they were to smaller fields of vision. Any help that Katz could offer in location of their targets would increase their prospects for success.

So many faces, jeering, shouting, animated by the violence of emotion. Katz began to think that he could sweep the mob all day without discovering the men he sought. Suppose they picked this day to watch the riot from a distance, rather than participating at the scene. What then? More to the point, suppose they were on hand, somewhere below, but he couldn't find them. Would Gourad accept the failure and continue to cooperate, or would he be enraged and slam the door in Katz's face?

The best way was to get it done, and never mind the options, keep on scanning, search the crowd until he spotted a familiar face and—

There!

He double-checked, referring to the mug shots, making sure. When he was satisfied, Katz palmed his walkie-talkie and pronounced the orders for a total stranger's death.

HASSAN GOURAD felt nervous, like a new bride on her wedding night. His palms were moist with perspiration, and it felt like worms were wriggling in his stomach, threatening to bring up his meager breakfast.

He had been a fool, Gourad decided, to entrust his fate to strangers. If the plan went wrong, somehow— or if it was successful, and his name was linked to the event—a prison cell was waiting for him, possibly a firing squad. A clean hit would be murder multiplied, perhaps with other charges like sedition tacked on as an afterthought.

What did he really know about these foreigners, presumably employees of the CIA or some such outfit? They had saved his life, of course, but that would count for nothing if they turned around and got him killed or slapped in prison. It was likely that they had their own agenda, and Hassan might well be sacrificed if he didn't protect himself.

At that, the plan was his idea. The enemy sent strangers to his country, stirred up mayhem, left their bloody tracks around the countryside and it seemed fitting that Hassan should do the same. If he could use these foreigners to purge the capital of dangerous provocateurs, so much the better. If it cost him dearly in the end, at least he would know that he had done more for his country than the feeble politicians who stood by and shook their heads in impotent dismay.

Gourad was stationed with a troop of soldiers on the sidelines, watching as the action heated up. From shouted threats and insults, the Afar and Issa had proceeded to a pelting rain of stones, the odd glass jar or bottle shattering in jagged shards on impact with the pavement, stinging naked feet and legs. The hostile lines were undulating, almost like a tribal mating dance, and he could see the uniformed policemen brace themselves for an assault.

It would be hard on the police, but he had made his mind up to withhold support for several minutes, let the two sides mix and mingle as they liked, until the foreign spotters had a chance to do their jobs. His men were getting restless even now, but they would follow orders, and Gourad could always say that he misjudged the situation, thought the civil officers were better able to control the crowd. His troops would move, of course, before the riot got entirely out of hand, but for the moment he didn't want any soldiers in the line of fire.

So, this was what it felt like to participate in a conspiracy outside the law. For all his life, Hassan Gourad had taken pride in his position as a law-abiding citizen—and later as a servant of the state, in uniform. He wondered if the course that he had chosen for himself this day would haunt him, either in his waking hours or in dreams.

If so, then he would live with it, believing he had done his best.

The most effective course of action didn't always lie between the covers of a rule book. Law and justice sometimes parted company, and while a civilized society demanded regulation, there were times when it wasn't enough for men of conscience to stand by and quote prevailing statutes as a reason for inaction.

He was ready, and let the chips fall where they might.

A shout went up from both sides of the crowd at once, and the opposing ranks rushed each other, the defending line of uniforms trapped in between. The officers lashed out with their batons, a couple of them hurling tear gas canisters, but they were quickly overwhelmed and brushed aside. The best that they could hope for, in the circumstances, was to fight their way clear of the crowd and thereby save themselves.

Gourad's lieutenant leaned in close to him. "Should we advance, sir?"

"On my order." Standing firm, Gourad said nothing more.

He felt the eyes of the lieutenant and his other men upon him, waiting, curious at the delay. He stolidly ignored them, staring at the mob scene several yards away. Stones clattered almost at his feet, but he stood fast. A whiff of tear gas stung his eyes and nostrils, but he wouldn't budge.

The tears that glistened on his cheeks weren't produced by noxious gas alone.

Gourad wept for his country and the circumstance that made him party to assassination, wondering if he could ever purge the dark stain from his soul.

Or whether it was even worth his time to try.

Too late to save himself, perhaps, but there was still Djibouti, his beloved homeland. If he could help prevent a national catastrophe, it would be worth the sacrifice.

It would be worth his life.

THE RIFLE WAS a Galil sniper's model, manufactured in Israel, with a folding stock, adjustable bipod and a 20-round box magazine. Unlike the parent assault rifle, the sniper version had a heavy barrel fitted with a muzzle brake, together with a recoil pad and cheek rest on the wooden stock. The action had been set for semiauto only, keeping distance work in mind. Its Nimrod 6× telescopic sight was designed to score head shots at 300 meters, half-body hits at 600, with full-figure hits between 800 and 900 meters. Fitted with a silencer, as this one was, the rifle had to use subsonic ammunition, but a lethal tag at ninety yards would be no sweat.

Assuming he could find a target, McCarter thought, peering through the scope and checking out the demonstration, one face at a time.

It was bad enough when the assembled demonstrators had been lined up on opposing sides of the square with cops in between, perhaps three thousand shouting, jeering faces, some of them disguised by colorful bandannas worn to hide identities or filter out the burning fumes of tear gas. It was impossible. He could lie up there all day and never spot a face he recognized, unless—

McCarter froze, went back an inch to double-check, unwilling to trust his senses on the first pass. There, in the blue shirt, carrying a megaphone. He spent a moment staring at the profile, then the target spun to face him, raised the megaphone and started shouting at his enemies across the square.

Or, was he speaking to the men and women massed around him, urging them to greater violence, calling out to them for blood?

No matter.

Recognition was achieved. The mark had grown a little straggly beard since he had posed unwillingly for mug shots, sometime back, but he hadn't changed otherwise. It was a lean face on a round head, giving the impression of a teardrop upside down. His eyes were bright with a fanatic's zeal, his lips drawn back from crooked teeth. His ears stood out like wings.

All things considered, then, McCarter wondered how it could have taken him so long to spot the Ethiopian provocateur who called himself Wendo Dashan. The name was probably a fake, but that was nothing to McCarter. He could call himself Joe Camel, if he wanted to, and it wouldn't prolong his days on earth.

McCarter had his finger curled around the rifle's trigger, counting down the heartbeats, when he lost his target. All at once, the crowd surged forward, rushing the police line from the east side of the square. Directly opposite, their Afar adversaries rushed to meet them, brandishing their signs and bludgeons, coming in behind a rain of stones.

It was a hopeless situation for the cops down there, surrounded, overrun and hopelessly outnumbered. Lashing out with their batons and lobbing tear gas when they had an opening, they would be lucky if they made it out alive.

McCarter left them to it, wished them well and tried to find Wendo Dashan. Blue shirts were popular among the Afar tribesmen, and he concentrated on the megaphone, the teardrop head, the straggly beard. He seemed to have no prospect for success, until he figured out what he was doing wrong.

The role of a provocateur, as indicated by the very term, is to provoke. He stirred things up, started trouble, egged his comrades into foolish, violent actions if he could, on the behalf of hidden sponsors. It wasn't his role to stand and slug it out, risk injury or death in a demented street fight. Rather, he was trained to hit and run, let others do the fighting, while he slunk away to rouse the rabble somewhere else.

With that in mind, McCarter swung his sniper scope away from the police line and the riot proper, searching the fringes of the crowd. It struck him that Wendo Dashan might want to linger and admire his handiwork, see who was winning in the square before he bugged out to his current hideaway. If so, he would be looking for a vantage point where he could watch without much risk of being dragged into the melee.

Checking out the north side of the square, the Briton found his man tucked back inside a recessed doorway, peering out, almost invisible within the shadows. Almost. He was safe from brawlers on the street, because they had their hands full at the moment, fighting for their lives, but he hadn't been counting on a rooftop spotter with a dedicated mission.

For the second time, the teardrop face filled McCarter's telescopic sight. He took a breath and held it, getting comfortable with the Galil and waiting for the perfect moment.

He could probably have fired without the silencer, considering the racket in the street below him, but it made no difference now. The light, subsonic load was more than adequate to drop a human target at the present range. No sweat. If necessary, he could use the whole damned magazine to nail his man.

The recessed doorway was a deathtrap, and Dashan had picked it for himself.

McCarter had him, waited for the lean face with the straggly beard to rotate, peering left and right. When it was centered, looking in the direction of the struggling police, McCarter stroked the trigger and sent a single bullet on its way.

The slug ripped through Dashan's face, underneath one eye, and slammed him back against the wall. His legs were rubber now, unable to support him, and he slithered down the brickwork, leaving crimson smears behind to mark his passage.

Done.

McCarter palmed the walkie-talkie, keyed it, offered two words to the air: "Scratch Dashan."

THE TERSE ANNOUNCEMENT came as Gary Manning was about to gnash his teeth in grim frustration. He had figured out the need to check perimeters, instead of scoping on the epicenter of the riot, but it wasn't paying off. He was about to check the north side of the square when he received the news about Wendo Dashan, his earpiece whispering the name. A moment later, Manning spied the body, slumped back in a recessed doorway, seated in a pool of blood.

They had a working list of five provocateurs, but it wasn't believed all five would turn out for the demonstration in the square. Assuming there would be at least one rabble-rouser for each side, he still had three Somali agents to watch out for, plus another Ethiopian who might—or might not—have decided to attend.

It wasn't quite like hunting for a needle in a hay-stack; more like watching for a certain marble, being shaken in a tub with several hundred others, all identical, or nearly so, in size and color. Taken one by one, he knew, the rioters would easily be recognized as striking individuals, but in the swirl of combat, lashing out at one another in a frenzy, they all looked alike. Their faces masked, averted, blood-smeared, bobbing up and down erratically—it was enough to make his stomach queasy if he concentrated long and hard enough through the restricted viewpoint of the telescopic sight.

Relax. Swing wide and check the side streets. Look for individuals retreating from the riot zone before it started cooling down.

And then, he had them. Two of them, in fact. They were Somalis, sent to agitate among the Afar tribesmen. One—the taller of the pair—was known to the police around Djibouti as Mareg Farid. The other, several inches shorter and an easy ten pounds heavier, was called Halim Kismayu.

They were getting in a dusty compact car when Manning spotted them, a block west of the square. Kismayu sat behind the wheel, his partner standing by an open door, watching the riot as if he were reluctant to leave. Kismayu spoke, interrupting his reverie, and Farid ducked his head, sliding into the car on the passenger's side.

Now or never.

Manning framed his sights on Kismayu's face, thankful that a fine layer of dust kept the windshield from glaring. It was close to ninety yards, and he would have to make allowances for possible deflection by the safety glass.

He stroked the trigger twice and saw the windshield blur, his first round pulverizing glass, the second drilling flesh and bone an instant later. Kismayu was dead before he had a chance to raise a hand in self-defense, his body slumping toward the driver's door, blood spouting from his shattered face.

The good news with a semiauto, Manning thought, was speed. He swiveled toward the secondary target, caught Farid gaping at his comrade, trying to assimilate the grisly image and respond in timely fashion.

But he never had a prayer.

Round three burned through his temple with the impact of a hammer stroke. His head snapped sideways, bouncing off the padded seat before his muscles got the message and began to melt, his body sliding out of view below the dashboard.

"Scratch Kismayu and Farid," Manning told the walkie-talkie, switching off before he got an answer, packing up his rifle in the duffel bag that he had carried to his rooftop perch. With folded stock, its silencer removed, the Galil measured thirty-one inches overall, and it fit easily inside the bag. Eighteen pounds of hardware, with the loaded magazine and Nimrod sight, and Manning hardly felt it as he slung the duffel on his shoulder, moving toward the staircase that would take him down and out.

He had the feeling of a job well done, but there was no excitement in it. He didn't take satisfaction in the killing of another human being, although he understood that it was necessary, a predictable aspect of war.

Downstairs, he turned right and proceeded through a corridor that took him out the back door of a squat, four-story office building. He could hear the battle raging out in front, a storm of angry voices shouting all at once, with whistles blowing, sirens wailing in the distance, and the brittle sound of breaking glass. The alley where he stood was like an echo chamber, but the frantic action wouldn't touch him there.

He turned north, moving toward the street some eighty yards away. If anyone had found the dead provocateurs, it would take time for them to summon help. The uniforms already on the scene weren't in a position to take homicide reports just now, and Manning had no fear of being intercepted as he put the sniper's nest behind him.

By the time he reached the street, Gourad had sent his shock troops charging into the melee, swinging riot sticks and gun butts. Scalps were split and bloodied, tear gas wafted through the crowd, and slowly, by degrees, the action fell apart, like an amoeba subdividing, breaking into smaller units, the combatants scattering.

The Rover waited for Manning two blocks farther west, with Katz behind the wheel. Encizo had the shotgun seat, McCarter in the rear. Katz gunned the engine into life as Manning got in back, then they were moving, putting ground between themselves and the chaotic riot scene.

"Not bad," McCarter said, when they were rolling.

Katz glanced back at his companions in the rearview mirror, frowning.

"It's a start," he said.

CHAPTER TWELVE

Mogadishu

It wasn't your average family reunion. They had talked for hours, off and on throughout the night, with little sleep before the first gray light of dawn came peeping through the windows. The American—a black man, like himself—hadn't insisted that Samatar address Amrita in the English language, but he did so, for the most part, out of courtesy. The man had saved her life, while Samatar's covert work had nearly spelled the end of her. The guilt he felt inside wouldn't be easily assuaged.

Amrita had been saddened as he told the story of his covert work against the warlords, but she didn't seem surprised. In fact, beneath the obvious anxiety, he thought he detected something very much like pride. She would be thinking of her husband, his untimely death, and rooting earnestly for the destruction of the men who took his life.

Mohammed el Itale, Jouad ben Ganane—they were all the same in spite of minor variations in political philosophy. They robbed Somalia's people, left them destitute and starving, riddled with disease, while they inflated prices on black-market food and medicine, extorting weekly "taxes" from the merchants who were still in business after four long years of civil war.

Apologies were futile, in the circumstances, but Samatar had offered them, regardless. Amrita had forgiven him already, he could see it in her eyes, but it would take more time—if he could ever do it—for him to grant himself forgiveness.

It was full light when Amrita went to bed, a back room in the safehouse, and Samatar sat down alone with the American who called himself Carl Jones.

"I don't know who those jokers were, last night," Calvin James said, as they sat drinking coffee, "but we both know they weren't looking for your sister."

"No. It would appear I am exposed."

"Ideas?"

The shrug required an effort, weary as he was. "I deal with different groups," he said. "There must be six or seven private armies active in Somalia at the moment. I have contacts inside three of them. If anyone found out that I was helping the Americans, well . . ."

"Could you tell if we had names?" James asked.

"Perhaps. Of course, I don't know all the gunmen. There are many thousands."

"Worth a try, though. I can try and pull some strings, see what we hear from the authorities."

In Mogadishu, at the moment, that meant the United Nations military force in charge of keeping order and distributing relief supplies. Samatar assumed that the American had some kind of official link with the UN command, though he wasn't about to ask.

He would never cease to marvel at the power these Americans appeared to take for granted, the self-confidence they demonstrated as a matter of course, as if it were part of their birthright. And, he thought, perhaps it was. Their nation had been spawned by revolution, tempered in the fires of war that spanned two hundred years. The troubles in Somalia seemed minor, by comparison, but that wasn't the case when you were living with them day by day, when friends and relatives were sacrificed without good cause.

Samatar's own sister, lately widowed, had come close to being such a sacrifice. The fact she was still alive, against all odds, was due to this American, his courage and resolve. Attempting to repay that debt might cost the Somali his own life, but refusal never crossed his mind.

"When can I see them?"

James was up and moving toward the telephone. "Let's check it out."

If he recognized the dead men, then Samatar would be obliged to act. His family honor would demand no less. The bold Americans might help him; if they couldn't, then he would have to do the job himself.

He had already failed Amrita twice, by failing to avenge her husband's murder, and by placing her in jeopardy through his collaboration with the foreign agents. Now that a direct attempt had been made on her life, the Somali couldn't avoid his duty any longer.

Those responsible for the attack would have to pay, by one means or another. He would bring them down, destroy them root and branch.

Because he was a realistic man, Siad Samatar knew how the lopsided battle was likely to end. His death would be a small thing, if he left the world with honor still intact.

He would identify the dead, if possible.

And he would help increase their numbers, too.

El Bur, Somalia

LIEUTENANT COLONEL Ziyang Tse Chung was furious. His mind was seething, and a spot check on his pulse would have revealed that it was nearly twice the normal rate. It felt as if his heart were pumping liquid fire and venom through his veins. The painful pressure in his skull would have disabled lesser men, but Ziyang Tse Chung concealed his inner feelings from the world by force of habit. For a stranger watching him, completely uninformed about the contents of the message crumpled in his fist, it would have been impossible to tell that he was agitated in the least.

He didn't mind the loss of sixty-three Somali troops, so much as he begrudged the death of four Chinese assigned to their encampment near Serenli. The report had sparked a scramble to retrieve their bodies and dispose of them before the UN forces arrived and made the link between Mohammed el Itale's army and Beijing.

From all appearances, his orders had been carried out efficiently, but the successful cover-up didn't alleviate his rage. It would take time to replace the officers through covert channels, but he had an even greater problem on his hands.

Specifically he didn't have a clue to the identity of those responsible for the attack, and it was critical that he secure his operation now, before another sneak attack caused further damage. If he allowed the situation to degenerate beyond control, there would be anger in Beijing, and rightly so. His reputation—possibly his life—was riding on the line.

So far, the Chinese officer could only speak in terms of negative intelligence. He had a fair idea of who was *not* behind the raid. At a glance, it had been logical to place the blame on Jouad ben Ganane, but further reflection discredited that idea. Three known survivors from the camp agreed upon the presence of a helicopter gunship firing rockets, and Ganane had no such equipment in his arsenal. More to the point, one of the living was insistent that the raiders—or at least one member of their party—had been white.

The latter detail worried Ziyang Tse Chung the most, beyond all talk of helicopters, rockets, automatic weapons and the like. An arms race could be won, equipment smuggled to his clients, piece by piece if necessary. Lowly peasants could be taught to operate the most sophisticated weapons and equipment, given time... but there might be no time, if they were up against a Western military force right now.

His strategy, thus far, had been to shy away from contact with the UN forces, train Itale's men in relative seclusion and dispatch them on their raids across the border to Djibouti. If the British or Americans were on his track, then it could mean a world of trouble in the days ahead.

Of course the white man sighted at the compound could have been a mercenary. It wasn't beyond Ganane's means to hire selected triggermen, especially if he was feeling slighted by Beijing's attention to his major rival. He could even rent a helicopter for a few days, if he turned his pockets inside out. Employing white men would deflect attention from himself and add a brand-new variable to the grim equation, leaving Ziyang Tse Chung and his Somali clients to discover who was stalking them, and why.

He hoped Ganane was responsible for the attack, and yet the raid's efficiency, its sheer ferocity, ruled out Ganane in the colonel's view. These local war-lords were adept enough at killing peasants, taking random shots at one another, but the past four years of civil war had passed without one true, decisive battle being fought. If anyone possessed the skill and courage to attempt such action now, it should have been Mohammed el Itale's men, with their support and training from the People's Revolutionary Army. Now, instead of pushing on to victory, those very men were filling shallow graves.

The message crumpled in his fist was coded, but the colonel had memorized its contents. Brief and to the point, it gave him time, location, estimated body count. The few remaining details, speculative as they were, had come to him by scrambled telephone transmission. White men coming out of nowhere with machine guns, helicopters, rockets.

Turning from the window with a snarl, he flung the wadded paper toward a nearby trash can, missed and watched it bounce across the concrete floor. It was a no-frills office, nothing in the way of carpeting or decorations on the walls. He had a metal desk and mismatched swivel chair that had seen better days, a filing cabinet with a combination lock and two wooden chairs for his infrequent visitors. A folding table in the corner opposite his desk, behind the door, was piled with maps of eastern Africa, including Ethiopia, Somalia and Djibouti.

It was all he needed to conduct his business in the backward, war-torn land...or so he had believed, at any rate, until his client troops were slaughtered in the middle of the night.

Retaliation was essential, for morale of the surviving troops, if nothing else. Before he struck, though, he would have to find a target. That meant talking to Mohammed el Itale, trying to decide if he had any secret enemies, of whom Colonel Chung was unaware. If they agreed upon Ganane as the likely culprit, action would be taken to repay the injury.

The colonel wasn't a quitter, but he caught himself fervently wishing that his duty in Somalia was completed and behind him. He was tired of dealing with these strangers and adapting to their savage ways.

Above all else, surprising even to himself, Chung found that he was troubled by the thought of dying there, so far away from home.

Dikhil, Djibouti

YAKOV KATZENELENBOGEN settled in his folding chair across the table from McCarter, Manning on his right, Encizo on his left. The map spread out in front of him, weighted at the corners with their coffee mugs, displayed the eastern half of Ethiopia, Djibouti and perhaps three-quarters of Somalia. Katz reached out with the shiny metal claw of his prosthesis, and scratched a ring around Korahe, in the eastern horn of Ethiopia.

"Right here," he said. "As far as we can tell, the Cuban military staff is operating from a villa on the edge of town, and it appears they're not alone."

"What's that supposed to mean?" Manning asked.

"Russians," Katz replied, enjoying the surprised reaction from his men. "A few, at least. The Company came clean with Stony Man last night, or maybe it was news to them, as well."

"Fat bloody chance," McCarter scoffed.

"Whatever, we're advised to watch for one or more alumni from the old KGB, assisting Castro's people with the raids against Djibouti."

"Unofficially?" Encizo asked.

Katz shrugged. "It sounds that way, but who can tell? The party line from Washington specifically denies suspicion of aggressive Third World moves from Moscow. These guys are free-lance. The bottom line—if we find unofficial Russians working with the Cuban military, we can take them out."

"Sounds fair," the big Canadian remarked.

"Of course, we have to find them first."

"You have the villa marked?" McCarter asked.

"Affirmative. It's on the north side of Serenli, near the river. We can airlift to a point upstream, then come down overland or on the water. Take them by surprise."

"Reconnaissance in force?" Manning asked.

The gruff Israeli veteran frowned. "The truth is, I had something else in mind."

"Such as?"

"Our ace, right now, is stirring up dissension. If we keep the heat on, we can make them work against each other. Running down a clean sweep now, we lose the option of manipulation."

"What's the game plan, then?" McCarter asked.

"Disruption and harassment," Katz replied. "It won't need all of us. A two-man team can pull it off, with backup from Grimaldi."

"This is where we volunteer, I guess," Encizo said. The Cuban wore a rueful smile.

"I'm going," Katz informed them. "All I need is one man for support."

"You always hog the easy jobs," McCarter interrupted, feigning irritation. "There's a better way to settle it."

"I'm listening."

The former SAS commando reached across the table and deposited a tiny deck of playing cards directly in the middle of Djibouti. "Never leave the house without them," he declared.

"You want to play a hand for who goes out?" Manning asked.

"High card, low card," McCarter said. "Fair is fair."

Katz scanned the faces, waiting for objections, knowing there would be none. "Are you all agreed?" he asked at last.

They nodded, none of his companions in the least put off at trusting their fate to the turn of a card.

"Fine with me," Manning said.

"I feel lucky," Encizo replied.

"All right, then. I'll go first."

McCarter fanned the deck and waited while Katz worked a card out with his left hand, faced it to reveal the four of diamonds.

"Next?" McCarter said.

"I'll go," Encizo told him, reaching out to palm one of the miniature cards. He checked it, grinned and showed them all the king of spades. "I told you I felt lucky."

"Me, next," Manning interjected. He was plainly disappointed as he faced the ten of clubs.

McCarter frowned and drew a card, exposed it to the others as he dropped it in the middle of the table. They were looking at the deuce of hearts.

"I'm low," he said. "Encizo's high."

He turned to Katz. "Looks like you watch this round from ringside, Chief."

"I should have made you shuffle," Katzenelenbogen said.

"It wouldn't help. They're my cards, after all."

"Remind me not to play with you for money," Manning said.

"I'm not inviting you to play with me at all, old son."

They laughed at that, but it was whistling past the graveyard. Each man present knew the "lucky" two were pushing it and risking everything to score a psychological advantage on their enemies. If they went down in Ethiopia, the effort would be worse than wasted. Following their orders to the letter, they wouldn't have taken out the hostile leadership, but their exposure would inform the enemy that he was dealing with a wild card, maybe give him time to cut and run.

So much at stake, and they were smiling, cracking jokes.

Katz was reminded of their selfless courage in that moment, and the reason that he trusted each and every man among them with his life.

Stony Man Farm

IT WAS A SHORT HOP from Dulles International in Washington to the Virginia hardsite. Hal Brognola made the journey once a week on average—more often, if there was a major crisis in the works. This morning made his second visit in the past four days. He paced the War Room like a guard dog on a leash, too nervous to relax.

"They're clean, so far," Barbara Price said, aware that reassurances would make no difference in Brognola's mood.

"'So far,' is right," the Justice man replied. "We didn't know about the Russians yesterday."

"They'll handle it," Kurtzman told him, watching from his chair behind the console that controlled the War Room's visuals and lighting.

"It's a whole new wrinkle," Brognola said. "If they're free-lance rogues, okay. We take them out, and everybody's happy."

"Everyone except their clients and the Russians," Price stated.

"But if they're *not*," the big Fed continued, ignoring her, "if they were sent by someone in Moscow with official orders, then we're in a different ball game."

That was obvious, of course. Officially the cold war was defunct, a closed chapter in the history textbooks. Still, the jousting match of East and West—the Reds versus red, white and blue—had dragged on for more than seven decades, encompassing two world wars and a score of undeclared "police actions" ranging from the Caribbean to Southeast Asia. It was hard to close the book on all that blood and bitterness, especially when you met a team of Russians in the field, intent on mobilizing native troops for yet another brushfire war.

"We're waiting on some word from Langley," Kurtzman said.

"Good luck," Brognola groused. "They couldn't find a mole at their own counterintelligence desk, but they've got the lowdown on East Africa. I love it."

"We're still on track," Price said. "Our people know about the Russians, and they're taking action. Nothing too extreme, from what I gather. Something in the nature of a wake-up call."

"Ex-KGB, they're saying." Kurtzman's tone was cautious, even skeptical.

Brognola stopped his pacing, fumbled in his pocket for a pack of gum. "That could be wishful thinking," he replied. "If Langley missed them going in, it stands to reason that their analysts would try to minimize the screwup. Missing one or two rogue mercenaries might be understandable. You miss a Russian strike team, it's a disaster. Someone has to take the heat, and Langley would prefer to pass it on."

The running feud between Brognola and the CIA was old news to the team at Stony Man. For Price's part, she leaned toward cautious trust for Langley, holding back enough to realize that any federal bureaucracy will cover its mistakes, if given half a chance. The Company had secrets that it hoarded from its own director, from the President himself. Some never saw the light of day, and maybe that was for the best.

Or maybe not.

Reliability was Job One in Intelligence, and too much secrecy reduced analysis to a pathetic guessing game. From Stony Man's inception, independent sources had been cultivated so that no external agency—the FBI, CIA, NSA, DEA, you name it—could control the flow of data pouring in. She liked to think relations with the other agencies were cordial, but reality, as Price realized, was often very different from the public face.

This time, until the Company was proved wrong, she felt inclined to trust their judgment on the Russian team in Ethiopia. With all the problems Moscow faced at home, it made no sense for anyone to waste time plotting minor revolutions on another continent.

Still, policies had been approved and actively pursued by both sides in the past, with no apparent logic or regard for common sense. At one point, ranking staffers at the CIA had dreamed of putting LSD inside Fidel's cigar, or dusting his clothes with a depilatory that would make his famous trademark beard fall out. The Soviets, for their part, had thrown support to terrorists who murdered Communists; at home, they executed so-called "traitors" on the flimsiest of evidence chagrined in many cases when the charges were disproved after the fact. More defectors had run to the West in fear of their lives than from dissatisfaction with living conditions in Moscow or Minsk.

"We'll know more later on this afternoon," she told Brognola, knowing as she spoke that it would be no consolation.

"Right. The trouble is, we need to know it now."

And he was right, of course, but there was nothing she could do about it from the Blue Ridge Mountains, even with her satellite connection to the warriors fighting on the far side of the globe. Without the crucial information they required, the best that she could do was watch and wait, report developments and keep a log of field reports.

It was a helpless feeling, sometimes, but at least it kept her busy. If she simply had to sit and wait, she knew that she would lose her mind.

"They've got it covered," she announced to no one in particular. And wondered even as she spoke, if she was trying to convince Brognola, Kurtzman or herself. "They'd doing fine."

And heard the echo in her mind.

So far.

CHAPTER THIRTEEN

Fafan River Valley, Ethiopia

The drop was three miles due north of their target, on the outskirts of Korahe. Traveling by water gave them speed and shaved the odds of meeting soldiers on patrol—or stray civilians, for that matter—who would blow the whistle on their game before McCarter and Encizo even had a chance to play.

They traveled light, with their Kalashnikovs, spare magazines and side arms, fighting knives, garrotes—two warriors in a rubber boat that they would leave behind, a riddle for their enemies since it was manufactured in a country of the former Eastern Bloc.

It was supposed to be a simple in-and-out...or not so simple, as the case might be. The NAVSTAR linkup brought Grimaldi to the drop without a hitch, and satellite photography had given them a layout of the neighborhood, together with a fair count on the soldiers present, but a hundred different things could still go wrong. The kind of hit-and-run they had in mind could blow up in their faces, and they might never even see it going wrong until it was too late.

In that case, they had both agreed, all bets were off. Plan A called for harassment of the enemy, with no tag on the major players. They could live with that, if it was going smoothly, but a foul-up changed the rules of play. Without consulting Katz, McCarter and Encizo had decided they would pull out all the stops in the event of a disaster. Make their dying count for something, at the very least.

That meant elimination of the Cuban officers, their Russian playmates—anyone and everyone the Phoenix Force warriors had a chance to tag before they went down in a blaze of something less than glory.

Gliding with the current now, and staying low inside the light inflatable, McCarter didn't like to think about the worst scenario. He didn't like it, but he thought about it anyway, made sure that he was ready for the showdown, if and when it came.

When he was serving with the SAS, one of McCarter's comrades had described him as an "irrepressible pessimist." And the description fit like a glove, as far as it went. No defeatist, by any means, McCarter believed in preparing for the worst—expecting it, in fact—each time he took the field. That way, when things went sour, he was ready. And if bad news failed to materialize, he was always pleasantly surprised.

It was a grim philosophy to live by, but it did the job.

They caught a break as far as witnesses, passed no one on the trip downstream, and thus were spared the need of silencing civilians. From the aerial surveillance shots, they knew when they were getting close. Encizo recognized the screen of trees that came down to the river's edge, within a hundred yards of their selected target. Paddling swiftly, they were back on solid ground in seconds flat, the rubber boat concealed halfheartedly. Whatever happened in the next half hour, they wouldn't be using it again.

If they had floated for another mile or so along the stream, they would have reached a neighborhood where children frolicked in the river, women carried water for their cooking, men came down to fish. The north side of Korahe was a more exclusive district, though, and peasants were discouraged from trespassing there, unless they were employed as gardeners or servants. So it was that no one saw the Phoenix Force warriors come ashore, discard their rubber boat and move in the direction of their target.

From satellite surveillance photos, they expected twelve to fifteen soldiers on the property, along with several Cuban officers ... and now, the Russians who had joined the game. Their plan was worked out in advance—McCarter following the river southward, while Encizo veered off to the west and worked his way around the target for a distance of two hundred yards or so. By that means, they would catch their pigeons in a cross fire without jeopardizing each other or preventing Rafael from falling back when it was time to go.

They barely spoke in parting, no vain wishes of good luck, Godspeed. Each warrior was dependent on his skill and courage, his equipment and the battle plan they worked out in advance. If anything went wrong from this point on, they either had to cope with it or die.

Two very different men, they shared a common background in their military service, waging long, relentless war against a list of deadly enemies. They had survived this long by taking pains with everything they did and manufacturing their own luck in the process. Any doubts they might have had about the mission had been put on hold.

It was time to rock and roll.

AT FIFTY-FOUR YEARS OLD, Dmitri Kuybyshev was pleased to find that he could start from scratch, as the Americans would say, and build his life anew. Of course, his reputation from the "old days" was a help in that regard, considering the nature of his customers. The KGB had been officially reorganized and purged of Party loyalists, but the memory of its achievements would survive wherever saboteurs and terrorists or Third World rebels needed some direction and advice, a modicum of expertise.

It was ironic, when the Russian thought about it, that his latest mission—physically identical to others he had once performed on orders from Dzerzhinsky Square—made him an outlaw in the eyes of Moscow's present ruling clique. Times change, of course, and Kuybyshev wasn't one to ignore the warning signs. While others in the old KGB were fighting last-ditch, rearguard actions to preserve the status quo, he had devised a means of getting out alive with every ruble he could lay his hands on in the process.

It was never quite enough, however. He would always have a need for more, and when he thought about it, in his private moments, there was something else. A lust for action and intrigue, the opiate that hooked him in his years of active service to the state, and that he still craved to the present day.

The game in Ethiopia had been both profitable and amusing, up until now, despite the fact that he was forced to work with Cubans.

Facing Kuybyshev across a wrought-iron table in the villa's patio was Major Raul Rodriguez, representing Castro's government in Ethiopia. The Cuban presence was supposed to be a secret, but they took no pains to hide. If anything, their flagrant posturing was a relief to Kuybyshev, because it helped *him* pass unnoticed, hanging out behind the scenes. His personal assistant, young Igor Storenko, was in Addis Ababa this morning, huddled with a team of military officers to find out what had happened to the latest batch of Cubans.

It was bloody business, all the more unfortunate because they didn't have a clue to the identity of the assailants. Kuybyshev believed Rodriguez was unnerved by the attack, and who could blame him? For the past few months, his "war" had been a string of border raids in which his seasoned troops attacked and looted native villages, annihilating unarmed peasants. It would be a shock for them, and no mistake, when someone started shooting back.

The Russian sipped his strong black coffee, wondering if it was time for him to disengage and find another battleground. He thought back to Afghanistan, the horrors he had witnessed on both sides, and while the graphic pictures in his mind didn't unnerve him, neither was he anxious to become one of the casualties.

"Your men were not disheartened by the news?" Kuybyshev asked.

Rodriguez frowned at the suggestion. "They are worried, some of them, but they will follow orders. None of them are cowards, Comrade Kuybyshev."

It took an effort of the will to keep from laughing in the Cuban's face. Rodriguez used the "comrade" line as if there were still a Soviet Union to support his escapade in Ethiopia. Some people, Kuybyshev reflected, never seem to grasp reality until they were compelled by force.

"We still have business in Djibouti, Major."

"I am well aware of that," Rodriguez answered, huffing. "We have suffered losses, but I still have men enough to carry out the mission."

"Good."

Kuybyshev wouldn't be paid from Addis Ababa unless the Cubans carried out their portion of the contract, and the deal wasn't complete until they had provoked an incident of suitable proportions with Djibouti. Once that line was crossed, permitting an invasion in the name of "self-defense," the Russian's work in Ethiopia was finished. He could take some time off for himself, relax along the Riviera and begin to seek another theater of war.

"It would be beneficial, I believe," Kuybyshev said, "if they resumed activities tonight—tomorrow at the latest. We must not allow their doubts and fears to spread."

Rodriguez raised his coffee mug but didn't drink. "You have a special target in mind?" he asked.

"Perhaps."

In fact, Kuybyshev had several, the kind of isolated border villages that made such easy pickings for Rodriguez and his men. Next time—or soon at any rate—it was essential that they manufacture evidence suggesting an incursion from Djibouti, something that would mobilize the Ethiopians in righteous outrage and demand retaliation.

Something in the nature of a Reichstag fire.

But first, the shaken Fidelistas needed to regain their confidence. An easy victory, perhaps with women to be mauled, should do the trick. Kuybyshev made a note to check his map again and choose a village large enough to offer ample targets, while avoiding any risk of serious resistance. If they suffered any further losses, in their present state, the Cubans might begin to fall apart, perhaps rebel against their officers. The last thing any of them needed at the moment was—

The sudden, crackling sound of automatic weapons startled Kuybyshev. He sat bolt upright in his lounge chair, reaching for the pistol that he wore beneath his jacket. There came a shout of warning from the guards on the perimeter, immediately answered by another burst of gunfire.

"Down!" he snapped, already suiting words to action as Rodriguez rolled out of his chair and lay prone on the patio.

The last thing any of them needed at the moment was another whipping by an unknown enemy, but something told the Russian he was just about to witness such a setback for himself.

THE TWO MEN ON THE PATIO were obviously brass, though neither wore a uniform. The one on Encizo's left, as he faced toward the house, was an Hispanic, almost certainly a Cuban officer. His tall, gray-haired companion had a Slavic look about him, something in his face, his bearing. There was military training in the gray man's background, definitely, but he could as well have been retired for several years.

One of the Russians.

From his vantage point, some fifty yards due west of where they sat in mottled shade, Encizo could have killed them both with his Kalashnikov. An easy tag, full auto, dropping both of them before they recognized a hint of danger in the wind. It was a tempting thought, but discipline prevented him from acting on the impulse.

They were working on a shake-up, turning on the heat, but taking out the hostile leadership had been deferred until another time—unless the probe went sour, and they found themselves with no way to escape. For now, unless it fell apart, Encizo knew that he would have to be content with potting sentries from his hiding place among the trees and undergrowth that rimmed the villa's spacious yard.

He had four Cuban soldiers spotted when the clock ran down. McCarter ought to be in place, but there was no point waiting for him, either way. Encizo shouldered his Kalashnikov and chose a target from among the soldiers walking post. There would be others in the house, relaxing or asleep, but they would rally when the fireworks started.

Coming up.

Encizo took the nearest sentry first, because he posed the greatest threat in terms of swift retaliation. Lining up the shot, he squeezed the rifle's trigger gently, taking up the slack. A short burst, dead on target at a range of thirty yards, and he could see the rounds strike home. A splash of crimson, and the Cuban soldier went down, sprawling lifeless on the grass. His visible companions swiveled toward the sound of gunfire, while the two men seated on the patio went instantly to ground.

Not bad.

Encizo heard McCarter open up a heartbeat later, but he had no time to think about his friend. The other soldiers in his field of vision were reacting now, one breaking toward the patio, as if to guard the prostrate officers, while two moved in the general direction of Encizo's hiding place.

They didn't have him spotted yet, but it would not take long. The trick was killing both of them before they had a chance to bring him under fire.

As with his first choice, Encizo picked out the nearest of the three survivors, understanding that proximity improved the chances of a lucky hit. He met the runner with a rising burst that stitched him from his groin up to his larynx, punching him over backward in a boneless dive. A long burst from the dead man's automatic rifle was directed toward the cloudless sky.

The third lookout was firing now, and coming dangerously close, as Encizo swung back to face him. Lying prone, he heard the bullets whisper overhead, a rain of mutilated bark and clipped leaves falling on his head and shoulders.

He waited, lining up the perfect shot.

He knew it at a glance and stroked the trigger, sending half a dozen rounds downrange to meet his fellow countryman. The Cuban gunner seemed to stumble, pitching forward with his arms thrown out to catch him, dead before he hit the ground.

And that left one, at least in theory. Turning back to strafe the patio, Encizo saw a line of soldiers bursting from the villa, grappling with their weapons as they ran to join the fight. He wasted no time counting heads, but swung around to rake them with his AK-74, dropping two at the head of the line, watching the rest scatter for whatever sanctuary they could find.

Encizo wished them luck—all bad.

One soldier doubled back in the direction of the house, but he couldn't outrun the 5.45 mm bullets pouring from Encizo's automatic rifle. Staggered by the impact of a burst between the shoulder blades, he managed two more steps before surrendering to gravity and sprawling on his face.

Encizo spotted two more soldiers racing for the patio. He led the forward runner slightly, squeezing off a burst that caught him in midstride and dropped him in the second Cuban's path. The two of them went down together, one man limp in death, the other struggling to his feet, abandoning his weapon in a desperate bid to save himself.

Too late.

Encizo tripped him with a burst at ankle height and kept on blasting as the soldier fell across his line of fire. The stream of bullets kicked him over on his back and made him shimmy as he died. The rifle's slide locked open on a smoking chamber, and Encizo ditched his empty magazine, replacing it with another from his bandoleer.

The smell of blood and cordite made a heady fragrance, summoning the memories of other battlegrounds where the Phoenix Force warrior had risked his life. For greater stakes, or less? Could such a thing be quantified?

Encizo put the sterile question out of mind and concentrated on the killing zone. He still had work to do, before their time ran out, and no firm guarantee that he would leave the field alive.

McCARTER HAD A TARGET in his sights when Encizo began to fire, perhaps two hundred yards away to the southwest. At once, the Cuban sentry he was covering spun back in the direction of the villa, picking up his pace, intent on seeing action. What he got, instead, was three rounds to the chest, a burst that dropped him to his knees and dumped him over on his side.

The decorative undergrowth was thick here, Mc-Carter's field of vision limited. He had a wedge-shaped portion of the villa covered, and a path that led back from the tree line to the house, but he could see only about one-quarter of the manicured lawn. The patio was just beyond his range of vision, but the firing concentrated there.

The Briton knew that he would have to move, unless he planned to miss the best part of the fight.

He broke from cover, moving in a combat crouch, his finger on the automatic rifle's trigger. Ready. Following the narrow path, he stepped around the body of his first kill, homing on the whitewashed house. It seemed to shimmer in the brilliant sunlight, almost radiant, a mockery of the corruption housed inside.

McCarter was prepared for anything, and so wasn't surprised by the appearance of a soldier on the path, directly in his way. The Cuban spent a crucial moment gaping at him, trying to decide what he should do, and by the time he hit on a reaction, he had lost the chance to save himself. A short burst from Mc-Carter's weapon gutted him and left him thrashing on the trail, his tremors fading gradually as his life ran out through gaping wounds.

The firing from Encizo's quarter was sustained and heavy, several weapons blasting all at once. McCarter came upon the scene from eastward, following the garden path, and found himself behind two Cubans who were hunkered down and firing toward the tree line, eighty yards away.

In Hollywood, the script would clearly have demanded that McCarter warn them of his presence with a cute one-liner, give the bad guys time to turn and fire before he took them down. In real life, where survival was the top priority, however, different rules applied.

He shot them in the back, a raking burst at something close to point-blank range, and felt no trace of guilt as they collapsed together, lifeless. Given half a chance, he knew they would have done the same to him.

He edged around the recent dead, ignoring them, his senses focused on the battleground in front of him. That had to be Encizo, firing from the trees, while several Cubans jockeyed for position, trying hard to pin him down. McCarter checked his wristwatch briefly, saw that it was almost time to cut and run.

He could alert Encizo to the time, perhaps unnecessarily, but that would only help distract him from the job at hand. In fact, it just might get him killed. The wiser course of action, McCarter thought, was to help him with his adversaries and withdraw while they were reeling, never mind if some of them were still alive.

His job had been to shake the Cubans up, not wipe them out.

McCarter had a glimpse of two men crawling on their stomach, trying to escape the patio. He left them to it, knowing Rafael could easily have dropped them if he wanted to.

A Cuban corporal blundered into range from somewhere on McCarter's left, another exit from the house. He ran across the former SAS commando's line of fire without a backward glance, unconscious of the danger on his flank. The Briton grimaced, shot him in the legs and pelvis, finishing him when he was down.

It was becoming butcher's work, but that was SOP for hit-and-run guerrilla warfare. Had there ever *really* been a battle fought by gentlemen, according to established rules? You read about it in the ancient textbooks, with their woodcut illustrations, but McCarter had a sneaking hunch the truth was something else entirely. When the chips were down, and soldiers faced each other on the battlefield, they did their bloody work with any tool at hand, employed the most effective means available. From Genesis to Desert Storm, a soldier's job was killing, plain and simple, in defense of those who lacked the courage or ability to do it for themselves.

McCarter saw three Cubans rushing Rafael's position, one cut down immediately, on the left. He took the gunner on the right, stitched half a dozen rounds along his spine and saw him go down on his face. Encizo nailed the third man with a short burst from the shadows, and the field was briefly clear.

The Briton tried to keep it that way with a frag grenade. He yanked the pin and lobbed the bomb in the general direction of the patio. Not close enough to nail the creepers if they kept their heads down, but a number of the windows went to hell when it exploded, spewing shrapnel.

By the time it blew, McCarter was already moving, running back the way he came. Grimaldi would be airborne, skimming toward the pickup point, and he couldn't afford to wait around all morning for his passengers.

Come on! McCarter urged himself to greater speed. Come on!

Another strike behind them, but the game was far from over.

It was merely getting warm.

CHAPTER FOURTEEN

Mogadishu

Sometimes, a leader had to lead. Rank had its privileges, and Jouad ben Ganane was accustomed to dispatching a subordinate to do his dirty work, but hard times called for hard decisions. The attacks upon his men within the past two days were a direct affront and challenge to his leadership. If he refused to meet that challenge personally, there was danger that the men who served him might begin to doubt his courage, his ability to lead. And once those doubts took root, Ganane realized, the end would be in sight.

That afternoon found Ganane driving through the streets of Mogadishu at the head of a procession that included half a dozen vehicles, all bristling with weapons. It was doubtful he would find Mohammed el Itale on the street, but in the absence of his moral enemy he would content himself with any of Itale's soldiers he could find. The trick was not so much in finding targets as avoiding the United Nations troops who would undoubtedly attempt to seize Ganane, with his men and weapons, if they had the chance.

His style of preference was hit-and-run, no great pitched battles that would give the UN soldiers time to mass and intercede. The stop-and-go technique also reduced the risk of friendly casualties, a point of vital interest at a time when Ganane had already lost so many men.

The first stop was a private "social club" monopolized by members of Itale's personal militia. It wouldn't be crowded at this time of day, but there were always several watchmen on the premises. If nothing else, it would be adequate to set things rolling in Ganane's quest for sweet revenge.

His caravan pulled up outside the club at 1:05 p.m. They left the engines running, nothing to retard evacuation when their work was done. A signal from Ganane, and his men unloaded in a rush, three gunners from each vehicle with automatic weapons and Molotov cocktails. They formed a line along the curb and opened up in unison, their bullets ripping through the club's facade, imploding window glass, the red door splintering and sagging on its hinges.

From his seat in the command car, Ganane had a glimpse of figures dodging back and forth inside the club, a desperate effort to evade incoming fire. He saw one man go down, arms flailing, and couldn't suppress a smile. So let his adversaries perish, all the fools who dared defy his leadership.

There was a sudden lull in firing, several of his soldiers pausing to reload, and two stepped forward with their cocktails, wicks already smoking. Ganane watched the firebombs wobble out of sight, one through the open door, another through a window, busting into flame on impact with the floor.

He blew a whistle and saw his men fall back to their respective vehicles in perfect order. Flames were spreading in the club, and just before Ganane gave the order to drive on, a figure burst out through the doorway, swathed in fire, a lurching scarecrow trail-

ing sparks. It would have been a kindly act to shoot
him, so they drove away and left him reeling down the
narrow sidewalk, blind and screaming.

The sweet aroma of revenge.

Their next stop was located in a residential neighborhood, the home of a lieutenant in Itale's army.
There were two young guards outside, but they were
slow and clumsy, groping for their weapons as the
caravan pulled up outside, too late to save themselves. A roaring broadside dropped them where they
stood, Ganane's soldiers charging from the street,
across a tiny yard of dirt and dried-out grass, immediately fanning out to ring the house. Ganane heard
more shooting from the rear, then his troops were
crashing through the front door, shouting, cursing,
firing shots into the walls and ceiling.

Ganane stepped out of his vehicle and waited, leaning against the fender with an automatic pistol in his
hand. A moment later, several of his men emerged,
half-carrying a man whose battered, blood-streaked
head sagged limply forward, chin on chest. His shirt
was torn, and there were blood spots showing on his
khaki trousers from the beating he had taken.

He was barely conscious when the soldiers brought
him to Ganane. At a nod, one of them grabbed his
ears and twisted, laughing as the sudden pain revived
their prisoner. A sharp kick brought him to his knees
before Ganane, and the soldiers stepped back out of
range, uncertain what they should expect.

Ganane reached out with his free hand, cupped the
prisoner's weak chin and forced his head back. One
eye was already swelling shut; the other stared up at
Ganane with a look of abject fear.

"Where is your master?"

"I don't know." The wounded soldier tried to shake his head, but Ganane held him fast. The pistol rose, its muzzle settling against his forehead.

"Is it worth your life to keep his secret safe?" Ganane asked.

"Have mercy! I cannot tell what I do not know!"

"Perhaps you're right," Ganane said, and shot him in the face at point-blank range.

The impact punched his captive over backward, blowing out a fist-size portion of his skull in back. A couple of his men were chuckling, the others looking on with grim expressions on their faces, understanding that Ganane had lost nothing of his strength or ruthlessness.

"We go!" he snapped, and turned back toward his staff car.

There were others he could ask, and one of them was bound to have the answer, if it took all night.

In fact, the longer the time required to learn Itale's whereabouts, the more of his subordinates Ganane could eliminate. There was no rush, he thought.

No rush at all.

THE ORDER for retaliation had come down at one o'clock. It took another hour for Ali Sekota to collect the soldiers he would need, make sure that each of them was armed and had extra ammunition. Finally they loaded into several vehicles and set out hunting for their enemies.

Sekota knew whom he was looking for, but tracking down Ganane and his soldiers in the streets of Mogadishu was another thing entirely. There were UN troops to be avoided, certain neighborhoods it might be dangerous to visit, even with a squad of gunmen at his back. The capital—or parts of it, at least—had been a battleground for years, now. Several districts posted guards around the clock, some armed, all capable of raising an alarm that would bring men and women racing from their homes with any weapon readily at hand.

Sekota owed his life and everything he had at this point to Mohammed el Itale. He had risen through the ranks as others gave up their lives for the cause, and he wasn't afraid to do the same, if necessary. Life was cheap in Mogadishu these days, and a number of his closest friends were in the ground already, casualties of civil war.

They started with reports of various attacks around the city, seemingly committed by a roving band with Jouad ben Ganane at its head. Sekota knew that it would be a feather in his cap to bag the man himself, a bonus he hadn't expected when he called the troops together in response to the command from his superior.

They visited the scene of one attack, the burned-out social club, but found the UN troopers there before them. Turning down a side street, they were out of sight before the soldiers in their sky-blue helmets could react or recognize the caravan for what it was.

So much for playing catch-up. It was time to try a new approach.

There was a small hotel, a half mile due north of the former presidential palace, that had been converted into something like a barracks for Ganane's soldiers living in the capital. At any given time, it sheltered several dozen gunmen, but Sekota reckoned some of them would be out riding with their leader at the moment, leaving him a relatively easy target. Not too easy, though. A bloodless victory wouldn't inspire congratulations from his master.

It wouldn't be easy, sneaking up on Ganane's troops. Sekota had his driver park a block east of the target, waited for the other vehicles to kill their engines, spilling men into the street. He issued orders swiftly, splitting up his force to ring the former hotel in a pincers movement, cutting off evacuation from the rear in case their adversaries chose to run, instead of fighting. Leaving four men with the vehicles, to keep them safe, Sekota led the group that would assault the hotel from the street. The loaded Uzi in his hands felt feather-light.

They were thirty yards from the hotel when they came under fire. There were no lookouts on the street, but someone had to have seen them from an upstairs window, blasting with an automatic rifle. Hasty rounds went high and wide, but it might still have been enough to rout Sekota's soldiers if he hadn't rallied them by sheer ferocity, demanding that they follow him to battle.

Firing from the hip, he led the way, his Uzi stuttering, the bullets chipping brick and mortar from the drab facade of the hotel. He didn't wound the sniper, but at least he drove him back and out of sight. Another moment found him on the hotel's doorstep, rushing forward with a pair of his commandos, heedless of the danger, kicking in the double doors.

The lobby had a musty, mildew smell about it, even with the sunlight streaming through broad windows. One of Ganane's soldiers stood behind the onetime registration desk, a shotgun in his hands. Sekota sprayed him with the Uzi, splattered blood and brains across the wall behind his target, smiling as the man went down.

His first kill of the day.

"Upstairs!" he shouted to his soldiers. "None of them must get away!"

The race was on, his troops ascending in a rush, with angry shouts and curses, firing as they went. Ganane's men returned fire from the floors above, but they were already losing ground, fleeing to the upper floors, from which there could be no escape.

Sekota fed his Uzi a fresh magazine and followed his men upstairs, taking the steps two at a time. It was a shame to rush the moment but he had no choice. The UN soldiers would be coming soon, responding to the sounds of gunfire.

And Sekota wanted to be present for the kill.

THE DAY HADN'T GONE well for Colonel Winston Moseley, currently in charge of the United Nations military force in Mogadishu. Not that any of his time abroad was good, in the accepted sense, but things had gotten worse the past two days, with bloody violence breaking out in districts long since "pacified." The warlords had been taking a vacation from their fratricidal slaughter recently, content to move their contraband and make a tidy profit, but the truce had lately broken with a crash that echoed all the way back to the UN Plaza, in New York.

It would be Moseley's job to keep the lid on and restore a modicum of peace...assuming he was equal to the task. Just now, with bodies scattered everywhere, fires burning, new reports of mayhem pouring in, the UN officer felt anything but capable.

He was, for all intents and purposes, indulging in a futile exercise. The proud Somali people seemed intent on killing one another, maybe wiping out the race, and there were days when Moseley wondered why he even bothered stopping them. It wasn't his place, playing God. He was a relatively humble soldier, trained to fight for an objective—or, in this case, to defend a principle. The trouble came when those he was defending didn't give a damn about the principle themselves and kept on killing in defiance of their own best interests.

It was madness, and the colonel had already seen enough in Mogadishu to suspect it was beyond a cure.

If he was wrong, so much the better. It would be a thrill—and quite a boost to his career—if he could pacify the natives in Somalia and become the hero of the hour. At the moment, though, he was too busy chasing fresh reports of bombings, drive-by shootings, paramilitary-style assaults on home and public buildings. He didn't have men enough to lock the city down, which left him playing catch-up with the opposition forces, getting nowhere fast.

Standing in the street outside the ruins of a former social club—charred timbers now, and roasting bodies, by the smell of it—he listened to the radio reports of new and greater violence several miles away. His enemies might be illiterate, unschooled in military arts, but they were highly mobile, and they killed with an enthusiasm that made up for any lack of formal training.

He had begun to hate Somalia. Colonel Moseley had a wife and teenage daughter back in London, praying for his safe return, and here he was in godforsaken Mogadishu, chasing homicidal maniacs around the streets as if it were some kind of bloody parlor game.

He didn't really care about the people anymore. He had a job to do, of course, but if it came down to a choice, the colonel would be opting for his own survival, rather than a nameless, faceless stranger. Three more months to go, before his tour of duty ended, and he meant to make it home alive at any cost.

"We've got another one," said Captain Joiner, coming up on Moseley's blind side.

"Bloody hell, what now?"

"An old hotel," Joiner stated. "Several dead, from what I understand. They've had a proper dustup."

"Christ! We'd better have a look. Leave one car here to keep the scene secure. We'll swing around and pick them up when we get done."

"Yes, sir."

The four BDX armored personnel carriers were lined up and waiting, two-man crews and ten armed soldiers each. Each vehicle mounted a .50-caliber machine gun in its turret, weighing in at 10.7 tons, powered by a Chrysler V-8 180-horsepower engine. The top speed was sixty-two miles per hour, but it hardly mattered when the BDX was cruising through a riot zone, absorbing punishment and spitting sudden death.

Or, as in this case, keeping the peace.

Colonel Moseley was puzzled, too, by the recent meddling in his business of American Intelligence. The Yanks had pulled out of Somalia back in 1994, officially, but now one of their alphabet agencies was asking for Polaroid photos of four men killed the previous night, another unsolved case that would doubtless remain so. Moseley had no problem delivering the photographs, but it surprised him when a black American came by to pick them up.

It made him wonder what in bloody hell was going on.

He would have been a simpleton to doubt the possibility of a connection with the recent spate of violence in Mogadishu, but suspicion was one thing, and proof was something else. He couldn't go accusing the Americans of anything without hard evidence—and what would be their motive, now that all their troops except a tiny palace guard around the embassy and diplomatic compound were removed?

The colonel climbed into his BDX and found a seat. Surrounded by his men and layers of armor plating, he felt safer than at any time since his arrival in Somalia. If the choice were his, he would have lived inside the BDX, emerging only when he had to take a shower or respond to calls of nature. Park the BDX inside a compound ringed by twelve-foot walls, with razor wire on top, and he would let the damned Somalis kill one another as they pleased.

Except that he could get away with no such thing. He had a duty to perform, however vain and futile it appeared to be. He was supposed to "keep the peace"—as if there were a peace in Mogadishu to be kept.

So be it. He had been a soldier all his adult life, and it was too late now for him to change. His life consisted of a million different orders, handed down from his superiors, passed on to his subordinates.

"Drive on," he said, and felt the BDX lurch into motion, cruising at a stately fifteen miles per hour.

With any luck, Moseley thought, he could chase the phantom gunmen all night long and not catch anyone at all.

FROM HIS POSITION in the vanguard of the convoy, Jouad be Ganane had a fleeting glimpse of final victory. His mind's eye saw the countryside laid waste before him, while the capital was fortified and colonized by his militia, driving out pretenders to the throne. When life was stabilized in Mogadishu, he would set about establishing a puppet government, apply to the UN for recognition as a sovereign state, fill bank accounts in Switzerland and Liechtenstein with profits from the systems of taxation he imposed.

The Red Cross would be welcome to continue sending food and medicine, of course. Ganane knew the Western fable of the golden goose and understood its moral perfectly. A strong man at the helm wouldn't alleviate the poverty his people suffered, or the droughts that plagued Somalia's agriculture. Thankfully the crisis wouldn't end when he assumed control.

But he would finally, at long last, be rid of his mortal enemies.

Beginning with Mohammed el Itale.

That breakthrough wouldn't occur today, of course, but he had made a start. At least two dozen of Itale's soldiers were dead so far, and it was early yet. The UN troops were busy cleaning up behind him, totally unable to predict his moves and thereby head him off. They might as well go back to camp, for all the good they were achieving, but Ganane knew that was too much to hope for.

He would have to keep on playing hide-and-seek.

A mile north of the great athletic stadium, unused for years except by vagabonds and squatters, they were passing through a major intersection when all hell broke loose. A Shorland Mk3 armored car, immediately followed by a dusty flatbed truck, pulled out to block the street, machine guns mounted on both vehicles erupting in a storm of armor-piercing rounds and tracers.

"Stop!" Ganane shouted to his driver. "Turn around!"

Too late.

Behind them, cutting off retreat was an ancient Russian BA-64 light armored car. It had come out of nowhere, parking in the middle of the street to bring them under fire. On either side, Ganane had a glimpse of infantry emerging from the narrow alleys. All were armed with rifles, shotguns, submachine guns, firing as they came.

It wouldn't be correct to say that Ganane's whole life flashed before his eyes, just then. Self-centered as a man could be, he focused solely on the here and now, the options for escape at any cost to his opponents or subordinates. His lightly armored staff car was already taking hits, the outside gunner wounded, screaming like a woman in the throes of labor. If they didn't make a move, and quickly, they would all be killed.

"Turn left!" Ganane snapped.

"There is no street!" his driver answered, panic-stricken.

"Turn left now! Across the sidewalk, there."

The driver cranked his wheel around and stood on the accelerator. They were moving, but it seemed to be at a snail's pace, veering out of line and toward the sidewalk, putting riflemen to flight and crushing one who wasn't quick enough to leap aside. For just a moment, Ganane thought they had a chance... and then a burst of armor-piercing rounds tore through the cab, his driver twitching, going limp behind the wheel.

Ganane tried to drive the staff car from the shot-gun seat, as there was no way to dump the driver's body without opening the door and showing half a dozen riflemen his face. He stretched for the accelerator with his left leg, but he couldn't work the clutch, and in the instant it took for them to bounce across the low-slung curve, the staff car's engine stalled.

Ganane had been frightened in his life before that moment, often, but the terror that he felt just then eclipsed all other frights that went before. He felt his bowels let go, ignored the ripe aroma as he pictured firebombs raining on the staff car, trapping him inside a metal coffin while he slowly burned alive.

He scrabbled at the inside handle of his door and got it open on the second try. The warlord had no thought of how he would defend himself outside the vehicle. His mind was frozen on the image of the burning man outside Mohammed el Itale's "social club," the blackened, blistered face his own. Praise God, if he only had the chance to run.

Ganane hit the pavement, managed all of two long strides before converging streams of automatic weapons fire ripped into him. He felt the first half-dozen bullets, stunning hammer strokes, then he was nothing but a lifeless puppet, twitching through a jerky little dance, held upright by a three-way cross fire that prevented him from falling.

Seconds later, when his adversaries lifted off their triggers and moved on to other targets, Ganane crumpled to the pavement in a spreading pool of blood. It would be late next morning when his mutilated body was identified, too late to make a difference in the action that ensued.

His dreams of glory stained the sidewalk and began to dribble down the gutter, one by one.

CHAPTER FIFTEEN

Mogadishu

The computer monitor, three inches square, was bright with amber characters as Bolan drummed his fingers on the tiny keyboard. He was using "shortline," the compressed language designed for small-screen imagery, to communicate with Phoenix Force in neighboring Djibouti. The five-foot silver dish antenna had been mounted on the flat roof of the safehouse, linked up to the landsat that would bounce his short transmissions back to a receiving unit manned by Katz or one of his companions.

He typed: CNTACT W/ ENMY CNFIRMD? RUSS PRESNT W/ CUBNZ?

A touch of the transmission key, and Bolan's query was beamed skyward in a microsecond. Moments later, the reply came back in that peculiar shorthand that required his eyes and mind to fill the blanks.

AFRMATV CNTACT KRAHE–CAUC MALE OBSRVD W/ CUBN OFICR– EST 98 PRCNT CONFDNCE RUSS/CUBN COLABRATN–STATUS UNCLR.

Bolan frowned at that. Sometimes, a confirmation of suspicion made things worse, instead of better. With at least one Russian on the scene, he had to think about the possibility of an official Moscow presence in the game, no matter how improbable that seemed.

His fingers flew across the keyboard.

PROGRES MOGDSHU SATSFACTRY–BEGIN NXT STEP ASAP–ADVISE XTREME RISK TO ASSOC ONSITE–ALL COST AVOID XPOSUREST TIME TO BEGN.

He sent the message to its halfway station in the heavens, waited for another terminal in the Djibouti capital to catch the "squirt," unscramble it and print it out. The answer came back to him with surprising speed.

HAVE LOCL ISSUE TO RESLVE–SOLUTN WORKING–EST AVAILABLTY FOR NEXT STEP 2/3 HRS XCLUDNG TRANSPRT/ONSITE PREP–SPSFY TRGT COORDS.

He had a fair idea of what the "local issue" would involve, around Djibouti, but he balked at picking out the final target from so many miles away. They needed experts on the ground to pull it off, including the co-operation of their military contact and the muscle he could bring to bear if he was in the proper mood.

Again, the warrior started typing: SEEK LOCL ASSTNS TRGT SLECTN–SE QUAD A1 AXSS ETH/SMAL–NEED HELI AXSS–ADVNCE SUPRT PREFRD THIS MOVE–CAN DO?

There was a longer hesitation this time, probably some heated consultation on the other end. He was requesting that Phoenix Force select the final killing ground, cooperating with their local contact, and arrange for military backup on the play. It would be no small order, with their ally under scrutiny by his superiors, but there were ways to pull it off, and Bolan trusted Katz to work the problem out.

His confidence was bolstered by the Phoenix Force's reply.

CAN DO–WILL TRNSMT SITE COORDS 4/5 HRS–77 PRCNT CONFDNCE LOCL SUPRT–EST NXT TRNSMSSN 1730 HRS–PHENX OUT.

Bolan typed his sign-off—STRIKR OUT—and cut the power to his terminal. He palmed the compact walkie-talkie from the table, raised it to his lips and said, "We're done."

Two minutes later, Jack Grimaldi brought the gear down from the roof, the dish antenna folded to resembled an umbrella. It was hard to picture the equipment flashing signals into space and back again, but the technology was fairly standard, fallout from the race to other worlds that had been sidetracked into military applications.

"How's it look?" Grimaldi asked, when he had parked the gear and settled in a chair across from Bolan.

"Still on track," the Executioner replied. "We've got at least one male Caucasian hanging out with Cubans at Korahe. If he's not a Russian, I'll be very much surprised."

"You think it's unofficial?"

"That would be my guess. The snarl they've got at home, it's hard to picture anyone in Moscow looking for a piece of Africa to chew on."

"That's a help, at least."

"You know it."

If the Russians hanging out in Ethiopia were unofficial—rogues—they could be dealt with swiftly, ruthlessly, no second thoughts about a possible response from Moscow. Next time Phoenix Force saw the stranger's face, they could feel free to take him down.

"How long until they wrap up in Djibouti?" Grimaldi inquired.

"They're estimating two, three hours. We can use the time to shake things up a little more right here."

"And then?"

"We'll get Siad to make some calls and put the final ball in play, but first we need coordinates."

"You asked about the backup?"

"They'll be working on it, once they get the odds and ends nailed down."

"I hope it's handy. That's a long walk back, if we run out of fuel."

"Consider it a challenge," Bolan told him, smiling without humor.

"Like I need the exercise," Grimaldi said.

"Let's try some warmups, stretch our legs a little. I've still got spots on my wish list."

"If they're standing."

"One way to find out."

It was Grimaldi's turn to smile. "I thought you'd never ask."

Korahe, Ethiopia

WHEN CLEANING UP the refuse of an ambush, it is always helpful to have local government officials on your side. The explanations are less bothersome that way, if any are required in fact, and it is relatively easy to dispose of evidence—including bodies.

Bury them, or ship them out.

Raul Rodriguez knew that he was fortunate to be alive. For a second time, his soldiers had been taken absolutely by surprise, and this time he was on the scene, not only watching as they died, but dodging bullets with the rest of them. He was a combat officer, of course, but by its very definition that meant he was years away from crawling on his belly in the mud and trading rounds with unseen enemies. An officer, most customarily, sat well behind the lines and told his soldiers where to go, whom they should kill.

The usual.

He was embarrassed by his personal reaction to the ambush at the villa. Not that he had soiled himself or otherwise become a public laughingstock, but it had set a bad example for his men to see him prostrate on the patio, with Kuybyshev, instead of on his feet and leading them to victory. The good news was that most of those who saw him drop and crawl were dead now, and the others had been busy chasing shadows through the trees.

They had retrieved a rubber boat, some distance from the house, its stamp and markings pointing to a factory in the former state of Czechoslovakia. Rodriguez didn't think the gunmen had been Czechs, of course, or even Slovaks. They were clever, though, and knew exactly how to agitate his nerves.

The Russian, meanwhile, didn't seem tremendously concerned. A change of clothes, a glass of wine, and he was seated on the patio once more, discussing the attack with a colonel of the Ethiopian army, watching while African soldiers helped the Cubans haul their dead away.

Rodriguez had their names, but they wouldn't be going home. Fidel believed that it demoralized his people to see coffins coming back from foreign battlefields. In his philosophy, if revolutionary warriors blessed a place by pouring out their life's blood, the place they fell—or a facsimile—became their final resting place. The parents, siblings, wives and children would be satisfied with notice from a sergeant bearing gifts of fruit and candy.

The Russian cleared his throat. Rodriguez glanced back from the busy lawn and found the Ethiopian had left them. If you didn't count the two guards standing twenty feet away, they were alone.

"As I was trying to explain before the interruption," Kuybyshev began, "we need a swift, impressive victory. Now, more than ever. You agree?"

"A victory would be a pleasant change," Rodriguez said.

"And at the moment, you still have sufficient numbers to achieve it, yes?"

The Cuban major thought about it, finally nodded. "Yes, I think so. It depends, of course, upon the target."

"Certainly. And since we have our choice, the target should not be a problem."

That would mean another border raid. Rodriguez didn't mind, in principle. In six months dodging back and forth across the border with Djibouti, he had only lost one man in combat—and to friendly fire, at that. The peasants had few weapons, and they were easily surprised and terrorized. The border raiding yielded an impressive body count for his reports back to Havana, and his soldiers liked the native women for a change of pace.

"We're getting nowhere with the villagers," Rodriguez said. "Aside from spreading fear, we've come no closer to the incident required for all-out war."

"My friend, that simply means it's time to escalate. Instead of killing peasants, we need contact with the military."

"Face the army?" Skepticism and surprise were mingled in the major's voice.

"A single unit, more precisely. Something for your men to overwhelm and capture. Bring the vehicles and bodies back across the border into Ethiopia and stage a scene. Leave no doubt as to the identity of the aggressors."

It was such a simple thing, the way he spelled it out, but still Rodriguez frowned. "So, we go looking for the soldiers this time," he remarked, "instead of trying to avoid them."

"With our contacts in Djibouti, it should not be difficult to find a target," Kuybyshev replied. "In fact, I have an officer in mind."

Rodriguez knew the name before he heard it spoken. "Ah," he said. "Hassan Gourad."

"The very same."

Gourad had been an obstacle from the beginning of their border raids. He couldn't head them off, of course, but he collected evidence and filed reports. The files were growing in Djibouti, ammunition for complaints to the United Nations, and the fact that they hadn't been used before was due in no small part to the connections Kuybyshev maintained across the border. Sympathy for Ethiopia was strong among the Afar tribesmen, some of whom had found their way into the government and military. Every nation has its traitors lurking in or near the corridors of power, picking up a conversation here, a piece of paper there.

"You can arrange his transfer to a border area?" Rodriguez asked.

"I'm more inclined to bait a trap," Kuybyshev replied, "and wait for him to stumble in. If word got out, for instance, that we planned to raid a certain village, and Gourad had time to lead his unit from Djibouti, we could have him to ourselves."

That "we" must be a euphemism, Rodriguez thought, for the Russian certainly wasn't about to risk himself in combat.

"If he knows we're coming," said Rodriguez, "he will order reinforcements."

"We will *ask* for reinforcements," Kuybyshev replied, correcting him, "and the request will be denied. It does not take a full division to investigate a rumor, after all."

So, that was it. The Russian had a man inside the general staff—or close enough, at any rate, to keep Hassan Gourad from beefing up his normal unit when the chips were down. Still, with the men Gourad had standing by, Rodriguez knew that he would have to field his Cubans as a bloc, no holding back reserves.

It was a gamble, and he didn't take it lightly.

Neither did he have the option to refuse.

"My men are ready," he informed the Russian, hoping it was true.

Mogadishu

AMRITA FOUND HER BROTHER gone when she awoke, but the American who called himself Carl was waiting for her in the smallish kitchen of the house where she had spent the night.

"Good morning. Coffee?"

"Yes, please."

It was strong and black, much like the man himself.

"Who are you, really?" Amrita asked, after they were seated at the table.

"Just a soldier."

"I don't think so."

"Everyone's entitled to their own opinion," Calvin James replied."

"That is not always true in Mogadishu."

"Yeah, I noticed."

"You are here to help us, I believe."

James nodded. "That's the plan."

"But, why?"

"Why help you?" If the question took him by surprise, it didn't show. He shrugged and answered, "It's my job."

"Some person hired you, then," she said. "You fight for money? Like a mercenary?"

"Not exactly." He was slightly irritated now, but it didn't detract from his charisma. "I get paid for what I do, but I'm not chasing wars."

"You pick and choose?"

"Whenever possible."

"What made you choose Somalia, Mr. Jones?"

He blinked, as if the name were unfamiliar to him, but the moment passed almost before it registered. "You're on the short end of the stick," he said, "in case you hadn't noticed. No one's helping you to a significant degree. I mean, the Red Cross sends in food and medicine, the UN tries to guard it, but the warlords rip it off, regardless."

"That's been going on for years," Amrita said. "What brings you to Somalia *now?*"

"Back home, they like to work 'through channels.' Nice and legal—on the surface, anyway. It takes awhile for someone with authority to get the message that their plan's not working, then they have to take a breather, think some more and start from scratch. I get a call around the time they've used up all their other options, and they've got egg on their faces."

"Egg on faces?"

"Meaning they're embarrassed," James explained. He hesitated for a moment, weighing what it might be safe to tell her, then continued. "Plus, on top of that, you've got the warlords spreading out there days."

"Djibouti." When she spoke, it didn't come out sounding like a question.

"There you go."

"And what role does my brother play in this?" she asked.

"You talked to him," James said.

"He told me next to nothing."

"Then I really couldn't say."

"You mean you won't say."

James responded with another shrug, but smiled to soften the effect. "Same thing," he said. "it's not my place to talk about his private business."

"Even with his sister?"

"Even so."

"You are a man of scruples then." There was a sharp edge to her voice, but James didn't appear to take offense.

"I try."

"And killing fits within your value system."

"I'm a soldier," James replied. "I do my job."

"Last night was just a job of work to you. I see."

"We talked about that once already. I was waiting for your brother. It's a lucky thing for you that I was there."

"I'm sorry," she said relenting. "I do not wish to appear ungrateful. You must understand that I am worried for Siad."

"I see that, but he's only got one little job to do before he's done—with my folks, anyway. It won't take long. The risks are next to none, and if it all works out, the two of you should be home free."

"In Mogadishu," she reminded him, "no one is ever quite 'home free.'"

"Things change," the tall American replied. "These problems didn't hit you overnight. It's bound to take some time to clean things up."

"With the UN?" Amrita smiled and shook her head. "They come as referees, and nothing more. American Marines could not restrain Mohammed el Itale with their guns and tanks. How are the people to control him now?"

"It might not be a problem. Wait and see."

"You mean to kill him?"

"Me?" James smiled. "I never met the man, you know? It wouldn't be so bad if someone capped him for his trouble, would it?"

"I would not weep at his funeral," she admitted, "but I do not think his death will solve my country's problems, either. Someone will replace him, and the war goes on."

"Or, maybe not."

"You have more faith in the Somali people than I do," Amrita told him.

"No," he answered, putting on another smile. "I just keep hoping things will work out for the good guys, now and then."

"Well," said Amrita, as she matched her smile to his, "it does no harm to dream."

El Bur, Somalia

MOHAMMED EL ITALE did not like reporting to a foreigner as if the two of them were equals, much less with the implication of his own inferiority. Itale had invested years and countless human lives in rising to his present status, and it galled him to be summoned like a peasant by his master in the old times. It was all the more humiliating that the man who summoned him should be Chinese.

Ziyang Tse Chung wasn't the easiest of men to tolerate, with his abrasive tongue and lordly attitude. For someone who believed in "people's revolution" and the brotherhood of men, he acted more like an aristocrat. One more good reason, in Itale's view, for the expulsion of all Asians from Somalia, once he ruled the roost.

Just now, however, he still needed the Chinese, for the material support and training they provided. In a few more months, if all went well, he would have soldiers ready to begin instructing new recruits, plus all the guns and ammunition he would need to end the four-year civil war. When that day came, the Red Chinese would have outlived their usefulness, and he could deal with them as he saw fit.

Beijing would be in no position to complain, he thought, since their involvement in Somalia was a secret from the world at large. Their very presence in his country mocked United Nations rules and resolutions, leaving the Chinese without recourse if he decided to eliminate their emissaries. They couldn't protest in public, and reprisals would expose them to the wrath of the UN.

The thought of executing Ziyang Tse Chung improved Itale's humor as he moved past hard-eyed Chinese guards to enter the lieutenant colonel's private office. Chung didn't rise from his desk to greet the new arrival, nodding toward an empty chair as if displays of common courtesy were foreign to his nature.

Which, Mohammed el Itale knew from previous experience, was very likely true.

Itale sat and crossed his legs, regarding Chung with what he hoped was an impassive face. He waited for the Chinese officer to speak, since Chung had made the summons. It was his job to begin and state the business of their meeting.

"You have lost more men in Mogadishu," Chung remarked, as if the fact would be unknown to his reluctant guest.

"It's true," Itale said, "but we were lucky, also. One of my informers tells me Jouad ben Ganane is among the dead."

Chung raised an eyebrow, frowning thoughtfully. "Your most persistent enemy."

"I am attempting to confirm it, as we speak. My source knows better than to lie about a thing of such importance."

"My congratulations." Chung refused to smile; it would have made his face look alien, deformed. The man was born to frown. "Unfortunately even victories may leave an army weakened and encourage opposition from outside."

"I am prepared to deal with any fool who tries to challenge me."

"Perhaps," Chung said, "there is a better way."

Itale waited, knowing the lieutenant colonel wouldn't keep his words of wisdom to himself.

"A gesture," Chung repeated, when he realized Itale didn't plan to question him. "A show of strength to dazzle your surviving enemies, bring new, potential adversaries into line."

"What kind of gesture?"

"You require an incident to help unite the country under one man's leadership," Chung said. "A strong man who has proved himself in battle. If the threat came from outside Somalia, the United Nations could not argue with your methods when it comes to self-defense."

Itale wasn't sure about Chung's logic, but it made an interesting story. He kept listening, a noncommittal grunt to let the Chinese officer know he was keeping up.

"If your home country is invaded—by Djibouti, for example—it is only common sense for you to punish those responsible. Seize territory, as a form of reparation for the damage and the loss of life. No one can argue with the justice of your choice."

Again, Itale held a different view, but he was captivated by the thought of managing an empire. They had talked about Djibouti in the past, launched several minor raids across the border for the hell of it, but he could see Chung's larger strategy emerging now. The colonel was looking for a conquest of his own—or for Beijing.

Itale smiled, imagining the rude surprise he had in store for Chung.

"I can't imagine that Djibouti would invade Somalia," he replied.

"It might appear so, to the world in general," Chung said.

Itale took pride in his ability to feign ignorance, when it was called for. "How could that be, Comrade Chung?"

The foreigner was buying it. He almost smiled. Almost.

"There is a way," Chung said, "if you are willing to cooperate."

"Of course, to help my country."

And to help myself, Itale thought.

"Ah, good. In that case..."

By the time Chung finished outlining his plan, Itale had a new respect for the man. And he knew that Chung would have to die.

CHAPTER SIXTEEN

Djibouti

The central headquarters of the National Union Party was located in downtown Djibouti, six blocks from the scene of that morning's riot. It was relatively small, considering its total impact on the nation, but it paid, sometimes, to keep a low profile in Djibouti, between demonstrations. There were enemies abroad in the land, and a group as controversial as the National Union Party could expect bomb threats and vandalism, arson and assault, perhaps attempted murder of its staff.

The NUP was organized around the hard core of the Issa faction in Djibouti, agitating for "reunion" with Somalia. Officially the group didn't encourage terrorism, but its members never shied away from trouble, either, and a healthy number of them were in prison, charged with acts of violence linked to tribal politics. They clashed most often, as that very morning, with their rivals of the large Afar community, but they weren't above attacking government officials if the mood was right.

A part of Yakov Katzenelenbogen's bargain with Hassan Gourad to wrap up the trouble in Djibouti was cooperation by the men of Phoenix Force in crushing violence by the Issa and Afar. Their first step had been taken in the riot, rubbing out the foreign agents who were sent from Addis Ababa and Mogadishu to incite more violence in Djibouti. Rounding off the play, before Gourad would help them bait the final trap and throw his military weight behind the effort, they were pledged to put a major crimp in the subversive actions of the native Issa and Afar.

To Katz, that meant a full-scale blitz with everything he had: four men, himself included, with a fair amount of hardware and a bit of cover from the troops commanded by Gourad. They couldn't expect direct assistance from the army, but it was a comfort—more or less—to know that they wouldn't be hunted through the streets by men in uniform. Ideally Katz was hoping to conclude their bloody business in the next two hours and proceed to laying Striker's snare, but he would have to cope with first things first.

They had three targets, altogether, but he had refused to send a single man for any one of them, which meant that they would have to make good time. Katz checked his watch again and hoped that Rafael had found his place behind the smallish storeroom office. Ready or not, it was time to put the ball in play.

He left his car and crossed the street, the little MP-5 K submachine gun feeling bulky underneath his arm. The jacket covered it, but Katz was sweating by the time he reached the sidewalk, glancing left and right before he barged in through the door.

Katz had a photo lineup memorized, six faces linked to documented acts of terrorism in the capital or in the countryside, but he wasn't about to take unnecessary risks. He had the little buzzgun in his left hand as he cleared the threshold. The male receptionist rose behind his desk his hand groping for a weapon in the middle drawer.

The Phoenix Force leader hit him with a 3-round burst that dropped the stranger in his swivel chair. He left him there, proceeding down a narrow hallway to the rooms in back. A crash from somewhere out of sight announced Encizo's entry through the back door, cutting off the only exit hatch. A rattle of staccato automatic fire from that direction, followed by a gargling cry, and Katz kept hunting.

Suddenly a door popped open in front of him, two men spilling out into the hall. Katz recognized the second of them from the photo lineup, knew that he was linked to bombings in Djibouti and Dikhil. The short man with him was a cipher, but they both had pistols in their hands and frightened, panicky expressions on their faces.

Dust to dust.

Katz hit them with a sweeping burst that tracked from left to right and dropped them where they stood, limbs tangled in the semblance of a last embrace. He stepped across the bodies and checked the office they had come from. Empty.

To his right, another door stood halfway open, no one visible inside. He kicked it back and entered in a crouch, the MP-5 K leading. Scuffling sounds behind the desk alerted him to danger, and he swung in that direction, ready when a shadow shape burst into view and started pumping wild rounds in his general direction from a handgun.

Katz responded with a rising burst that slammed the shooter back against a metal filing cabinet, pinned him there for just a heartbeat, then let him slither to the floor. Before he sank back out of sight, the Israeli recognized another visage from Gourad's collection of suspected terrorists.

Two down, and they were running out of time.

Returning to the hallway, Katz met Encizo coming from the opposite direction, reloading his SMG on the move.

"How many?"

"Two," Encizo told him. "One guy from the photos."

"That makes three," Katz said. "We're out of here."

"Suits me."

They had another target waiting, and the gunshots would have drawn a crowd by now. The ethnic breakdown in Djibouti meant they couldn't lose themselves among bystanders flocking to the scene. They had to get away, and swiftly, while they had a chance.

The Phoenix Force warriors found themselves surrounded as they left the office, but they kept their weapons visible and cleared a lane without resorting to further bloodshed. As they drove away, the crowd filled in behind them, massing in the street.

"You think we're doing any good?" Encizo asked.

"We made a deal," Katz said. "We're sticking to it."

"Right."

And they were on their way to target number two.

HASSAN GOURAD was troubled by the thought that he had made a devil's bargain, but he saw no other way to save his country in the present crisis. It grieved him that his actions would result in escalating violence in the short run, but he salved his conscience with the thought that he was helping to protect Djibouti and her people from invasion and the greater ravages of war.

And all he had to do, for now, was go along behind his allies, picking up the pieces. Later, possibly that very night, he would be called upon to risk his men, his very life.

But that was later. He would deal with one thing at a time.

His second in command emerged from the offices of the National Unity Party, frowning and shaking his head. A ring of uniforms and guns restrained the crowd of several thousand people that had gathered to observe, shout questions and absorb the general atmosphere of death.

"Survivors?" Gourad asked.

The young aide shook his head. "Six dead, sir. Three of them I recognize from our investigations into sabotage and terrorism."

"Which?"

"Dolo Agere, Bako Mandera and Kurmuk Asose."

"All dead."

"Yes, sir."

Gourad was nodding, trying to suppress a rush of satisfaction at the news. He worried that it made him something less than human to exult in the destruction of another man, but these three were responsible for thirty-seven deaths between them, to his certain knowledge. None of it was provable in court, but truth and evidence were sometimes very different things.

"Descriptions of the gunmen?"

"They were white, sir. Two of them were seen, with automatic weapons, as they left the office. It will take some time to know if there were others."

"Time is all we have, Lieutenant," Gourad said. "I would not care to rush a case of this importance.

Question every witness thoroughly before you broadcast a description of the killers."

"Sir?"

"My point, Lieutenant, is that we risk stirring up a firestorm if we say that white men were responsible, but we have no more information. Do you want the Issa rioting outside the embassy of the United States? Great Britain? Russia?"

"No, sir."

"Very well, then. Finish your interrogations. Leave no stone unturned. Report to me before you furnish any information whatsoever to the press."

"The men responsible—"

"Are not available for questioning themselves. Until they are, we must attempt to separate the facts from idle gossip and distortion. Is my order understood, Lieutenant?"

"Yes, sir."

A salute, before the young man turned away. He was suspicious, growing more so since the morning's riot, when Gourad had restrained his troops and kept them from the hidden snipers' line of fire. No challenge yet, and with a bit of luck the matter would be finally resolved before it came to that.

Gourad couldn't expect great sympathy if it was learned that he had cast his lot with foreigners to violate the law. It would be tantamount to treason, and the price could be his life if he were tried, convicted by a military court. The fact that it would be a lawful sentence didn't keep Gourad from trying to avoid that awful end.

He could explain tomorrow, when the smoke had cleared—if he was still alive. There were officials in the government—and army brass above him—who were pledged to the Afar and Issa, traitors in their own right, but they managed to conceal their treason. Maybe, when the helping hands they prayed and plotted for were swept away, they would be easier to topple from their pedestals.

Or maybe not.

Gourad would take that chance, but he would have to take it one step at a time. The foreigners were risking everything on his behalf this afternoon, and it would soon be payback time. When they were finished in the capital, if they all managed to survive, Gourad knew he couldn't refuse their personal request for help.

And if the final conflict cost his life, so be it. He would go down fighting, like a soldier, in the service of his homeland. If it came to that, his name would be unsullied when they put him in the ground, the pension secure for his family. More critically, with any kind of luck at all, his country's mortal enemies would be exposed for all the world to see.

It would be worth his life for that.

But it would be better yet, if he could find a way to stay alive.

As THE ISSA ACTIVISTS were organized in the National Unity Party, so zealots of the Afar tribe had joined ranks in the Freedom League. To them, however, "freedom" had a somewhat novel definition, linked to union of their homeland with the state of Ethiopia, controlled from Addis Ababa. If any citizens of present-day Djibouti were opposed to annexation, they were free to leave the country with whatever personal belongings they could carry—or, in the alternative, they had the choice to stay and fight against a force consisting of their neighbors, Ethiopian militia, and the Cubans who had come halfway around the world to "help."

The Freedom League had spent the past two years preparing for that struggle, caching arms and ammunition, staging raids against the Issa diehards, wreaking havoc with sporadic acts of sabotage around the salt mines. In a nation where fifty-two percent of the population was illiterate, they spread their message via word of mouth, employing threats where necessary to control the faithful. Blood was thicker than water in Djibouti, but it sometimes flowed more freely in the streets.

The morning's riot had been costly—five men dead, including two important organizers, and at least three dozen jailed—but spokesmen for the Freedom League had already declared a victory against the Issa bandits. As the story spread by word of mouth throughout the countryside, it would become a great pitched battle, with the opposition scourged and put to flight in disarray.

That is, if they had time to spread the word.

McCarter stood atop the flat roof of the Freedom League's two-story headquarters, a stucco blockhouse on the western outskirts of Djibouti. Manning would be on the fire escape by now, prepared to enter through a window they had chosen in advance for access to the area where weapons were illegally concealed.

One minute left, and counting.

He had tried the access door already, found it locked and used a knife blade to defeat the flimsy latch. The way stood open, and he double-checked his Uzi submachine gun, feeling for the extra magazines to guarantee that he could find them in a hurry, under fire.

All set.

He slipped into the murky stairwell, closed the access door behind him and descended nine steps to the floor where members of the Freedom League were known to bunk at night, if they were working late or hiding out from the police. He glanced both ways along the hall and waited, counting off the final seconds, letting Gary make his way inside.

Time, now, and he veered off to check the four rooms on his right as they had planned. The first two doors stood open, no one visible inside. McCarter passed them by and found the last two closed, a muffled sound of voices coming from the bedroom on his left.

He walked in as though he owned the place and found two gunners cleaning AK-47 rifles at a folding table. They had stripped the weapons down, and there was no way to reassemble them before McCarter cut loose with his Uzi, stitching them from left to right and back again. The Parabellum manglers made them jerk and twitch before they fell together, stretched out on the bare wood floor already stained with blood.

Across the hall, a door swung open as McCarter left the two dead gunners. Number three was gaping at him with a look of stunned surprise, retreating in a rush, too late to slam his door again before a stream of bullets blew him away.

Three targets down, and none of them was recognizable from any of the mug shots handed over by Gourad. McCarter knew there was a chance that they might come up empty on the hit list, but they couldn't turn back now.

He caught a glimpse of Manning, moving toward him down the hall, before the shock of an explosion rocked the building. That would be the arsenal, a plastique charge destroying military hardware stockpiled by the Freedom League for use against their many enemies.

"Look out!" McCarter shouted, bringing up his Uzi as a shadow lumbered into view at Manning's back. The big Canadian went down and swiveled back to face his adversary, leveling a submachine gun of his own.

They fired together, probably a dozen rounds between them, and the shadow shape collapsed without a whimper. Manning ran to check him, came back smiling while McCarter watched the stairs.

"That's one," he said. "Nose ring and cornrows."

"Right. Let's go."

They charged downstairs, McCarter leading, Manning covering his back. Above them, flames had taken hold and smoke was filling up the second floor. In moments there would be the stench of roasting flesh, aside from wood smoke and the smell of plaster dust.

McCarter glimpsed a ring of faces at the bottom of the stairs and came down firing, bodies twitching, keeling over as his bullets found their marks. A blank, familiar face stared up at the Briton with sightless eyes as he leapt over huddled bodies, following a wounded member of the group to finish him.

The runner turned to face McCarter, brandishing a shiny automatic pistol, but his aim was off, and his first two bullets hit the ceiling overhead. The Briton nailed him with a short burst to the chest and slammed him over on his back, a final tremor of his limbs before the man went limp in death.

And that was all.

McCarter heard a voice raised in the direction of the street, and others quickly joined it, drawing nearer. They would have a mob scene if they lingered, but the car was parked out back in the alley.

"We're done," he said to Manning, catching a nod from the Canadian, and broke in the direction of the back door, fifty feet away. Emerging into sunlight, he couldn't help thinking of Encizo and Katz, the final target on their hit parade.

The clock was running down, and it would soon be time to stage their final play, for all the marbles. As he slid behind the steering wheel, McCarter hoped that they would all be there to see it when the storm broke loose and swept Djibouti clean.

WAITING TAUGHT YOU patience, Rafael Encizo knew from long experience, but there was still an urge to jump right in and get things done, to hell with caution and the risks involved. He had to put the ultimate objective out of mind and drag his thoughts back to the here and now, stay sharp and focused. No mistakes.

The first hit had been relatively easy, in and out before the targets really had a clue of what was happening. It wasn't pretty, but Encizo had seen worse— much worse—and would again, before a new day broke across Djibouti.

He was counting on it.

They were still three faces short of clearing out the Issa photo lineup, no way to be sure the targets would be present at this final stop, but it was worth a shot. If nothing else, they would have helped Hassan Gourad enough that he was in their debt and bound—if honor still meant anything, these days—to help them with the last phase of their plan.

The target was a walled estate, and getting in had been less trouble than Encizo had anticipated. Up and over at the northeast corner, in the shadow of some looming trees, and they split up to flank the house. The grounds were guarded, but the young men picked as sentries were a careless lot, imbued with youth's delusion of immortality. Encizo dealt with two of them before he came within a stone's throw of the house and started ticking off the final moments, counting down to doomsday.

Katz was on the far side of the house and closing in by now. Encizo waited for his signal, cradling the folding-stock Kalashnikov and marking time. In front of him, no more than fifty feet away, a set of sliding doors stood open on a smallish patio. Inside, as far as he could see, the sitting room was occupied by three or four men having drinks, something with ice that rattled in their glasses, audible from where he waited.

The explosion, when it came, was muffled by the intervening walls. Encizo saw his targets drop their tumblers, scramble to their feet and grab weapons that were close at hand. It looked like five men, now that they were on their feet and moving, but he couldn't let the numbers slow him down.

Encizo charged the open doorway, sprinting for it, praying that his enemies wouldn't glance back and see him for another second, maybe two. When he had closed the gap to thirty feet, he opened up with the Kalashnikov on full auto, dropping two before they realized that they were under fire.

It went to hell from there, his three remaining targets breaking left and right, a couple of them flinging wild shots toward the sliding doors and missing by a mile. Glass shattered on his left, bright slivers catching sunlight, tinkling on the patio. Encizo didn't have the space or inclination for evasive action, boring in without refinements, spraying bullets left in a deadly arc that cleared his path.

He saw a third man stumble and go down thrashing as the tumblers swept him off his feet, dead before he hit the floor.

Another shooter had Encizo covered on the right flank, working on a decent shot when the Phoenix Force warrior squeezed off a burst that cut his legs from under him and dropped him on his back. A short burst finished it, and that left one.

The last man up was running for his life. It would have been a decent strategy, except that he had nowhere to go, and nothing in the way of cover that would help him get there. Encizo was up and after him before the runner made it halfway to the nearest exit, triggering a burst that slapped his target's back between the shoulder blades, and flattened him against the nearest wall.

Reloading on the move, Encizo made a quick check on the dead and recognized one face among the five. A little heavier than in the mug shot, with some recent facial hair, but it was unmistakable.

He tracked the sounds of gunfire, homing in on Katz, and found his comrade as the gruff Israeli finished off a wounded adversary. Two more bodies lay behind Katz on the threshold of another room, with cordite heavy in the air.

"I bagged one coming in," Katzenelenbogen said. "You?"

"That makes a double. Are we done here?"

"Just about. I want to leave a small memento."

As he spoke, Katz took a fist-sized plastique charge out of the satchel slung across one shoulder, crossed the room and wedged it in the nook where two load-bearing walls were joined. He set the timer, giving them a lead, and started toward the exit.

"Ready when you are."

A sentry met them on the front porch, looking dazed, too late to save himself before they opened fire in unison and cut him down. The way was clear from there, a short jog to the gate and out, along the road to reach their waiting vehicle. When they were half-way there, the house behind them shuddered, rocked on its foundation by the C4 charge.

"They'll need some decorating work," the Cuban said.

"At least."

So much for the preliminaries, Encizo thought. Dusk was coming, and they had work to do before the final trap was sprung. It might be wasted effort, but they damn well had to try.

With everything they had.

CHAPTER SEVENTEEN

Mogadishu

The news of Jouad ben Ganane's death reached Bolan shortly after 4:00 p.m., accelerated by Siad Samatar's reluctant visit to the city morgue. From that same visit, Bolan knew that one of the assassins taken out the night before by Calvin James had been a member of Mohammed el Itale's private army.

It was all the information the Executioner needed, in the final hours of his play.

He was about to close the game in Mogadishu, move on to the last phase of his plan, but there was time to spread a little more confusion in the opposition ranks. Itale would be jubilant at the elimination of his chief competitor, inclined to celebrate, perhaps believing that his troubles were behind him.

But the Executioner was out to rain on his parade.

For Bolan's purposes, it was essential that the warlord understand his error, realize that he was still confronted with an enemy who meant to see him dead, his petty empire laid to waste. It would require an extra shove to send Itale on the warpath, put him right where Bolan wanted him, but it could still be done.

The fuse was lit. He simply had to fan the flames a little and make sure the charge went off on schedule.

Starting now.

The target was a warehouse in the old port district, a quarter mile northeast of the fortified French embassy. Itale stored a fair amount of contraband at the location, mostly food and medicine awaiting distribution through black-market channels to his ailing fellow countrymen. The cargo came from Red Cross shipments, for the most part, pilfered on arrival from the docks, or robbed at gunpoint from relief centers spotted around Somalia's capital city.

Bolan was about to shave the warlord's profit margin by an estimated twenty-one percent.

He parked a hundred yards north of the warehouse, took an olive-drab satchel from the space behind the driver's seat and placed it on the hood. He double-checked his weapons—the Beretta and the Uzi submachine gun on its swivel harness—making sure that both were fully loaded, with the safeties off. When he was ready, Bolan locked the car and walked back through the muggy heat to reach his destination.

Closing in, he saw no sentries covering the warehouse. Was it possible Itale had already dropped his guard, or was the warehouse not considered a priority? In either case, it wouldn't bother the warrior if his adversary made things easy for him, just this once.

He found a ladder bolted to the north wall of the warehouse, granting access to the broad, flat roof. There was a row of skylights and a massive air conditioner, the latter silent now. It would be stifling hot inside the warehouse, Bolan thought, but then again, the real heat hadn't started yet.

He chose a skylight in the center of the roof, knelt and peered in through the lightly tinted glass. Below him, double rows of wooden crates were stacked ten or twelve feet high, approximately halfway to the rafters. Bolan had to guess at the specific contents, but it made no difference to his plan.

He tried the skylight and found it latched. No matter. Opening his satchel, he removed a thermite bomb and weighed it in his palm. He ditched the safety pin but held the spoon in place as he removed the sleek Beretta from its shoulder rig and thumbed the hammer back.

Two rounds broke the heavy glass, and he leaned forward, dropped the thermite can and watched it fall. The warrior stepped back before it burst, already moving toward another skylight as the white-hot coals of phosphorus began to do their work. It took a special foam to douse their heat, and Bolan rightly guessed that none would be available in Mogadishu— or, at any rate, not soon enough to salvage anything of value from the warehouse.

Number two went in on target, and the Executioner kept moving, smashed another skylight and released his third incendiary bomb before a minute had elapsed from number one. Beneath his feet, Itale's merchandise was burning brightly, giving off a pungent cloud of smoke. In places, where a thermite coal had reached the ceiling, sparks were bleeding through the metal of the warehouse roof.

And it was time to go, before the building started melting out from under him. He grabbed his satchel, jogged back to the ladder and descended swiftly to ground level. He was almost to the loading dock when three men burst out of the warehouse, coughing smoke and fumes, their leader brandishing a pistol in his hand.

The gunman caught a glimpse of Bolan through his tears and tried to shout a warning, choking on it as his gun came up and wobbled into target acquisition. The warrior wasn't waiting for the guy to make his shot, the Uzi sliding out of cover, spitting Parabellum rounds almost before it cleared his lightweight jacket.

Bolan dropped the shooter with a 4-round burst that opened up his chest, kept firing as the others tried to break for cover, cutting both men down in awkward attitudes of death. He waited for a moment, half expecting more to follow, but the trio seemed to be alone. When he was satisfied that no one was about to surface, firing at his back, he turned away and jogged to his waiting vehicle.

El Bur, Somalia

THE PLAN WAS TYPICAL of Ziyang Tse Chung, a mixture of simplicity and guile. The basic premise called for members of Mohammed el Itale's private army to invade Djibouti one more time, engaging a selected— and presumably outnumbered—military force, which could be overwhelmed and captured, or at least encouraged to pursue them back across the border to Somalia. It wouldn't take a genius to detect the ruse, but by the time investigators went to work in earnest, Chung would have his war, with the potential for enveloping Djibouti.

All Itale needed at the moment was a clear-cut victory in arms to clinch his reputation as the ruling warlord in the country. Once the battle for Djibouti had been joined, his ranks would triple or quadruple with enthusiastic volunteers, while competition from his rivals withered on the vine. Chung was satisfied that the arms and training he had managed to provide would make the difference in a showdown with Djibouti's peasant soldiers, and there would be more help for the dynamic "freedom fighters" once Beijing learned of his progress in the field.

Somalia had been a gamble to begin with—what the Americans would call a long shot. Chung's superiors were chafing at the harsh opinions voiced in Western editorials, at the United Nations in New York, all carping on the Chinese way of handling dissidents at home. It pleased the West to ridicule Beijing and call for "liberal" reforms, as if the Anglos understood a thing about the Chinese history and culture.

Chung's superiors were every bit as anxious for a victory as were his clients in Somalia, and they would gratefully reward the officer who gave it to them. If he managed to secure more territory for Beijing, perhaps a puppet state for them to play with, he could write his own list of demands. Promotion, possibly an office in the government itself, instead of serving on the firing line.

He hadn't chosen a specific target yet, but it was coming. It would have to be a village fairly near the border, to facilitate abduction or pursuit. In either case, Itale would be forced to hold some troops in reserve, against the possibility that he would have to spring an ambush on his own side of the boundary line.

It might look more authentic that way, Chung decided, but he would accept whatever happened. The perpetuation of a grand illusion was no easy task, and the colonel didn't expect the Western press to swallow it in any case. The UN troops would try to intervene, of course, in their own bungling way, but once the conflict started, they would have a hard time keeping up, much less controlling the events.

In days gone by, Chung could have relied on soldiers from Beijing to back his play, but times had changed. The cold war was a memory, and wars of "Liberation" had to be stage-managed with a bit more delicacy than the outbreaks in Korea and in Vietnam. It would be foolish—dangerous—for his superiors to feign a legitimate interest in Somalia, so far from their own native land, but covert aid was something else. The proud Americans were always doing it, especially in the Western Hemisphere. Deniability was everything, and Chung was a past master when it came to covering his tracks.

He had already managed to retrieve the bodies of his soldiers killed that morning, in the predawn hours, near Serenli. Relatives at home would be informed of losses in a tragic accident, but that could wait a few more weeks. Meanwhile, the soldiers were hyena food, their military gear collected and recycled or destroyed.

It was a relatively simple matter, cleaning up, if you were organized and passably intelligent. Chung, for his part, was a genius when it came to subterfuge. False modesty didn't pervade his thinking, even when the jealousy of his superiors forced him to mask his brilliance for the sake of other, tender egos.

He sat and scanned the topographic map, examining the best approaches and retreats, considering a dozen villages as he went shopping for prospective targets. Something fairly isolated, not too large, but populous enough to matter. It would help if he knew where the local troops were stationed, and he made a note to ask Itale, see if any of his contacts in Djibouti had the information Chung required.

The raid should be tonight, tomorrow at the latest. If they waited any longer, some new problem might arise and scare off Itale. A puppet had no value if he started to revel, or ran away to hide.

So much the better, then. Tonight.

Chung would prove himself to all concerned, and when the smoke cleared, he would be a hero of the People's Revolution. It was terribly immodest of him to anticipate the possibility, but he was frank enough to recognize the truth of his own brilliance.

Destiny was coming for him.

And he'd be ready.

Awdeyle, Somalia

JACK GRIMALDI had enlisted in the Army as a chopper jockey, polished off his training there and piloted a Huey gunship over Vietnam. His skill wasn't confined to helicopters, though—it was a rule of thumb at Stony Man that Grimaldi could handle anything with wings or rotors—but the whirlybirds still felt like home.

Especially when he went out hunting on his own.

It wasn't killing that excited the pilot, although it didn't turn his stomach, either. He enjoyed the chase, the thrill of fighting for his life a mile or two above the surface of the earth, or skimming close enough to count the leaves in treetops racing past beneath his aircraft when he dropped his high-explosive load.

The kick was flying, but it always seemed a trifle tame when he was simply going somewhere, with no prospect of a mortal showdown at the other end.

This afternoon, to Grimaldi's delight, he had been unleashed on a target west of Mogadishu, on the outskirts of Awdeyle, where Mohammed el Itale kept an arms dump hidden in a long-abandoned factory. The target had been fingered by their native contact, young Siad, and the Stony Man pilot had seen enough to trust him. If the kid was wrong, it meant that he would waste some fuel and ammunition, but he had enough on hand, back at the U.S. diplomatic compound, to complete their mission with a fair reserve.

The NAVSTAR homing system gave him time to think, in this case wondering about the diplomatic compound residents in Mogadishu, wondering what had to be on their minds as they observed his Cobra gunship taking off, returning, taking off again, at crazy hours of the day and night. The brass in charge would have their hands full scotching rumors, fielding questions, and he wished them well.

For Grimaldi's part, he would rather take the heat up front than handle cleanup chores behind the lines.

He had the Cobra armed with Hellfire missiles, two quad launchers, plus the lethal minigun and M-129 up front. The Hellfires were designed for antitank deployment, tipped the scales at ninety-five pounds each and used a laser guidance system, homing on a beam projected from the gunship to its target and reflected back to sensors in the missile's nose. In theory, barring interference from another laser, it would be impossible for him to miss his target at any range under five thousand yards.

In practical terms, he planned to be a good deal closer than that when he struck.

Like, right on top of them.

Grimaldi circled wide around his target, came from the west to keep them guessing, nothing for survivors to report in terms of where he came from. Military markings on the Cobra had been painted over, though his enemies could still identify the kind of whirlybird, for all the good that it would do.

He came in low and fast, a hundred feet above the deck. He spotted lookouts pointing at him, scrambling for whatever sanctuary they could find, but he wasn't concerned with strafing them. Not yet. He had the Cobra's laser tracking system zeroed on the factory-turned-arms depot, his finger on the trigger that would send his Hellfire missiles hurtling toward the target.

Closer...closer...

Now!

Two away, the fiery tails like giant tracers homing on the once-abandoned structure, boring in exactly where Grimaldi meant them to. They detonated with a double thunderclap, the west wall of the target lunging out to meet him in a cloud of smoke and flame. Grimaldi drew back on the stick and climbed above the conflagration, banked and circled back around to home in from the north.

He got new target acquisition, even through the drifting smoke. Another pair of Hellfires sizzled from the launchers mounted on the Cobra's stubby wings and rocked their target with a fiery one-two punch. From all appearances, the spreading flames had reached the ammunition and explosive stores, a string of secondary detonations ripping through the building as if giant fireworks had been dropped into the middle of the blaze.

It would be hell in there, Grimaldi thought, a miracle for anyone to make it out alive, unless they had an exit close at hand and used it right away. A few of those were streaming from the shattered building, running for their lives as he returned to make one final pass, just mopping up.

Grimaldi could have let them go. It was an easy thing to look the other way; some would have praised him for his evident humanity. The problem, when he thought about it, was that long experience had taught him that an enemy allowed to run away was always out there somewhere, maybe looking for a chance to even up the score.

He fell in line behind them, dropping lower, with his finger on the trigger of the minigun. Five runners, one of them already wounded, and Grimaldi counted off five seconds as he held the trigger down. The minigun sounded like a chain saw, spewing out a hundred rounds per second, mauling flesh and bone as if the moving targets had been dropped into a giant grinder. They went down together, in a cloud of dust, and none of them was moving when Grimaldi circled back to double-check.

It was enough. He was on borrowed time, and Bolan would be waiting for him back in Mogadishu. He would have to fuel and arm the big Sikorsky UH-60 Black Hawk for the flight that was supposed to wrap their mission in East Africa.

Supposed to, right.

But anything could still go wrong, and Grimaldi wasn't about to count his chickens yet. The whole play could blow up in their faces, if they started getting cocky.

It wasn't over in Somalia or Djibouti, yet.

Not even close.

Mogadishu

BOLAN WAS PREPARED to disengage in the Somali capital, but he couldn't let go without a parting shot to keep his major adversary guessing. By the time the sun began to set, Mohammed el Itale knew his problems hadn't ended with the death of Jouad ben Ganane, but he didn't have a fix on who was plaguing him. The answer, when it came, would hopefully propel him into self-destructive action.

At 6:00 p.m., the Executioner was perched across the street from a three-story building near the National Theater, several blocks south of the former presidential palace. Through the telescopic sight attached to his Galil sniper's rifle, he had a perfect view of the second-floor windows opposite and twenty feet below his rooftop stand.

Itale wouldn't be appearing at the office—not today, of all days—but it made no difference to the warrior's plan. A number of the warlord's functionaries and lieutenants moved around the two rooms he could see, some of them wearing jackets to conceal their side arms, two or three with weapons on display for all to see.

They would be keeping track of late reports from Mogadishu and environs, possibly relaying word back to their leader at his present hideaway. Within the next few moments, they would have a brand-new crisis to report.

He took a breath and held it, let his finger curl around the rifle's trigger, taking up the slack. A dark face filled his eyepiece, cross hairs centered on the forehead, holding steady. Bolan stroked the trigger, holding target acquisition as the rifle bucked against his shoulder and the 7.62 mm bullet sped downrange to find its mark.

The office window shattered, and his target vanished in a crimson blur, the rifle tracking toward its next mark while the handful of survivors stood and stared. He framed a profile in the eyepiece of his telescopic sight and fired again, rewarded with another scarlet splash, another straw man sagging to the floor.

The others were in motion now, each diving for the nearest cover—one behind the desk, another hunkered down behind a filing cabinet, yet another lunging for the nearest exit. Bolan helped the runner get there with a lethal slap between the shoulder blades, propelled him through the open door and into the reception area, a facedown slide across blood-slick linoleum.

He shifted to the other window, where Itale's men were visibly reacting to the sound of smashing glass and startled voices, still uncertain what the problem was. He helped them out in that regard, with two quick rounds that dropped the largest of them in his tracks, a boneless sack of flesh and blood collapsing as the bullets drilled his skull.

Next up, was a slender man who lunged in the direction of the telephone, as if that instrument could save his life. Round six from Bolan's weapon tore his lower jaw away and knocked him off his stride. He never reached the telephone, but went down on the far side of the desk and didn't rise again.

Three others reached the door as one, like something from a slapstick comedy, three stooges shoving one another, throwing elbows, blowing it in their unseemly haste. He nailed them where they stood with three rounds, left to right, and let the snarl resolve itself as gravity took over, dragging deadweight to the floor. Their blood was on the walls and doorjamb, bright and shiny underneath fluorescent lights.

He tracked back to the office on his left, found no one moving and decided he had done enough. A couple of survivors would be useful, talking up the strike and making sure Itale knew his troubles weren't over.

They were only getting started.

It would remain for Siad Samatar to drive the next nail in the warlord's coffin. Samatar had been anxious to go gunning for Itale on his own, once he confirmed ID on the men who had tried to bag his sister, but the Executioner had managed to convince him he could do more damage with a telephone.

Itale would be hungry for revenge, a chance to salvage something from the current mess in Mogadishu. He would grasp at straws to save his reputation as a strongman who exacted vengeance for the smallest insult. There was much to answer for, and he was running out of candidates.

He needed help.

The Executioner was feeling helpful at the moment, as he packed his sniper's rifle in the OD duffel bag. In fact, Bolan thought, he would gladly help Itale right into his grave.

CHAPTER EIGHTEEN

Mogadishu

It seemed to be an easy job, but Siad Samatar was
frightened something would go wrong. Specifically he
worried that Itale wouldn't speak to him, or if he did,
the warlord might dismiss his news as a pathetic hoax,
see through the trap and so redouble his attempts to
kill him.

To find and kill Amrita.

She was safe, at least while she remained with the
Americans, but how long could that last? They would
be leaving Mogadishu soon, perhaps as early as tomorrow or the next day, and the safety they provided
would be stripped away.

What then? If Samatar failed to help them stop
Itale, how would he survive? Where could he take
Amrita, with the little money they possessed, to hide
themselves away?

He must not fail. His story had to convince the
warlord, blend a clever mixture of the truth and lies to
sell Itale on the whereabouts and the identity of his
assailants.

He was stymied at the very start, with no idea of
how to get the warlord's private number, when the
man who called himself Belasko gave it to him, smiling as if it were nothing for him to possess one of the
most closely guarded numbers in all Somalia. By that

point in his brief acquaintance with the stranger, Samatar wasn't surprised to know he had contacts who could get him anything he needed, including information and weapons.

It was a wonder that Belasko didn't simply kill Itale, but the tall American had something else in mind, a scheme to crush the warlord's army in a single stroke, unless Siad was very much mistaken in his reckoning. Already, Jouad ben Ganane was among the dead, his forces whittled down and scattered to the winds within the past two days.

Black Africa wasn't the Stone Age realm depicted in the Tarzan films of yesteryear, but neither was it on a par with Europe and America, in terms of modern-day technology. Few private citizens—and virtually none among the peasant class—possessed a telephone, and service, even in the larger cities, might fairly be described as intermittent. Old equipment failed, an operator skipped his shift without arranging for a substitute, a wealthy citizen or politician hogged the line for hours on end.

It was a fluke, then, that Samatar was able to get through on one attempt. He made the phone call from a hotel lobby, dropping coins and reading off the number from a slip of paper he would chew and swallow when he finished with the call. No point in taking chances. There wouldn't be time for anyone to trace the call and run him down, but it would look bad, later on, if he was found with the unlisted number of a major warlord on his person.

Details.

Samatar stood and listened while the telephone rang twice, before a deep sandpaper voice responded.

"What?"

"I must speak to Mohammed el Itale."

"Who is this?"

"He wouldn't know my name." It was a lie, considering the warlord's very recent effort to destroy him.

"If he doesn't know your name, he doesn't want to talk," the flunky growled. "Who let you have this number?"

"Never mind. I want to tell him who has been responsible for all his recent trouble. Where to find them, if he wants revenge."

There was a brief silence, while the owner of the gruff voice thought it over, trying to decide what kind of suicidal trickster he was dealing with. "I don't know what you mean," he said at last.

"Then you are far too ignorant to serve Mohammed el Itale," Samatar snapped with just the proper edge. "He has been losing property and soldiers for the past two days. If you don't know that, you must be a very stupid man."

The flunky snarled, a wordless sound of fury, but he didn't slam down the telephone receiver. Instead, he stalled another moment, fighting to suppress his rage, then said, "If you know who has done these things, tell me. I will inform the master."

"And take all the credit for yourself, no doubt," Samatar shot back. "No, thank you. If he will not speak to me, then I must keep the information to myself...or maybe call him back another day, when he has lost more men, and tell him that you would not put me through."

"I'll see if he's available," the man replied reluctantly.

"I'll wait."

But not for long. In less than thirty seconds, Samatar heard a new voice on the line. He recognized it from the four or five occasions when he'd heard Itale speak in Mogadishu.

"Yes?"

"Forgive the interruption, sir." He was all humble courtesy, now that he had the Great One on the line. "I understand that you are searching for the men who have attacked your soldiers in the past two days."

"Perhaps." A cautious man, and still alive because of it.

"The information was not easy to collect. I must have something for the risk involved."

"Arrangements can be made, of course ... if what you have to offer is of value."

Samatar pretended to consider it, a false edge of anxiety creeping into his voice as he replied after several beats of silence. "I must trust you, then," he said.

He could almost hear Itale smiling at the other end. The soft voice prodded him. "The information?"

"They are mercenaries from Djibouti, operating with the military there. I have been told they blame your men for raids across the border."

"That's ridiculous."

"Of course, sir. I repeat what I was told, and nothing more"

"Go on."

"These mercenaries are supposed to meet with their superiors tonight in a village called Dolele, twenty miles across the border. Soldiers will be there, but not so many, I was told."

"What is the purpose of this meeting?" Itale asked.

"I cannot be certain. Possibly the mercenaries want their money, or perhaps they will receive fresh orders for a new attack."

"Your information might be useful," the warlord said cautiously, "if you could tell me when the meeting was supposed to happen."

"Midnight," Samatar answered him without the slightest hesitation. "I made sure to ask."

"You wish me to accept your word on faith, without a name or any knowledge of your source," Itale stated, pretending not to be excited. "Why, for all I know, you might be one of those responsible for my discomfort, small as it has been."

"I'm not a fool, sir. Anyone with good sense knows that your army is invincible, but mercenaries, well, they go where they are told."

"Your information might be helpful, if it is correct."

"You have my pledge, sir."

"How am I to thank you properly, if I don't even know your name?"

"I trust you, sir. When you have finished with your enemies, I will present myself and gratefully accept whatever thanks you find appropriate."

"A humble man. I like that."

"Service to the greater good supplies its own reward."

"How true."

"But I will keep in touch."

"Of course."

Samatar hung up the telephone receiver, smiling. It hadn't been so difficult, at that. Of course, he had no way of knowing that Itale would believe him, much less act on what he had been told. Belasko was supposed to be arranging for some kind of confirmation, something that would push the warlord past the point of no return. Samatar didn't know how he meant to do it, and he didn't want to know.

Right now, the less the Somali was told about the plan, the safer he would be. Amrita would be safer, too.

And that was all that mattered now, until the smoke cleared.

He could think about their new life afterward, when there was time.

Assuming all of them were still alive.

El Bur, Somalia

IT WAS THEIR SECOND meeting in a single day, unprecedented, but Colonel Ziyang Tse Chung was pleased to see Mohammed el Itale, all the same. The warlord had some fascinating information for him, if he gave it credence, and it meshed delightfully with Chung's own rudimentary plan.

"You trust this man?" Chung asked his client pointedly.

Itale shrugged. "My people come to me with information all the time. They ask for money, favors, jobs. They are afraid to lie."

That was a lie, Chung realized, but he wasn't dismayed. The would-be ruler of Somalia knew enough about his people and his business to decide which risks were worth the taking.

"Tell me more about this village," the colonel said.

"Dolele. It is...here." Itale pointed to a flyspeck on the map spread out between them. "Average size, perhaps four hundred people. Maybe less."

"Defensive capabilities?" Chung prodded.

"They are peasants. Farmers. They might have a few old guns for hunting game and frightening the birds away, but nothing serious."

"And what about the army? If your information is correct, these mercenaries have been called back to Dolele for a meeting with their military sponsors."

"I've considered that," Itale answered, smiling. "This is an illegal operation, carried out in violation of international law. The men responsible are not receptive to publicity. They chose a minor village, miles out from the capital, to keep their meeting secret. I believe that they will send a small force—certainly an officer or two, perhaps a dozen riflemen. We should have no great difficulty."

Chung played devil's advocate. "We have a problem if the force they send is too small. No one will believe a dozen men were sent out to invade Somalia."

"I already thought of that. We can always say the others managed to escape across the border. How many corpses do we need to prove the point?"

It was the perfect answer, and Chung was pleased. Mohammed el Itale had a fair head on his shoulders for a man who lacked the benefit of being born Chinese. He needed guidance, still, but that was understood between them. Arms and ammunition, training and supplies, would be provided to Itale's private army just as long as he obeyed instructions from Beijing. There would be trouble, swift and certain, if he tried to wing it on his own.

They had no problem, at the moment, and Chung didn't expect one. Not within the next few hours or days, at least. When they had staged the incident, responded to the "foreign threat" with stunning force, then Chung would have to think about his own position in Somalia, the inevitable UN protests. It wouldn't be out of line, he thought, for someone like Itale to request assistance from Beijing, when faced with an invasion of his homeland. The United Nations would be anxious to investigate, of course, but much could happen in the time it took that august body to debate an issue, and Beijing would have a veto waiting if the Security Council sought direct action.

It was nearly perfect, but he still had doubts about the source of information, the number of troops Itale was likely to meet when he got to Dolele. That, in turn, brought up another matter they had yet to clarify.

"You plan to lead the strike yourself, I take it," Chung said.

In fact, the warlord had said no such thing, and he was visibly surprised at the suggestion. "Well..." He hesitated, studied Chung and recognized the Chinese officer's disdain for cowardice. "Of course, for such a mission, I would wish to supervise my men."

It was the last thing that Itale wished, in fact, but he was trapped by the demands of saving face. He hated Chung for placing him in that position, but he could see no way out.

"I understand," Chung said, before his client could begin to think of an excuse for backing out. "Your courage does you credit. How many soldiers will you take?"

The warlord pondered that for several moments, calculating losses for the past two days, the time involved to gather reinforcements from the countryside.

"Perhaps a hundred," he replied at last. "I think a hundred should do nicely."

"With a small force on the border, in reserve, as we discussed?"

"Of course."

Chung was calculating time and distance. Dolele was twenty miles inside Djibouti, give or take, and El Bur was four hundred air miles from the border crossing point. Call it seven hundred miles one way to the border, if they were scrupulous in avoiding Ethiopian airspace. With the aging transport planes at his disposal, Itale could have his men massed on the border in three or four hours. Add two more hours, minimum, for the collection of men and equipment at the airstrip, which would put them on the frontier sometime between 10:00 and 11:00 p.m.

The rest of it was driving fast and striking hard, an overland assault that, hopefully, would have at least some element of surprise. The effort would be wasted if their targets slipped away and made good their escape.

It was a stroke of luck, Chung thought, that white men were involved in the disturbances at Mogadishu. A few Caucasian corpses would be useful in the days ahead, when the United States and Britain started their predictable, self-righteous whining over loss of life in Africa and the involvement of Beijing. Chung hoped the mercenaries would turn out to be American adventurers, a circumstance that his superiors could use to cast a pall of doubt on Washington in the event of an official protest.

First, though, it was necessary to obtain the "evidence" of an abortive raid into Somalia, targeting Itale and his men. Chung would have been more comfortable if the meeting at Dolele was the following night, but he was good at working under pressure—and his client's troops would have to bear the weight of combat, after all.

There was a risk inherent in his plan to have Itale lead the raid, but Chung thought it was necessary. The technique allowed him to exert control, remind his client of exactly who was running things behind the scenes. Itale was the sort of man who liked to see what he could get away with, test the rules to learn how flexible they were. He needed a reminder now and then about the limits of his personal authority. No public insults that would push him to rebellion in defense of stubborn pride, but something subtle.

There was always one chance in a thousand that Itale might be killed or wounded on the raid, but Chung had made allowances for that eventuality. He had connections in the warlord's camp, a private understanding with a pair of young subordinates in the militia. When the day came that Itale was removed, by fate or by design, Chung would decide which of his stooges to support as the replacement.

All in good time.

At the moment, the colonel had a campaign to supervise, pawns to direct. He was looking forward to the action and the profits it would bring to him, in terms of personal prestige. With luck, a decisive victory would hasten his exit from Africa and return him to his beloved homeland, with a promotion including new responsibilities and higher pay.

The Africans were good for something, after all.

Stony Man Farm

"IT'S ROLLING," Aaron Kurtzman said to Hal Brognola, leaning slightly forward in his wheelchair to facilitate communication through the speakerphone. A green light on the unit told him that the scrambler had them covered.

"What's the rundown?" Brognola asked.

"If it all goes down on schedule, Striker has it lined up for the opposition to connect around a village called Dolele, in Djibouti. He's got backup coming, as per the arrangement with his local contact."

"Will it do the job?"

"With Phoenix and Grimaldi, he seems confident."

"What kind of schedule are we looking at?"

"They're hoping midnight, local time. Six hours, give or take."

"Between the two of us," Brognola said, "I won't be sorry when we wrap this up."

"Me, neither."

"State has feelers out to the Chinese on their involvement in Somalia, but we're getting stonewalled."

"What did you expect?"

"The usual. I keep on hoping, though. One time, I'd like to hear a diplomat admit what he's been doing, and to hell with saving face."

"Don't hold your breath," Kurtzman said.

"I can't afford to." Coming back to the main topic of discussion, Brognola asked, "Did you say they've got both sides connecting?"

"That's the word. I'm not sure how they pulled it off, but Striker seems to think he'll have a decent turnout."

"That'll be some show. I'd better call the Man and tip him off."

"It couldn't hurt."

But that was wrong, of course. The problem with a covert operation, going in, was that it wound up being linked to diplomats and politicians, even when they didn't call the shots up front. The first hint of embarrassment for anyone who held elective office, and the soldier in the field could count on being second-guessed, reviewed and criticized by Monday-morning quarterbacks. The worst case was a full-blown inquiry by Congress, which meant everyone was screwed.

Rats didn't so much flee a sinking ship, in Washington, as look for someone else they could shove overboard. Scapegoating had been elevated to an art form in the nation's capital, and neither party was exempt from blame in that regard. "Loyal opposition" might mean something in the British Parliament, but in the States, the emphasis was all on opposition, never mind the loyal.

If Bolan and the Phoenix Force warriors blew it, somehow, Stony Man would be exposed, which meant Brognola and his seat at Justice would come under fire. The Oval Office would be quick to dust him off and blame the program on a previous regime, no doubt with doctored paperwork to prove the Man was ignorant of anything and everything that happened at the Blue Ridge Mountain hardsite.

"Keep your fingers crossed," Brognola said. "I'll be here for another hour, more or less. Beyond that, you can get in touch with me at home. I want to know what happens, right away."

"You got it, Chief."

He punched a button to eliminate the dial tone, and the green light on the scrambler switched to red, then winked out altogether. Kurtzman tried to picture Brognola, a caged bear in his office, wishing he could keep in touch directly with their agents in the field. Bring back the "good old days," when he had worked with Bolan one on one against the Mob, without official sanction from above, his life and future hanging by a thread draped over razor blades.

Times changed, and the big Fed was part of the establishment these days, albeit on the sly. Several presidents had called on Stony Man to cope with various emergencies around the world and in the States, without a leak that would have blown their cover in the media. Most mornings, Kurtzman woke up wondering how long their luck could hold.

But not today.

His thoughts were focused on Somalia at the moment, and he worried more about their soldiers in the field than job security. He had a pension sewn up as it was, thanks to his disability, and if they all wound up in Leavenworth, well, then, he wouldn't need the money, anyway.

For Bolan and the others, though, there was a great deal more at stake than personal embarrassment, or even liberty of movement. They were moving toward a confrontation that, if carried off on schedule and as planned, would pit their guns and wits against two hostile forces, possibly involving several hundred men. Whatever help they managed to secure from military forces in Djibouti, Kurtzman knew it would be marginal and strictly unofficial. One more danger for his comrades, if the roof fell in.

There would be no help coming from the States if they were captured, nothing but denials out of Washington, but Kurtzman knew that wouldn't be a problem. Striker, Jack Grimaldi and Phoenix Force would never let themselves be taken. That was definite, and it was all he had to know about the price of failure.

It was all or nothing, win or lose.

And Kurtzman still had six long hours to wait.

He poured himself another cup of coffee, punched in a query to check the weather in Djibouti, near the village of Dolele. If he had to guess, he would have bet that fewer than a hundred people in America had heard the name before, or ever would. The vast majority would rise and head for work tomorrow, never knowing what a handful of the finest had endured on their behalf.

Too bad, he thought.

It was a goddamned shame.

CHAPTER NINETEEN

Dolele, Djibouti

Grimaldi held the UH-60 Black Hawk steady on its northbound course across the border, flying low to beat the radar, using NAVSTAR for his bearing, even though he could have made the journey on his own by now. He recognized the landmarks on the arid plane below him, dappled gray in moonlight, with the long, insectile shadow of his aircraft skimming out in front.

"Five minutes," he advised his passengers. Behind him, Calvin James and Mack Bolan sat with crates of ammunition at their feet, secured against a sudden shift if he was forced to take evasive action.

It would be Grimaldi's second visit to the village of Dolele in as many hours. He had dropped the other men of Phoenix Force before he made the turn-around to airlift James and Bolan out of Mogadishu. The evacuation had been under way last time he left Dolele, and it should be done by now, with any luck at all. Ninety minutes remained before their adversaries were expected, and there should be no civilians in the line of fire.

No lights were showing in Dolele as the Black Hawk slowed for its approach. Grimaldi felt a tingling hint of paranoia as he hovered, setting down, imagining a ring of weapons blasting at him from the ground, a setup with the locals switching sides. But nothing happened, and another moment found them on the ground.

Hassan Gourad came striding toward the chopper with a group of uniforms behind him. James and Bolan handed out the surplus ammo, the Phoenix Force commando shouldering a case of frag grenades as he dismounted. The Executioner lingered for a moment in the chopper, turning back to huddle with Grimaldi in the cockpit.

"So, you've picked your spot?" he asked.

"All set," the pilot told him. "I'm a half mile north, beyond the foothills. Give a squawk, and I can get back here in two, three minutes, point to point."

"Stay frosty," Bolan cautioned.

"Right. Will do."

The village was bustling as Grimaldi lifted off and circled out of sight in the darkness. Bolan shouldered the case of grenades and went to join his comrades in their final preparations. They had roughly an hour and a half, assuming everything went down on time, and every moment of it would be needed to prepare the stand.

Gourad had managed to uproot the population of Dolele and remove them to a holding area ten or fifteen miles from the anticipated killing ground. As far as what might happen to their homes while they were gone, the military—or Gourad himself—stood ready to make good with reconstruction or a wholesale relocation when the smoke cleared. A number of the villagers had volunteered to stay and fight, but they were neither armed nor trained for combat of the sort that Bolan had in mind.

The last thing the warrior needed at the moment was civilians standing in his line of fire. The impulse to defend their homes was natural, but there was nothing they could do against the kind of guns and numbers he was counting on, except sacrifice themselves unnecessarily. Right now, the fewer targets he provided for his enemies, the better Bolan felt about their plan.

He tried to form a mental picture of the village as it would have looked in daylight, with the normal occupants on hand, pursuing mundane tasks, with children playing in the dusty street. Dolele struck him as a ghost town now—or worse, a crime scene, with the uniforms and weapons, flashlights poking here and there, as if in search of evidence. In this case, though, the crime hadn't occurred yet. They were making ready for a bloodbath, laying out the killing tools and calculating fields of fire.

Bolan estimated that their enemies would be arriving from the southwest and southeast, respectively—assuming one or both contingents made the trip at all. If he was wrong, or his intended targets got cold feet, then it was wasted time and effort. He would have to start from scratch, or scrub the mission altogether.

One thing Bolan knew for certain was that they were running short on time.

A lightning war like this could only be drawn out, prolonged, at escalating risk to all concerned. Grimaldi and Phoenix Force were prepared to give their lives if necessary, but a part of Bolan's self-imposed responsibility on these joint operations was to look out for his men, do everything within his power to ensure their safety. Every day he added to the campaign schedule made the task that much more difficult, if not impossible.

Gourad was waiting for him in the center of the village, standing next to Yakov Katzenelenbogen, with an automatic rifle slung across one shoulder. Bolan moved to join them, conscious of the native soldiers watching him and whispering among themselves.

And the warrior wondered which of them would be alive to see the break of dawn.

Ayana, Ethiopia

THE FINAL PREPARATIONS would be done in no time, soldiers double-checking their equipment, loading weapons, cinching their web belts and their bandoleers. The transport helicopters would be loading soon, five choppers with a dozen soldiers each.

Raul Rodriguez hoped that it would be enough.

He had no clear idea of what he would encounter in the village of Dolele, on the wrong side of the border. Kuybyshev was predicting a contingent of Djibouti regulars, but he was closemouthed on his source of information and insisted that Rodriguez would have no great difficulty overcoming the resistance that awaited him.

In fact, according to the plan, resistance was essential. How else could they stage the necessary incident, and thereby make their own invasion of Djibouti seem legitimate, an act of self-defense?

Rodriguez knew a good deal more about the Russian's methods than he let on when the two of them were talking face-to-face. He knew, for instance, that Kuybyshev had contacts in Djibouti, some of them in government, who fed him information on troop movements, pending legislation and the like. Some were Afar, with ethnic ties to Ethiopia, while others sold themselves for money to the highest bidder, leaking classified material whenever and wherever there was profit to be made.

One of those contacts, maybe more than one, had tipped the Russian that a troop of soldiers could be found that night, performing some unspecified duty in the village of Dolele. On the map, it barely rated mention, just a dot below some foothills. Talking to his Ethiopian associates, Rodriguez learned that about four hundred peasants occupied the village, tending crops and raising scrawny livestock. There were thousands like them, back in Cuba; they had lighter skin, in many cases, but their stunted dreams and aspirations were the same. They struggled to survive from day to day.

For some, this day would be their last.

Rodriguez glanced at Kuybyshev and found the Russian smiling as he watched the soldiers climb on board their transport helicopters. Looking at him in the moonlight, it was easy to imagine Kuybyshev in Moscow, moving as he had through the corridors of power at Dzerzhinsky Square or stopping by Lubyanka Prison to interrogate some dissidents. He had that air about him—part spy, part assassin—that you came to recognize from dealing with the lethal cloak-and-dagger crowd.

Reluctantly the Cuban officer approached his Russian ally. Kuybyshev saw him coming, held the plastic smile in place and greeted Rodriguez with a nod.

"You're leaving soon," the Russian said. It didn't strike Rodriguez as a question.

"Yes. I hope your information is correct."

"I trust my sources," Kuybyshev replied. "God knows, I pay them well enough."

It still amused Rodriguez, listening to die-hard atheists abuse the name of a deity whose existence they denied. They almost seemed like children, whistling past a graveyard in the middle of the night.

"We'll soon find out," Rodriguez said.

"You doubt your men?" Kuybyshev asked.

"They do as they are told," the Cuban replied, projecting more assurance than he felt.

"In that case, there should be no difficulty." Hesitating for a moment, Kuybyshev continued, "It is good that you are leading them yourself."

Rodriguez tried to find an insult in the Russian's words, then shrugged it off. "I want to see that everything is done correctly."

"Of course. They won't have any difficulty with the vehicles?"

"Why should they?"

It had been decided that a number of his men should drive back from Dolele in the captured vehicles of their opponents, bring the bodies with them to a preselected site in Ethiopia, where they would stage the scene of an "invasion." After that, it would be up to the authorities in Addis Ababa to press the issue, scheduling reprisals and demanding territorial concessions from Djibouti.

First, though, it remained for Raul Rodriguez and his men to score a victory—their final border raid, if all went well. The other strikes had been rehearsals for the main event, and he was ready, looking forward to the challenge.

Still, Rodriguez had his doubts. If Kuybyshev or his informants were mistaken, and there were no soldiers in Dolele, then the raid would be a waste of time. Conversely, if the numbers had been understated, it was possible Rodriguez and his soldiers would be overmatched, outgunned. In that case, it would be a disaster.

Were they waiting for him, even now? Was there a trap laid for him in the tiny village that so few had ever heard of?

No.

Rodriguez steeled himself against the parasite of doubt. He needed confidence and self-assurance now, if for no other reason than to present a bold front for his men. Tonight would be the first time since they came to Ethiopia that any of his soldiers would confront armed troops, instead of hapless peasants.

"Time to go," Rodriguez said. The helicopters had begun to rev their engines, rotors turning slowly at the outset, gaining speed until they whipped dust in his face and made Rodriguez squint.

"Good luck," Kuybyshev said before he turned away and walked back toward his car.

Luck might be useful, Rodriguez thought, as he climbed aboard the leading helicopter. But for now, he had to put his faith in guns.

Northwest Somalian Frontier

MOHAMMED EL ITALE, traveling with a Chinese adviser and a force of ninety soldiers, crossed the border at 11:17 p.m. He had been forced to dodge a small UN patrol outside Borama, but the brief delay shouldn't prove fatal, if they made good time across the flatlands spreading out before them.

Twenty miles to reach Dolele, and they should be on the scene by midnight, if they met no grievous obstacles along the way. The last few miles would call for caution, going in, to keep from warning off their targets, but Itale had experience at sneaking up on villages in darkness.

It was something of a trademark, after all.

He rode the second vehicle in line, a Renault VAB armored personnel carrier, with two crewmen, the Chinese lieutenant and eight soldiers. The point vehicle was a Russian BA-64 light armored car, three men inside, with a .50-caliber DSh KM heavy machine gun protruding from its turret. Following the VAB, Itale had four flatbed trucks with eighteen men in each. The tail of the procession was an Israeli-made RBY Mk1 armored reconnaissance vehicle, with five men inside and two .30-caliber machine guns mounted on the hull.

It was the largest single force that he had fielded in a year or more, despite the fact that he had several thousand men at his command throughout Somalia. Most of the engagements he pursued, especially since the UN soldiers had arrived, were hit-and-run attacks with fewer than a dozen men involved. His border crossings in the past had normally included twenty-five or thirty soldiers, maximum, against small villages with no defensive capability.

This would be different, and then some. Still, Itale told himself that he could handle it. The men opposing him would be the poorly trained and underpaid troops who were famous—or infamous—throughout East Africa, best known for laziness, corruption, negligence and inefficiency.

For all that, though, Itale would be grateful for the serious advantage of surprise.

He rode in silence, conscious of the Chinese officer beside him, knowing that Chung had sent his man along as an observer, to report on the performance of Itale's troops. So be it. He couldn't accept the money and matériel Chung offered and refuse to let Chung's officers attend the very show they paid for.

Not yet, at any rate.

The day was coming, though, when he would be in a position to expel the Red Chinese. For now, it was enough to know that anything could happen in a fire-fight, and the young lieutenant seated on his left might stop a bullet, just like any other fighting man.

In fact, Itale thought, he wouldn't be at all surprised to lose his Communist "adviser." He could almost guarantee it.

Not that he had anything against the young man personally. There was racial prejudice, of course—he didn't care for the Chinese—but it would be a private gesture, more than anything. Let Chung consider the result and wonder what had happened, never sure until the moment when it was, at last, too late.

That day was coming, sooner than Mohammed el Itale had expected. All the violence in Mogadishu had precipitated this event, and now he stood—or sat—upon the threshold of a grand new day. His greatest single enemy was dead, and he had found a chance to prove himself, expand his influence beyond the borders of Somalia and become a hero to his people.

He could almost hear the cheering now, as he mounted the steps to the presidential palace, surrounded by bodyguards and beautiful women. He would treat himself to a new wife, perhaps several, and make the most of his glory days.

But first, he had to win the victory that would ensure his fame.

Soon, now.

He leaned toward the driver and tapped him on the shoulder. "How much farther?"

"Nine miles, sir."

He nodded toward the BA-64, in front. "Remind them to be careful for the last five miles."

"Yes, sir."

As he sat back on the uncomfortable bench seat, he could watch his order being carried out. The driver palmed his microphone and started speaking rapidly, relaying the command to those who led the caravan. It was impossible for them to travel silently, but there were ways to minimize the noise without a total sacrifice of speed.

He thought about the mercenaries who had made his life so miserable for the past two days, imagining what he could do to them if they were unlucky enough to be captured alive. It pleased the warlord to consider different forms of punishment, excruciating in their torment, and he found that he was smiling.

The simple pleasures.

He would have his fill of blood tonight, and no mistake.

Tomorrow, he would begin a new and glorious adventure as the man who would be king.

Dolele, Djibouti

HASSAN GOURAD HAD thirty soldiers with him, for a total force of thirty-seven ground troops in the village. Spread among the vacant huts, with interlocking fields of fire, they covered three sides of the village, with the north effectively excluded as an angle of attack. The native troops were armed with FN FAL assault rifles, plus several FN MAG general-purpose machine guns, chambered for 7.62 mm ammunition with a variable cyclic rate of fire between 600 and 1,000 rounds per minute. To cover all their bets, a pair of Russian-manufactured DSh K-38/46 anti-aircraft machine guns had been added to the arsenal, their crews camouflaged beneath wide screens of netting.

Bolan thought the soldiers were as ready for the fight to come as they would ever be. As for himself, he shared a hut with Calvin James, both warriors armed with AKS-74 assault rifles, Beretta side arms, and grenades. An RPG lay close to Bolan's feet, but he would have to run outside to use it, if he did not wish to set the hut on fire.

Outside and two doors to his left, or east, Manning and McCarter had another hut staked out. Away to Bolan's right, or west, were Katz and Encizo. They hadn't paired off with members of Gourad's platoon, in view of language barriers and variations in equipment. As it was, the Phoenix Force warriors could communicate, exchange spare magazines among themselves and generally operate on instinct born of long acquaintance.

When the ax fell, Bolan understood, it would be something close to each man for himself.

He sat and listened for the sound of engines—vehicles or aircraft, take your pick. The enemy wouldn't be marching in, that much was certain. If it fell apart, the raiders would be looking for a hasty exit, pouring on the speed. He knew the Cubans had been airborne on their previous attacks across the border, and it seemed a fair bet they would try the same tonight—assuming they showed up at all.

"I never cared for this part much," Calvin James said. "The waiting."

"No."

It was a fact of life, though, in the hellgrounds. Hunting men was just like stalking any other kind of game. You spent the best part of your time on day-old trails or sitting in a blind, just waiting for the moment when you had that one clear shot.

Unlike an elk or moose, though, men shot back. Sometimes they smelled the trap, and either shied away or went with countermeasures worked out in advance. He thought of Vietnam, the occasions when a jungle ambush had been turned around or had blown up in his face.

Not often, but you never quite forgot the feeling...if you lived.

"I'd like it better," James reflected, "if we had some eyes out with the opposition."

"So would I."

Hell, yes, but there had been no opportunity for planting spies inside Itale's private army or the Cuban hardforce based in Ethiopia. Preliminary observations indicted that Itale had swallowed the bait, incited by the call Siad Samatar had placed from Mogadishu. But they had no feedback on the word relayed out of Djibouti by a double agent who had been "cooperating" with the Ethiopians and Cubans for the past six months.

Disinformation was a subtle art form. Outright lies were seldom good enough to do the trick. You had to mix a blend of truth and falsehood, using just the right amount of each, to make the end result believable. Like any bait, it needed an enticing smell; the bitter taste came later, when your prey had swallowed bait, hook, line and all.

It would be disappointing if they missed the Cubans, but Itale was a big fish in his own right, and it would be worth the effort just to take him down. When they were finished in Dolele, Bolan would have to split his force again, deal with the Russians and Chinese who let their front men do the killing for them. Only then would he be finished with the job in eastern Africa.

"What's that?" James asked.

A sound, still faint with distance, came from the south, southeast. A gentle breeze was in Bolan's face as he stepped outside the hut and listened, breathing in the night.

Machinery.

He couldn't count the engines, dared not even estimate their numbers from the first slight sound, but Bolan felt the quickening inside him as his enemies drew nearer. He had traveled halfway around the globe for this, to meet these armed and deadly strangers on a plot of foreign ground, with trusted comrades at his side.

"They're coming," the warrior said, as he stepped back inside the hut.

He didn't sound a general alarm, desiring no commotion when the enemy was close enough for every man to hear it for himself. Their safety lay in stealth, now. Spiders waiting for the wasp to test their web.

Gourad had parked the transports out of sight, a half mile east, where they were more or less accessible at need. Grimaldi waited to the north, but it wasn't time, yet, to call for air support.

The vehicles were getting closer, still invisible, but clearly audible. Bolan picked up his rifle and flicked off the safety. He stood and waited for the dark dance to begin.

CHAPTER TWENTY

When he heard the vehicles approaching through the darkness, Hassan Gourad was ready, standing in the entrance of a hut that had been occupied by half a dozen villagers three hours earlier. He hadn't introduced himself before he sent them east, but he would recognize them if they met again.

As an officer, traveling light, he carried a Swedish Model 45/B submachine gun in place of the FN FAL automatic rifle that was standard for his troops. Chambered in 9 mm Parabellum, the 22-inch weapon with its folding stock could empty its 36-round magazine in just four seconds of uncontrolled fire. He carried extra magazines, a Browning semiautomatic pistol and a two-way radio to let him keep in touch with his subordinates around the village.

The convoy was running without lights, of course, making the best time it could with a minimum of warning. There was no way to disguise the engine noise, though, short of dropping off the troops and forcing them to walk in from a mile or two away.

Gourad picked up his radio and said, "Be ready." He didn't expect an answer from his men; in fact, they had been ordered to keep silent until the battle had been joined, and even then to reserve radio traffic for the direst of emergencies. Gourad didn't intend to let his adversaries eavesdrop, or alert them to the trap if they hadn't already been forewarned.

His men were under strict command to hold their fire until such time as they had clear-cut targets in the village proper. They were not to duel long-distance with a force that might be larger and better armed, when they could wait and spring a trap to catch their enemies. Gourad stepped back into the shadows, waiting, wondering if Mike Belasko and the others would be good enough to make the difference.

The convoy stopped two hundred yards outside the village, several vehicles that looked like flatbed trucks unloading infantry while other, smaller war machines stood by with motors idling. At a silent signal, three of seven vehicles raced forward, fanning out to ring Dolele, while the infantry came in behind them, jogging double-time.

Gourad was anxious for the battle to be joined, but his opponents were still too far away for the 9 mm submachine gun to strike effectively. His riflemen could probably score hits by now, but they were following their orders, waiting, marking time.

The armored vehicles would be a problem, but Belasko and his men had rocket launchers, Russian RPGs. If they were good enough and quick enough, the armor should be neutralized before it did much damage.

In the final moments that remained, Gourad considered who these enemies must be. From the direction of approach, he gathered that they came from Ethiopia, to the southeast. Were the Somalis coming, too? If so, where were they? Would a late arrival swing the battle one way or another, lending the advantage to his enemies or throwing them into confusion, thereby giving him an edge?

There was no way to tell, and so Gourad dismissed the line of thought from his consideration, concentrating on the task at hand. His palms were slick with perspiration as he gripped his submachine gun, and he wiped them on his khaki trousers, each in turn.

A few more seconds. Waiting, waiting...

One of the scout cars opened fire, a .50-caliber machine gun spitting measured bursts into the darkened huts. It was the moment they had waited for.

He came up firing at the infantry, aware that he would waste his bullets on the armored vehicles. The troops were still some sixty yards away, but that was close enough. He had to greet them sometime, let them know that they wouldn't be walking through Dolele unopposed, and there was no time like the present.

All around him, guns were hammering, a sudden symphony of death. Gourad could barely hear his own thoughts, splitting into fragments, rattling around inside his head, and that was fine.

The sounds of battle were like music to his ears.

THE LOADED RPG WEIGHED eighteen pounds, but it felt featherlight to Bolan as he left the hut and dodged outside. The armored vehicles were circling, hosing automatic fire into the village, tracers winking in the night. If he left them to it, many of the thatch-roofed huts would be reduced to ashes in the next few moments.

He was ready, homing on the nearest vehicle, which bore the general outline of an RBY Mk1. It was Israeli-made, which meant 10 mm armor plating overall. No problem for the RPG at any range within five hundred yards. Of course, he had to score a hit to make it count.

The driver helped him there. As Bolan stalked the scout car, ducking under swarms of bullets fired by friend and foe, the armored car stopped short, some fifty yards away, disgorging riflemen.

It was the best chance he was likely to receive—if not a silver platter, then the next best thing.

He knelt and brought the rocket launcher to his shoulder, peering through the sights by moonlight, steady on the mark. His opportunity to nail the grunts on board was gone, but he was more concerned about the two machine guns laying down a heavy screen of fire on either side. Those .50-calibers were deadly; they could rip the native huts apart as if they were made of cardboard, kill the men inside before they had a chance to defend themselves.

He squeezed the trigger and watched the five-pound rocket blaze away downrange. It struck the armored vehicle exactly where the center of the windshield would be found on any normal car, punched through the armor plate and detonated in the driver's cab. A ball of flame rolled through the RBY's interior and shot out through the open loading doors in back, the slowest of the grunts enveloped instantly and dancing like a fiery scarecrow in the night.

Retreating, Bolan dodged more bullets, weaving toward the hut he shared with Calvin James. A burst of automatic fire erupted from the doorway as he came in view, James firing high to let his friend duck in and out of sight while his pursuers dodged for cover.

One vehicle down, perhaps three men eliminated, but the worst part of the battle lay ahead. He primed the launcher with a second high-explosive rocket, slipped his rifle sling across one shoulder and prepared to go outside once more.

"You're pushing it," James stated.

"That's why we're here."

"So, let me cover you at least."

"My pleasure."

Bolan waited while his comrade found a moving target, led it by a yard or so, squeezed off and brought it down. Exploding from the darkness into dappled moonlight, the Executioner ran stooped over in a crouch, legs pumping as he wove a zigzag course from one hut to another, seeking prey.

Two armored vehicles were still rolling, and he had to stop them cold before their automatic weapons killed or panicked any of the troops Gourad had mustered to defend Dolele. Armor was an edge that gave his enemies the upper hand, however briefly, and he meant to level out the odds.

Where were the Cubans?

He heard it, then, above the sound of engines racing, automatic weapons stuttering. A deep, familiar sound that resonated in the air and sent vibrations through his eardrums, rippling down his spine—the sound of helicopters fast approaching.

Welcome to the party, Bolan thought, and knew that it wasn't Grimaldi, since he hadn't flashed the signal yet. Too many engines, anyway, for one Sikorsky, and unless he missed his guess, these aircraft were approaching from the west—the general direction they would come from if their flight originated in Somalia.

Okay.

He paused just long enough to grab the compact walkie-talkie from his belt and thumb down the transmitter button as he gave the signal.

"Striker calling Phoenix Air. Let's do it!"

He returned the little two-way to its belt pouch and continued on his way. Grimaldi would be coming, by and by. Meanwhile, the fighting fell to soldiers on the ground, and they would live or die according to their nerve, tenacity and skill.

The Executioner was hunting, and he had no time to waste.

"SOME KIND OF FIREFIGHT going on," the pilot told Raul Rodriguez, forcing him to leave his seat and lumber toward the cockpit, feeling awkward as he always did while walking in a military aircraft. There was always a sensation—groundless, but intense—which warned him that the floor might open up beneath his feet and send him plummeting to earth, a sack of mangled, lacerated flesh and shattered bones.

Instead, he reached the flight deck safely, peering through the windscreen, noting the erratic, unmistakable display of muzzle-flashes from Dolele, dead ahead. He didn't have a clue how many weapons were involved, but they were numerous enough to make a deadly light show on the flat land where the village stood.

He was expecting troops, of course, but they were said to be on a routine patrol, some kind of an inspection tour. He hadn't come expecting war games, much less a pitched battle in the middle of the night, with the opposing sides unknown.

He should turn back, Rodriguez knew, but that would force him to explain when he confronted Kuybyshev again. The Russian lacked official standing, but he had the ear of men who pulled the strings in Addis Ababa. There would be accusations of negligence at best, and cowardice at worst. Rodriguez had perhaps ten seconds to decide how he could best avoid the inquisition, salvage something from a situation that was clearly getting out of hand.

"Proceed," he ordered. "Put the troops out there, just to the north, and stand by to provide air cover on command."

"Yes, sir." There was reluctance in the pilot's voice, but he was trained to follow orders, even when they went against the grain of common sense.

The flight of helicopters veered a little to the north, correcting for the latest destination chosen by Rodriguez. Lurching back in the direction of his seat, Rodriguez huddled with his second in command, explaining what had happened and ordered the captain to assume command once he was on the ground.

For his part, Rodriguez would remain aloft, maintaining radio communications with his men, directing them to victory. He told himself that it was only logical and prudent, part of a cohesive strategy for triumph. On the ground, his field of vision would be limited, his overall command ability severely compromised. On high, he could observe the battlefield at large and know exactly what was happening in every sector.

It was perfect.

It relieved his jangling nerves and let him breathe again.

Rodriguez kept his seat as they approached the landing zone and hovered, setting lightly down. His men unloaded in a rush, ducked low beneath the whipping rotors, falling into rough formation as the captain started shouting his commands in Spanish. Moments later, when the whirlybird was airborne, Rodriguez made his way back to the cockpit, leaning in to watch the action from his safer vantage point.

Below him, in the moonlight, he saw armored vehicles. One burning, while two more ran rings around the darkened village, automatic weapons spitting fire. Black infantry was everywhere at once, men running here and there as if without direction, firing on the move, some dropping in their tracks as they were hit. From every second hut, it seemed, bright muzzle-flashes spit death toward the men in uniform, a unified defense if he had ever seen one.

His men surged forward, the young captain at their head, advancing on the north side of the village. Less than fifty yards remained when automatic fire erupted in their faces, and he saw the line begin to waver, almost breaking ranks, before they rallied, charging toward the enemy.

From somewhere down below, a heavy-caliber machine opened up, its crimson tracers arcing toward the helicopters. God in heaven, they were being fired on! Where did peasants get that kind of weaponry in an impoverished village like Dolele?

"Take us higher!" he commanded. "Quickly!"

The pilot required no further urging, hauling back on his controls and snapping orders through the mouthpiece of his two-way radio. Five helicopters rose as one, like giant, prehistoric dragonflies, evading ground fire from the village.

It wasn't supposed to be this way. Rodriguez had expected some resistance from the troops he came to slaughter, certainly, but this was total chaos. Battle had been joined, somehow, before he ever reached the scene, and now his troops had been committed to a hectic three-way dogfight with an enemy that he couldn't identify.

Rodriguez watched the tiny shadow figures running to and fro, more of them falling all the time, and wished he could remember how to pray.

THE CHARGING LINE of khaki uniforms was forty yards away and closing fast when Yakov Katzenelenbogen squeezed the trigger on his AKS and dropped two soldiers thrashing in the dust. They kicked and writhed like broken things, reminding him of wounded reptiles, but he had no time to finish them before new targets urgently demanded his attention.

They would have to die and so cease struggling in their own good time.

In combat, mercy was a luxury few soldiers could afford.

Beside him, Encizo was unloading through a window in the east wall of the hut. There was no glass or screen to block his weapon as he squeezed off short, precision bursts, his spent brass pattering around him on the earthen floor.

An armored vehicle sped past, approaching from the east, or left, and disappearing on the right. Katz didn't waste his bullets chasing it, but ducked as automatic fire burst from the turret, bullets ripping through the dried mud of the walls around him.

Katz fired another burst of 5.45 mm tumblers, saw another soldier stumble and topple forward on his face. Death came from nowhere in a fight like this, when soldiers fought without direction, scrambling for their lives on unfamiliar ground. There had to have been a plan when they arrived, but it had quickly been discarded at the first sign of resistance, every warrior fighting for himself.

And it was time to move.

"I'm moving," he advised Encizo, crouching in the doorway with his rifle braced across one knee.

"Where to?" the Cuban asked.

"I'm not sure yet. They're flanking us. I won't sit here and wait for a grenade."

Encizo thought about that, then nodded. "Okay," he said. "I'm with you."

Another hut, Katz thought, or maybe they could make it in the open for a while. In the confusion of the moment, anything was possible, each option fraught with peril.

"Bailing out on three," Katz said.

"You count."

"That's one."

Encizo fired another short burst through the window. Katzenelenbogen graced himself to run.

"And two."

A bullet smacked the wall above his head, raining dust into his iron-gray hair. He clutched his rifle in a death grip.

"Three!"

He broke from cover, dodging to his left in the direction of a hut he knew to be unoccupied. Was it a mere illusion that the fire around him doubled, tripled, as he came out in the open? Could it be that every gunner in a radius of sixty yards was pouring bullets at him, even now?

Behind him, Encizo was firing, leaping from the hut and pounding after Katz. A khaki figure moved to cut him off, and Katz unleashed a rising burst from twenty feet away, the bullets ripping through his target, spraying blood that looked jet-black by moonlight, dropping him before he had a chance to fire.

There was more furtive movement in the hut, as Katz barged in. A muzzle-flash cut through the shadows, bullets going high and wide. The Phoenix Force leader hit a crouch and fired back for effect, his own rounds homing on target, ripping flesh and fabric.

Encizo stepped in cautiously, prepared for anything, relieved to find Katz on his feet. "This isn't much of an improvement," he suggested.

In trading one box for another, they postponed the end, but they didn't enhance their own defensive options. It was quite possible that they'd be better off outside. A soldier who could keep his wits about him would survive.

MCCARTER CAUGHT a lucky break and saw Death coming for him, with time enough to swing his AKS around and squeeze the trigger, even if he didn't have a decent chance to aim.

Three soldiers, black and burly, skin so dark their khaki uniforms seemed disembodied in the night, like stage props from *The Invisible Man*. Invisible they might be, but they weren't bulletproof, and there was nothing to protect them as McCarter opened fire from less than forty feet away.

He swept the three from left to right, the tallest of them catching four or five rounds in the chest and lurching backward, rubber-limbed and reeling. By the time he went down on his backside, number two was hit and spinning through a sloppy pirouette, his automatic weapon spitting slugs into the dust before he fell across his comrade's outstretched legs.

The third man almost saved himself by lunging to his left, but almost wasn't good enough. McCarter's bullets caught him in the side, ripped through his rib cage, lungs and heart. The man was dead before he lost his balance, toppled forward on his face, his rifle pinned beneath him.

Done.

McCarter edged around the corner, keeping to the shadows, conscious of the blazing gunfire all around him. In a few short moments, peaceable Dolele had been changed into a shooting gallery, and it would soon become a slaughterhouse. Whichever way the battle went, there would be death enough to go around.

At least the helicopters weren't attacking yet. They had unloaded to the north and hovered well above action, watching, waiting. There was little doubt that they were armed and capable of intervening when the order came, but for the moment they were relegated to the sidelines, hanging like the proverbial sword of Damocles above his head. Would they be packing rockets? Automatic cannon? How long would the battle last, once they dived into action, raining fire and death?

Not long, unless Grimaldi came to help them or the antiaircraft guns got lucky, spraying tracers toward the heavens. The defenders in Dolele were outnumbered four or five to one, but with the armored vehicles and helicopters, you could kiss the odds goodbye.

McCarter freed a hand grenade from his web belt and yanked the pin, baseballed the bomb toward a group of soldiers double-timing from the south. A couple of them spotted him and fired short bursts in his direction, but the Briton was already dodging back and under cover of the nearest hut before the angry hornets started swarming overhead. He hugged the ground and felt a tremor as the frag grenade exploded, spewing shrapnel. Somewhere, out beyond his line of sight, he heard men screaming, crying out for mercy that wasn't forthcoming.

He went out to join them with his AKS, full auto, milking short bursts from the weapon as he closed the gap, dispatching three rounds here, four there, to nail down the survivors who were scrambling for their lives. Blood mingled with the dust, parched earth absorbing it before the crimson tide could spread.

A glare of headlights blinded him, one of the armored cars returning for another pass, machine gun stuttering. McCarter dodged back toward the huts, slid into shadow as the vehicle drew closer, bouncing over prostrate bodies in its path, the big tires pulping flesh and cracking bone.

McCarter fumbled for another hand grenade, but knew it would take a miracle for him to score against the armored vehicle with any hand-thrown missile. Still, if he could slow it or blind the driver, even momentarily, perhaps one of the others would have time to use an RPG to good effect. If nothing else, at least he might divert the turret gunner and prevent himself from being chopped up into dog food.

Nothing ventured, nothing gained.

McCarter pulled the safety pin and held the frag bomb in his right hand, braced the AKS against his hip, the fingers of his left hand wrapped around the pistol grip. It was the best that he could do.

He came out firing, fighting for his life.

CHAPTER TWENTY-ONE

The target was a Russian BA-64 light armored car, a World War II design, still used in front-line service by the North Koreans and Albanians, who have been known to manufacture knockoffs for commercial sale in Third World nations. Relatively easy to disable, with its rubber tires and less than half an inch of armor plating, the ungainly vehicle could still clock fifty miles per hour over open ground, and its .50-caliber turret gun gave the BA-64 a fairly impressive reach.

But it was no match for the RPG.

The trick was getting close enough to score a hit in the chaotic killing ground. While Bolan knew that he could make the shot, if given half a chance, it wouldn't do for him to chase the vehicle in circles, dodging bullets all the way. He had to find a vantage point and wait, however difficult that seemed, and let the armored hunter come to him.

Right now, the BA-64 was chasing Cubans on the west side of the village, hosing stragglers with automatic fire. It had to have come as a surprise when they unloaded from their choppers, looking forward to another easy border raid, and stepped into the middle of a major firefight—rockets and machine guns, armored vehicles, the works. About this time, the Executioner imagined, some or all of them were wishing they were safe at home in Cuba.

It was too damned late to think of that, though. Too damned late for anything but do or die.

Crouched in the deeper shadows pooled between two huts, he watched and waited with the RPG beside him, cradling the AKS. A group of soldiers sprinted past him, Africans, and moments later, several Cubans ran the other way. He could have dropped them all, but at the moment he was more intent on waiting for the scout car, taking one step at a time.

The Cuban helicopters were another problem, but they hadn't started strafing yet, perhaps for fear of cutting down their own troops in the general confusion of the battle. They were out of range from ground fire, hanging back, but they were also burning fuel to stay aloft, and Bolan knew the pilots would be forced to pick an option soon.

Once Jack Grimaldi joined the play.

The squat, top-heavy armored car, so awkward in appearance, had been running rings around Dolele since the private soldiers of Mohammed el Itale made their first appearance on the scene. It was impossible to guess how many casualties the gunner had inflicted so far, but Bolan meant to cut him short before he ran up many more.

Another moment, and he heard the four-cylinder engine revving, coming closer. Bullets rattled off the scout car's armored hide, the .50-caliber responding with its raucous voice. A cry of pain was cut off as though a heavy blade had fallen on the wounded soldier's neck.

He laid the AKS aside and braced the RPG across his shoulder, bulky with the five-pound warhead jutting from its muzzle. Bolan peered around the corner, saw one of Hassan Gourad's men try to stop the armored car with nothing but his automatic rifle. It was over in a heartbeat: first, they shot him; then, the driver crushed his body under some twelve thousand pounds of steel and rubber.

Coming closer.

Bolan lined up the sights of his RPG and waited, ticking off the final seconds in his mind. The BA-64 looked big and almost square by moonlight, barreling along toward the warrior's hideout on a near-collision course, flame spitting from the turret-mounted machine gun. Red tracers had been slotted in the MG's ammo belt, one every six or seven rounds. Behind the armored car, a couple of the huts were burning brightly, thatched roofs set aflame by tracer rounds fired high and wide.

He lined up the sights, aiming just below the turret. A gentle squeeze, and Bolan felt the rocket go, a blast of heat behind him, sudden brilliance as the nose-heavy projectile flew downrange. It nailed the BA-64 and blew on impact, opening the frail 10 mm armor as a shotgun blast would ventilate a beer can. Smoke and fire belched out of hatches, portholes, signaling the grim fate of the three-man crew. A moment later, and the gas tank detonated in a secondary blast, touched off by hungry flames.

The stench of burning oil, charred flesh and melting rubber wafted into Bolan's nostrils as he picked up his rifle, then fell back to find another vantage point. Eliminating one more vehicle was helpful, but it wouldn't win the battle. They were still outnumbered, and the Cuban helicopters could deliver blazing death on cue, with nothing to prevent their leveling the village.

Nothing but Grimaldi, right.

And he should be there anytime.

THE UH-60 BLACK HAWK was not Jack Grimaldi's first choice for a dogfight, but experience had taught him to make do with what he had. If it lacked the smaller Cobra's speed and maneuverability, the Black Hawk still packed plenty of punch: dual mounts for Stinger self-defense missiles, air-to-air, a quad mount for the Hellfires and twin FN ETNA HMP/MRL70 pods, combining .50-caliber M-3 P machine guns with four 70 mm rockets each.

With any luck at all, it ought to be enough.

The signal brought him racing from his drop, a half-mile north of the embattled village. There was no way to predict exactly what was waiting for him at Dolele, but he knew that every second counted now. His edge, regardless of the numbers, would be catching his opponents by surprise.

He started picking up their cross talk on the radio when he was still a quarter mile from contact. Voices were speaking excitedly in Spanish, and he understood enough of it to know that one of them belonged to the commander of a Cuban strike force, trying to control his people on the ground. Responses from the firing line were fragmentary and chaotic, almost drowned at times by gunfire and explosions.

They were catching hell down there, but they hadn't yet seen the worst of it.

The worst was coming up behind them, giant rotors whipping at the night.

He saw the choppers moments later, counted five and knew that it would be a risky proposition—close to suicidal—if he tried to deal with them on equal terms. They could surround him, smother him with cannon fire and rockets if they had to, bring him down in flames.

He would be no damned good to Striker and the others in a heap of twisted, smoking wreckage. Something else was called for.

A surprise.

Grimaldi came in on their blind side, knowing someone was bound to spot him in a moment, praying that he would be able to begin the strike, at least, without a general alarm to spread his targets far and wide. He armed the Stingers, lined up his sights on the nearest chopper in the group and let one go from around eight hundred yards.

The Cubans never saw it coming—or, at least, they had no time to save themselves. There was a loud squawk from Grimaldi's radio, a heartbeat prior to impact, but it could have emanated from another helicopter in the group. It didn't matter to the dead men as their ship disintegrated, raining twisted, blackened steel and mutilated bodies on the desert floor below.

One day.

Grimaldi had a second chopper lined up in his sights as they began to scatter, launched another Stinger as he closed the gap. The missile's infrared guidance system took over on launching, and there was no way for the Cubans to shake it at that range, without flares or jamming equipment. Another flash, and target number two was plummeting to earth on a dead-end collision course.

How many dead, so far, with two strokes of the trigger?

Grimaldi had no time to try to calculate the numbers, no concern for those who placed themselves in harm's way voluntarily, while stalking others. They had come to play for keeps, and they were getting what they paid for.

Down below, Dolele was a madhouse, vehicles and infantry all blasting in the dark, two armored cars and several of the native huts on fire. Grimaldi's friends were down there, somewhere, but the only way that he could help them at the moment was to keep the Cuban choppers off their backs.

And in the process, he would try to stay alive.

MOHAMMED EL ITALE listened to the rain of bullets rattling on the armor at his back, imagining one drilling through to pierce his flesh at any moment. The Uzi submachine gun in his lap was little comfort at the moment. He could feel his soldiers watching him, prepared to move on his command, but they were clearly frightened, caught off guard by the ferocity of the response from their opponents.

It was meant to be an easy victory, but he could feel it slipping through his fingers. First, there was resistance from the village: rockets, automatic weapons, and grenades from every side. Now helicopters had appeared from nowhere, landing troops who rushed the village from the west, and who were they? They didn't seem to recognize Itale's troops, but they were firing indiscriminately, killing as they came.

Despite its shield of armor, the Renault now felt like a mobile prison to him. He longed to fall back with the trucks, but he couldn't afford to let his troops suspect he was a coward. It was bad enough the way his master plan had started to unravel, but his men were trying to recover something from the situation, fighting for their lives. If he deserted them, there would be nothing to prevent them fleeing in a rush, the effort wasted, all his aspirations going up in smoke.

The hog-nosed APC lurched forward, hammering at unseen targets with its .30-caliber machine gun. Seated with his elbows braced against his knees, Itale felt the young Chinese lieutenant watching, judging him, perhaps already formulating his report to Colonel Chung. It would go badly for Itale if he didn't act, and quickly, to assert himself and save the day.

Assuming it could still be saved, and they weren't all doomed to sudden death within the next few moments.

"Stop!" he told the driver, hunching forward, shouting to be heard above the sounds of battle that surrounded them. The armored vehicle stopped dead, its motor idling, the machine gun overhead still rattling off staccato bursts.

"What is it?" the Chinese lieutenant asked.

"We're getting out," Itale told him. "I can't lead my people from inside this box."

There was no clear-cut reason to believe that he could lead them from the outside, either, but the warlord had his pride to think about. There had been other situations, in the early days, when he had found the odds against him, and he always pulled it off with nerve, audacity and ruthless courage.

He could do the same again.

One of his soldiers reached across, reluctantly unlatched the door in back and kicked it open. Instantly the sounds of combat doubled in intensity, the APC transformed from a protective shelter to a kind of echo chamber. Slugs and shrapnel had free access to them now, if anyone should fire upon them from the rear.

The time had come to move, and quickly, while they had the chance.

"With me!" Itale shouted, half-surprised himself as he leapt off the metal bench and waddled toward the open hatch. His soldiers followed him on instinct, the Chinese lieutenant bringing up the rear. It pleased Itale that his watchdog was the last to leave the vehicle, appearing tremulous as he emerged.

The village was in flames. Not all of it as yet, but several nearby huts were burning, and the air was fouled with smoke. The tracer rounds had done it, he decided, and it struck him that a raging fire on this side of the border undermined his credibility in terms of claiming that a strike force from Djibouti had been caught inside Somalia.

At the moment, though, it made no difference how the world at large perceived the night's events. Itale might not live to see the sunrise, and a dead man's reputation only mattered to his heirs. Survival was the top priority, right now, with victory a distant second on the list.

Still, they might travel hand in hand, he realized. One way to make sure that he left Dolele safe and sound would be to massacre his enemies. No small achievement, in itself, but it wasn't beyond his grasp. Not yet.

Itale hadn't risen to his present station by surrendering when things got tough. He was a fighter, even if he still preferred the ambush to the stand-up fight. An unarmed, sleeping enemy was easier to kill, but he had dealt with every sort of adversary in his day.

He chose a target, totally at random, beckoning his soldiers froward.

"This way! Follow me!"

And so they did.

Itale knew that it could be the greatest moment of his life . . . or it could be the last.

THE SECOND HUT, as far as Rafael Encizo was concerned, was no improvement on the first. It hadn't been constructed with defense in mind, and it was nowhere close to bulletproof. The walls would crumble under any kind of steady fire, and it would only take a tracer round or two to set the dry thatched roof ablaze.

So much for safety.

Katz was clearly having second thoughts himself, as he crouched down beside the only window, waiting for a target to present itself. Encizo had the door, but he could see only a portion of the street, two other huts and nothing much besides.

Restricted visibility and field of fire.

Strikes two and three.

"We're better off outside," he told Katz sharply.

As he spoke, a khaki soldier came in view, dragging a wounded leg, and Encizo dropped him with a short burst from his AKS. Behind the dead man, two more gunners instantly appeared, one laying down a screen of automatic fire while his companion cocked one arm to lob a round, black object toward the hut.

"Grenade!" Encizo shouted. He was firing for effect and scoring hits, but not before the grenadier had made his pitch. Encizo saw the dark egg wobbling toward him, glinting wickedly in the reflected firelight, falling short and wobbling toward the open doorway like a tiny football.

Katz went through the smallish window with agility and speed surprising for a man his size. Encizo's choices were to stay inside the hut or take a chance on hurdling the grenade and getting out of range before it blew.

He made his break, still blasting with his AKS, and almost lost it in the loose sand as he came down on one heel, veered left and caught himself before he fell. His boots found traction, strong legs pumping as he tried to put the hut between himself and the grenade, with only seconds left to spare.

He almost made it.

The explosion lifted the Phoenix Force warrior and hurled him through a forward somersault. He landed on his back, the breath slapped out of him, and felt as if he were drowning as he waited for his lungs and diaphragm to come around, recover from the shock. A moment later, he was breathing, checking out his limbs and back for shrapnel wounds. His nose was bleeding, and he had a headache like the worst hangover of all time, but he could find no open gashes, nothing that appeared to be an entrance wound. His arms and legs were functional, and he could move, despite a dull pain in his lower back.

Chalk that one up to luck, Encizo thought, as he retrieved his AKS and looked around for Katz. There was no sign of the Israeli at the moment, but that didn't mean that he was down. More likely he had kept on moving to evade the blast—as Rafael himself had planned to do, had he been quick enough.

The hut wasn't entirely flattened, but its roof was sagging sharply where the front wall had imploded, white smoke curling from the thatch as sparks took hold and blossomed into flame. Encizo had no time to think about the former occupants, their loss. He had survival on his mind and it required his full attention.

Shadow shapes approached him from two sides, all toting rifles. Where the hell was Katz? The others? Crouching near the shattered hut, unmindful of the radiating heat, Encizo waited to be sure the men approaching him were enemies. Another moment, and he knew for sure. Three Cubans were on his left, two Africans advancing on his right.

There was another hut directly opposite, its doorway facing toward the back wall of the ruined structure he had lately fled. Encizo saw his chance and recognized the odds as something less than fabulous. Still, he would have to try it, if he didn't want the enemy to kill him where he was.

He drew his side arm, held it in his left hand with the hammer back. The AKS was heavy in his right hand, set for semiauto fire. A hit would be a bonus, in the circumstances. What he needed, at the moment, was sufficient flash and noise to start a chain reaction with his enemies.

Encizo broke from cover, lunging toward the shelter opposite, unloading rounds in both directions as he ran. At once, the Africans and Cubans were returning fire, their brief glimpse of a moving target instantly eclipsed by muzzle-flashes from the weapons of their enemies. Five men unloaded on one another at a range of less than twenty yards.

The Phoenix Force warrior poked his head out when the firing stopped, found four men down and one, a dark Somali gunner, kneeling in the dirt. The African was still alert enough to see Encizo coming for him, but his arms wouldn't respond to signals from his brain. Encizo put a mercy round between his eyes and punched him over on his back.

Not bad, but he would have to do a great deal better to reduce the killer odds.

Beginning now.

THE HELICOPTER HAD BEEN absolutely unexpected, coming out of nowhere with its rockets blazing. Raul Rodriguez gripped his seat and fought to keep from trembling like a frightened child.

Two choppers left, and one of them was his.

He started shouting orders at the pilot, then decided it would only make things worse and shut his mouth. The man at the controls had every bit as much incentive to escape as had Rodriguez. It was his life, too, if they went down in flames, and he was doing everything within his power to evade the flying demon on their tail. Rodriguez barking at him on the intercom would only serve as a distraction, maybe doom them all.

They had a fifty-fifty chance, he reckoned, with the other transport helicopter a potential target for their adversary. They were armed, as well, but he wasn't convinced his Cuban pilot had the speed and skill required to turn upon their adversary and destroy him.

They had separated from the other helicopter as the third went down in flames, Rodriguez terrified to look to see if they were being followed. Now, it seemed their enemy had flown off to pursue the other ship, allowing them the extra time they needed to escape. The sudden thought of freedom, safety, was exhilarating, but Rodriguez caught himself, a sudden flush of shame hot in his cheeks.

His men were trapped without the helicopters to remove them from the village, some three dozen doomed already, no room on the two remaining aircraft. If he ran away and left the others now, how could he face himself again? What would become of pride and honor, if he simply ran away?

Conversely Raul Rodriguez knew he couldn't face himself at all if he was dead. Pride made no difference to a corpse, unless you cared about the memory you left behind. A lifelong Castro atheist, Rodriguez cherished no illusions of an afterlife, reward or punishment beyond what he would reap or suffer here on earth.

Still, he had been a military man since he was old enough to wear the uniform. Survival would mean less than nothing if he went back to Havana in disgrace, an officer whose men were sacrificed through cowardice. He had to make some effort, hope for luck. There was a chance, however small, that he could turn disaster into triumph, salvage something from the wild, chaotic scene below.

Rodriguez stood up from his seat, lurched toward the cockpit as the helicopter made a banking turn. He grabbed the pilot's shoulder, squeezing hard.

"Turn back!" he ordered. "We must stay and fight!"

The pilot and his second in command exchanged uncertain glances, but they knew enough to follow orders. In the air, at least they had a chance. Ignoring orders, even if they made it back to base alive, would mean a military trial, perhaps a firing squad.

No choice, then.

Solemnly the pilot nodded, hauling back on the controls. Rodriguez nearly lost his footing as the helicopter swung around and faced back toward the village of Dolele. Red lights winked on the instrument panel, as the pilot armed his guns.

So much for running.

Raul Rodriguez might not be a hero, but he wouldn't be a whining coward, either. There was still a chance to carry out his mission—capture vehicles and drive back to the border, if he had to—and he meant to see it through.

If only he could manage to suppress his numbing fear.

CHAPTER TWENTY-TWO

Hassan Gourad had dressed his soldiers in civilian clothes to foster the illusion of a normal peasant village, and because he feared his adversaries might be wearing uniforms that would confuse the issue in a close, chaotic fight. It helped him now, as he observed that the Somalis were in khaki, while the Cubans, out of Ethiopia, wore tiger-striped fatigues.

Three of those Cubans were approaching his position at the moment, moving cautiously, hunched over automatic weapons, daring glances back and forth in all directions as they came. The battle of Dolele had fragmented into dozens, scores of smaller actions, individuals and groups of varied sizes grappling for a hut, a ditch, a stand of trees.

He watched the Cubans through the fixed sights of his Model 45/B submachine gun, scarcely breathing. They were well within effective range, but he wanted no mistakes, no complications. Things had gotten rather badly out of hand already, and he had no wish to die here, even in a righteous cause.

It still might come to that, of course, but he was taking every possible precaution, swallowing his impulse toward fair play and taking any shot that promised him a kill.

Waiting.

Thirty feet, and there would never be a better time. The Cubans had begun to separate, the one immediately on his left about to veer off from his comrades and inspect another hut. The move would put him out of sight, beyond the line of fire in seconds flat.

Gourad squeezed off a burst that raked his enemies from left to right, 9 mm Parabellum manglers ripping into them with force enough to rock the Cubans on their heels. The soldier on his left was first to fall, a stiff drop to his knees, then over on his side, where he lay twitching in the dust.

The gunner in the middle took four bullets in the chest and toppled backward, firing wildly as he fell. His automatic rifle kicked free as he hit the ground, fell silent with no finger on the trigger. Spent brass gleamed like new coins scattered on the ground around the fallen soldier.

Number three was fast, but not quite fast enough to save himself. He turned to run, an easy pivot on one heel, and fired a short burst in the general direction of his enemy, for cover. As it was, he managed one long stride before the bullets found him, ripping through his flank, across his upper back.

The Cuban staggered, fighting hard to keep his balance, even as he died. Three lurching, limping steps, and he appeared to be unstoppable. Gourad was ready for another burst, when suddenly the man collapsed face forward, sprawling lifeless in the dirt.

A loud explosion overhead distracted him, and he glanced up in time to see a rain of fire and shrapnel coming down. One of the helicopters had exploded, from the look of it. Was that Belasko's friend, the flier, toting up another kill—or was it his ship, coming down in flames? Gourad couldn't keep track of what was happening around him on the ground, much less account for what might happen in a dogfight overhead. He knew the odds were four or five to one against the brave American, but something told him there was more to it than simple numbers.

Much, much more.

The airman might save all of them, in fact, but for now Gourad had more immediate concerns. His soldiers were outnumbered, overmatched with armored vehicles and hostile warships in the sky. It was his duty, his responsibility, to see that they survived . . . or gave a fair accounting of themselves, at any rate.

Sometimes, he knew, it was impossible to beat the odds, but that didn't excuse a man from trying. There would be no shame in losing, if they did their best. The shame would lie in giving up, surrendering without the maximum expenditure of effort to succeed.

He fed the Swedish SMG a fresh magazine, stepping cautiously from cover, seeking targets. They were out there, waiting for him. All he had to do was find them, keep the battle going.

Time and fate would dictate who emerged triumphant in the end.

The best Hassan Gourad could do was try.

IT WAS A PURE FLUKE that he missed the armored car from sixty yards. He had the RPG lined up, his finger on the trigger, taking up the slack, when someone made a lucky shot—or stray, he never knew for sure— and dinged the launcher's barrel as he fired. The RPG jogged hard to Bolan's right, and he was dodging backward, searching for the shooter, as his final rocket flew wide of the mark, streaking across the open desert, finally exploding when it struck the earth, three hundred yards beyond the outskirts of the village.

Dammit!

He couldn't tell if the driver recognized his danger, but it made no difference either way. The APC kept going, picked up speed, machine guns hammering away as it swept out of sight, proceeding on its circuit of Dolele.

Bolan left the useless rocket launcher and took his AKS as he retreated to the shadows of a nearby hut. He scanned the night in search of wily snipers, but there was no follow-up to the initial round that saved his enemies. If someone out there had him marked, they were apparently content to let it go and look for other targets while he watched and waited, hiding.

Not that he had any dearth of targets in the village. They were everywhere, dark figures running, crouching, shooting in the firelight, little to distinguish them except their uniforms. The Cuban troops were lighter-skinned, of course, but in the circumstances there was no opportunity to check complexions. It was now or never, kill or be killed, and he blessed the instinct that had led Hassan Gourad to dress his soldiers in civilian clothes, thus helping somewhat to reduce confusion.

It was time to move, he knew, and never mind the phantom sniper. Death could come from anywhere, at any moment, and he wouldn't let himself be sidelined by the prospect. Carrying the battle to his adversaries was the only way he knew to play the game.

He melded with the shadows, hunting now. He didn't need sophisticated tracking gear to find his prey; the challenge would be picking targets that advanced the friendly cause without getting killed in the process. No small challenge.

Ten seconds later, he was standing in the shadow of another hut and watching four Somali gunners dueling with a friendly light machine gun crew. Gourad's men held their own, but they were getting nowhere, with their field of fire restricted to the open doorway of their hut. The four Somalis, meanwhile, were at liberty to circle wide around them, try new angles of attack and keep them penned up while the hut was slowly, inexorably reduced.

The nearest gunner never heard Death coming up behind him, cautious footsteps covered by the crackling sounds of automatic weapons' fire. The man's first intimation of disaster was the touch of Bolan's Ka-bar blade against his throat, immediately followed by a hot spray from his opened carotid artery.

One down, and three to go. The others wouldn't be so easy to approach, but they were all in sight as Bolan put his knife away and raised the AKS. Once he began to fire, he couldn't hesitate, or the survivors would have time to nail him. No trick marksmanship was required at this range, even if they weren't the finest riflemen Mohammed el Itale had.

He dropped the first one easily, a short burst to his left side from a range of thirty feet. Four rounds punched through the gunner's rib cage, slammed him over on his side and left him squirming in his death throes.

He tracked on to number three, an easy flow of motion, never lifting off the rifle's sights. A gentle squeeze, and Bolan watched his human target stagger, going over backward in a boneless sprawl. His dead hand, frozen on the trigger of his submachine gun, sprayed the dark sky overhead with wasted rounds.

And that left one.

The sole survivor of the strike team knew that there was something wrong, by now. He spun in Bolan's general direction, looking for a clear-cut target, firing wild because it made more sense than simply waiting for the ax to fall. His bullets came within a few yards of the Executioner before a short burst stitched across the gunner's chest and took him down.

So far, so good.

But he was far from finished, yet. The bodies scattered here and there around the village told him little in regard to how the fight was going. Both Cubans and Somalis had been taking hits, but he had no idea about Gourad's commandos. They had been outnumbered at the start, and every loss reduced the odds against success.

All he could do was to keep on fighting, kill as many of their adversaries as he could and try to turn the odds around. If it happened to be a losing game, at least he would have tried.

He turned away and left Gourad's machine-gun team to help themselves. The fight was heating up, and they had far to go before the battle ended, one way or another. Victory or death.

GRIMALDI LOOSED the Black Hawk's final Stinger from a hundred yards and watched it home in on the airborne target, curving slightly to the right, or east, and following the Cuban helicopter's engine heat. Explosive impact sheared the chopper's tail off, spewing wreckage, plumes of burning fuel. The crippled whirlybird nosed over, fighting hopelessly for altitude, hell-bent on a collision with the ground.

One chopper left, and he was looking for it, wondering if it had managed to elude him, when he saw the armored car below, machine guns hosing the huts at random, tracers streaking through the night. Gourad's men would be catching hell down there, Grimaldi knew. If he could help them out...

He made another swift check for the final gunship, spotted nothing and revised his course to swing around behind the armored car. It was a waste of time for him to try to make an ID on the type of vehicle. There was a fairly standard armor gauge for APCs, and none Grimaldi knew of could withstand the Hellfire rockets he was carrying.

He came in from the blind side of the APC, his laser sight engaged and locked on target, index finger curled around the trigger that would send his enemies direct to hell without a detour.

Five seconds.

He skimmed in on target, low and fast.

Four.

The gunners didn't see him coming, focused as they were on strafing huts along their line of travel, turning up the heat.

Three seconds.

At a hundred yards, he had them cold, with no possibility for them to save it.

Two.

On one, he squeezed the trigger, holding steady on the laser sight to guide the Hellfire on its way. Too late, one of the gunners in the APC appeared to recognize his danger, swiveling around in time to scream before the rocket found him and exploded in a ball of oily flame.

The APC disintegrated, veering sharply from its course before the fat tires melted down and left it sitting in the sand, a blazing hulk. Nobody made it out, but he hadn't expected any of the crew to save themselves. The Hellfire's high-explosive warhead and a secondary detonation from the fuel tank ruled out any hasty exits from the vehicle.

That stripped Itale's raiders of their mobile guns, but there were still the flatbed trucks employed for transport, standing by to help them get away. Grimaldi made another quick check for the Cuban helicopter, failed to spot it and proceeded south at speed to visit the Somali motor pool.

His comrades on the grounds might not be able to annihilate Itale's soldiers, but Grimaldi had a chance to strand them miles from home, on foot. It was an option too inviting to ignore.

Four trucks, a quarter-mile south of the village, sat in the moonlight while their drivers watched the firefight from a distance. Did they have a clue which way the fight was going? Would it make a difference if they did?

Not now.

Grimaldi approached from the eastern flank, a loop that placed them perfectly in line. He came in at an altitude of ninety feet, unloading with the starboard FN ETNA pod, a stream of armor-piercing .50-caliber rounds and four 70 mm rockets rippling from their tubes almost in unison. The flight of high-explosive arrows spread slightly on their way to impact with their targets.

It looked like the Fourth of July down there, all kinds of heavy fireworks going off. One of the flatbeds reared up like a bucking horse; another tumbled over on its side, engulfed in flames. A burning tire rolled out of the inferno, bouncing off across the desert, out of sight.

Too easy.

The pilot swung back in the direction of the village, hunting for the final helicopter, knowing it should be there somewhere. He couldn't afford loose ends right now, especially when they came complete with rockets and a 20 mm cannon that could drop him from the sky. He was no good to Bolan and Phoenix Force if he was dead.

Grimaldi would consider it a challenge to remain alive and see the mission through.

THE BULLET STRUCK within an inch or two of Gary Manning's face and stung his cheek with slivers of adobe—or whatever dry, baked mud was called in this part of the world. He grimaced, ducked and returned fire with his AKS. A muzzle-flash some thirty feet away betrayed his adversary in the darkness, which had been compounded in the past few minutes by a drifting pall of smoke.

The whole damned place was burning by the look of things. No less than half a dozen flaming huts were visible from where the Phoenix Force warrior crouched in shadow, and he also smelled the unmistakable aroma of burning gasoline, motor oil...and human flesh. A snapshot of Dolele would come close to capturing the mood of hell, he thought, but there were no war correspondents on the scene.

Just war.

His unseen enemy was still alive and firing, semi-auto rounds that whispered over Manning's head or cracked against the mud wall of the hut where he had taken shelter. There was no safe place to hide throughout the village, when you came right down to it, but fleeting cover was available if you kept moving, watched your ass and kept a finger on the trigger.

He had dropped five men, so far, that he was sure of. It was often difficult to verify a kill in battle. Two sides firing back and forth—or even three, like now— and there was no opportunity to stroll around the killing field and make a body count. You fired at moving targets; some of them went down, but you could seldom know for sure if they were wounded, dead or simply lying low. Did someone else's bullet make the tag? How many of the wounded would survive?

No matter.

At the moment, Manning had survival on his mind, and that involved disabling as many of the raiders as he could. Grimaldi had reclaimed the sky, as far as he could tell, which took one worry off his shoulders, but the ground was still a scene ripped out of Dante's wildest nightmares. All they needed were some flying demons armed with pitchforks to complete the stage set for the lower depths of hell.

He had the gunner spotted once again...or, so he thought. The guy had shifted several paces to his left, around the corner of a hut whose thatched roof smoked and smoldered, still some moments short of bursting into brilliant flame. The problem with the shooter's weapon, though, was that it didn't have a flash-hider attached. Each time he squeezed the trigger, Manning's adversary told everyone exactly where he was.

And this time, when he fired, the big Canadian was ready for him, squeezing off a 6-round burst, full automatic. He was reasonably confident of scoring, tickled pink as he beheld his target lurching out of cover, clutching at a belly wound and brandishing his rifle overhead, as if it were some kind of ritual.

Another short burst finished it, and Manning put the dead man out of mind. He might recall his adversary later, weeks or months from now, but it would never haunt his dreams. A soldier who couldn't suppress the ghosts should find another line of work.

He went in search of other targets, hunting in the smoky darkness, knowing that a clean sweep or the next best thing would be required to see him out the other side and safely home.

Six down, so far. How many left to go?

The Phoenix Force warrior reckoned he would know when he was finished. In the meantime, he would concentrate on killing, so that he could stay alive.

ITALE FIRED A SHORT BURST from his Uzi, watched his target twitch and stagger, going down, all flapping arms and legs. The dead man wore civilian clothes, like any other peasant, but he carried military hardware. Staring at the FN FAL, Itale recognized the standard-issue rifle of Djibouti's army, but what did that tell him? Civilians were barred from owning military weapons, but the same was true—more or less—for Itale's own men in Somalia.

He had come in search of soldiers, meeting with a group of mercenaries who had done their best to spoil his life the past two days. The man who lay before him now, the others he had seen so far, didn't appear to fit in that scenario.

A trap!

He had suspected it the moment that Dolele's "villagers" had opened up with automatic weapons, rocket launchers and grenades. Somehow, his raid against the village was anticipated, and his present adversaries—soldiers or guerrillas, it made little difference now—had gathered to receive his men.

As for the others, with their helicopters, he couldn't begin to guess, nor did he care, as long as he was able to destroy them, or at least escape unharmed, while they dealt with the gunmen of Dolele. He was past concern about his reputation now, but getting out appeared to be more difficult than coming in.

In fact, from where Mohammed Itale stood, it just might be impossible.

For one thing, he had lost his vehicles, the flatbeds blown to pieces with the armored cars. Pure logic told him there were others to be had, somewhere within a short hike of the village, but he couldn't start to look for them while he was fighting for his life.

Without wheels, even if he fled right now, it was a grueling hike of twenty miles back to the border, farther still to reach the nearest friendly village in Somalia. Dawn would overtake them long before they reached the border, and Itale knew his men would never have a prayer if they were being hunted over open, unfamiliar ground.

Their only hope, then, was a victory right here, against their adversaries in Dolele. Overcome the odds, seize vehicles enough to carry the survivors and retreat with all deliberate speed. When he was safely home, there would be time to deal with the Chinese.

He had already dealt with one of them, in fact. The young lieutenant wouldn't be reporting back to Chung, unless he did so in the afterlife. Itale thought about the dead man, and he felt the satisfaction of a job well done.

Of course, it wouldn't do him any good if he was killed.

A hand grenade exploded somewhere to his left, and someone screamed in pain before the echoes died away. Smoke burned his throat and nostrils, brought tears to his eyes and made it difficult for him to see. The warlord thought that he was walking north, six of his men lined up behind him, but he could have been mistaken in the chaos of burning village. Little did it matter if he lost direction, anyway, because his enemies were all around him now.

Somewhere in front of him, a light machine gun opened up. Itale hit the deck and tasted sand, the bullets rattling past above his head. One of his men cried out, fell heavily across the warlord's legs and pinned him down.

Itale cursed and struggled, thrashing underneath the deadweight of his former soldier. Bullets kicked up dust around him, spitting grains of dirt into his eyes. He tried to wriggle backward out of range, but once again the bulk across his legs prevented him from moving freely. Several of his men were hastily returning fire, spent cartridge casings pattering around him on the ground.

It seemed to last forever, then someone had freed his legs and hauled Itale to his feet. They started brushing off his uniform, as if that mattered, and he slapped the helping hands away. A moment wasted could be all it took to get them killed, and he wasn't prepared to die.

Not here. Not now.

Another hand grenade went off, and they were running. Where? Itale didn't know or truly care. The only way out of Dolele was directly *through* his enemies, and over their dead bodies.

He was getting there, the warlord told himself, but he had far to go.

THE TROUBLE WITH a three-way firefight, Calvin James decided, was simply trying to stay alive in the midst of chaos. In a normal scrap—whatever that was—there were lines, positions, strategy. It helped a soldier get his bearings when he knew the enemy was "over there," a concrete presence, even when the troops were on the move.

When there were three or more contenders, though, all coming in from different sides, things had a tendency to fall apart. The whole damned battlefield became a cross fire, no such thing as sanctuary with your adversaries all around you, out for blood.

But two could play that game, and it would be no easier on Calvin's enemies, although their numbers were superior. The Cubans and Somalis had to deal with one another, not just Phoenix Force and the Djibouti troops. The raiders had been taking heavy hits, and James was moved to wonder if they still held a majority, excluding dead and wounded from the head count.

Never mind.

It only took one man, one bullet, and the former Navy SEAL knew he would have to watch his back until the final curtain fell across Dolele, one way or another. He was doing fine, so far—a graze across his ribs, left side, but nothing major—and he counted nine men dead: four Cubans, five Somalis.

Race wasn't an issue in the present situation, though he knew some disaffected veterans who would have drawn the line at firing on another black, regardless of the cause. It was "political," to them, a tag that covered a reverse discrimination James could never stomach. He preferred to look beyond skin color, judge a man by words and deeds instead of pigment, profile or the angle of his eyes.

Savages came in all shapes and sizes, all colors and creeds. When you stripped away the mask, the only thing they really cared about was power and manipulating others to assert themselves. The only language that they understood was force.

James crouched between two huts, one of them smoking from a tracer round, the other housing two dead members of Gourad's defense team. James had glimpsed them, passing by, saw there was nothing he could do for either one of them, and kept on going.

Dead was dead.

Right now, he had his eye on two young Cubans who had ambushed a Somali soldier, pumped him full of lead and frisked the body in a search for anything worth stealing. When they came up empty, James watched them drift away in search of other targets, moving closer to the point where he was waiting, sighting down the barrel of his AKS.

The Cubans never saw it coming. They were talking back and forth one moment, and the next he hit them with a raking burst that stitched both men across their chests and dumped them over backward, squirming on the ground. James stood back and watched them, waiting. In another moment they were still.

A helicopter thundered overhead, and James glanced up, immediately recognized the Black Hawks' silhouette. Grimaldi on the prowl, and that was something to be thankful for. Air cover could make all the difference in the world.

But it wouldn't stop bullets, or prevent a soldier on the ground from getting killed if he was careless, standing in one place too long. James broke from cover, gliding through the dappled shadows, clearing two more silent huts before he went to ground again.

The sounds of combat sputtered in Dolele, fading here, redoubling there, until it was impossible to chart the ebb and flow of battle from the ground. Grimaldi might have some idea of what was happening, with his exalted bird's-eye view, but even that was doubtful in the circumstances.

You could always tell the winners when the smoke cleared. They were still alive and ready to continue fighting, if it came to that.

James meant to be among their number, no mistakes to get him killed. And one mistake, he knew, was showing mercy to your enemies.

He fed the AKS another magazine and started scanning for another target. The game was hunt and kill, without distinction. Any Cuban or Somali was fair game.

James thought about the slogan he had seen on T-shirts in the States: Kill 'em all and let God sort 'em out.

His war hadn't come down to that, not yet, but it was getting close.

The shadow warrior rose and went in search of someone else to kill.

CHAPTER TWENTY-THREE

The two Somalis came at Bolan in a rush, no thought behind it, snarling like attack dogs. If they had been thinking clearly, planning out their moves, they could have dropped him from the shadows with a single well-placed bullet, but they chose to do the job by hand, instead.

It was a critical mistake.

Between the two of them, they weighed perhaps three hundred pounds, while Bolan weighed two hundred on his own. In terms of combat training, after basic marksmanship, the pair had next to none. They charged without coordination, telegraphed their move with grunts and growls, intent on clubbing Bolan with their rifle butts and finishing the job when he was down.

They never got the chance.

He heard them coming, spun to face them in a heartbeat, ducking underneath the gun butt that his left-hand adversary swung in a terrific roundhouse toward his face. The Executioner responded with a short jab from the muzzle of his AKS beneath his adversary's ribs, and squeezed the automatic rifle's trigger as he struck. Three rounds ripped into his assailant and blew the startled soldier backward ten or fifteen feet before he hit the ground.

The dead man's stunned companion tried to make the best of it. He lunged at Bolan, brandishing his ri-

fle like a club and making the Executioner wonder if
the gunners had already spent their ammunition,
forcing them to grapple hand to hand. Whatever, he
was braced and ready for the charge, a butt stroke to
the slim Somali's solar plexus, pivoting to crack his
forehead with an uppercut that stretched him out unconscious on the ground.

It should have been enough, but Bolan took no
chances on a sleeper rising to snipe him from behind.
One round between the eyes to finish it, and he moved
on.

The tide of battle had begun to turn. Despite their
numbers, the assault teams had begun to falter, losing ground. They had inflicted casualties on the defenders, but their losses had been piling up, the more
so since Grimaldi joined the fight. Jack could have
done the job alone, perhaps, but Bolan was intent on
making sure the raiders were annihilated, nothing in
the way of stragglers to alert the man who sent them
here.

He still had business with the men behind the guns,
but it would have to wait until the issue on Dolele was
resolved.

Soon, now.

A Cuban in his early twenties almost stumbled into
Bolan, checked himself too late to save it and swung
up his folding-stock Kalashnikov. The Executioner
was there ahead of him, his AKS erupting in a short
burst from the hip. The Cuban private staggered
backward, seemed to stumble on his own feet, going
down. He lay unmoving as the tall man stepped
around his prostrate body, passing on.

Bolan heard Itale's flatbed transports blow, turned
back in that direction as Grimaldi pulled out of his

strafing run. The trucks burned brightly in the desert, like a beacon drawing rootless wanderers from miles away.

The warrior paused to wonder who might see that fire and come in search of answers. Never mind, if they were walking; it would all be over by the time they got there. Otherwise, Hassan Gourad had cleared the way with his superiors. There should be nothing in the way of interference from the military.

They were on their own.

He turned his back on the impressive funeral pyre and moved back toward the center of Dolele, where the fighting still raged on. It couldn't last much longer, and he wanted to be present at the finish. When they started counting bodies, Bolan hoped he wouldn't find his friends among the dead, but he was braced for anything.

HASSAN GOURAD was running when the bullet hit him, drilled his shoulder, spinning him around and down. There was no pain to speak of, not at first. The impact stunned him, and he lost his breath when he collided with the ground. There was a warm, wet, sticky feeling on his chest, where blood was streaming from the wound, but still no pain.

He wondered if it felt like this to die.

The thought revived him, brought him struggling to all fours. One of his soldiers tried to help him, grabbed his wounded arm, then the pain kicked in. Gourad lashed out as best he could, lurched upright on his own and let the shaken trooper guide him toward a nearby hut that had survived the fight, so far.

The smell of smoke was thick inside, although the hut wasn't on fire. An atmospheric trick, Gourad decided, slumping down beside the open doorway so that he could breathe a semblance of fresh air.

It would be days before the smell of fire and death evaporated from the village—if it ever did. He idly wondered whether anyone would ever come back here to live, or if the ground was cursed now, soiled with human blood. It made no difference to him, one way or the other, just as long as he succeeded in the conquest of his enemies.

Dolele, as a village, was a small price for the larger good.

He hadn't planned to sacrifice himself, but if it came to that, he was prepared. If he was dying even now, Gourad wouldn't begrudge the loss. He simply had to hold on long enough to know his men had won the victory.

Two soldiers crouched beside him in the darkened hut, incongruous in their civilian clothes. They looked like bandits, anything but military men, despite the automatic rifles in their hands.

Gourad still had his submachine gun, even though he would be forced to fire left-handed now. He was considering the awkward problem when the soldier on his right snapped a warning.

"Soldiers coming! Six or seven I can see."

Gourad allowed the private on his left to help him up, avoiding contact with his wounded shoulder this time. Peering through the open door, he saw a group of men approaching, all of them in tiger-striped fatigues.

The Cubans.

"Wait," he ordered. "Let them come a little closer."

As he spoke, Gourad was shifting toward the nearest window, lining up his shot. The baked-mud windowsill could brace his submachine gun's barrel, help him to control the weapon when he fired one-handed. It wasn't the surest way to score a kill, but he appeared to have no choice.

His men were in the doorway, rifles poised.

"Don't fire until I do." His voice was steady, a surprise that gratified. His palm was sweaty as he clenched the Model 45/B's pistol grip, his index finger curled around the trigger.

Coming closer. One step at a time.

He didn't speak, but simply squeezed the trigger, rattling off a burst that used up half his magazine at once. His soldiers started firing at the first sound from his submachine gun, pouring fire into the Cuban squad from less than fifteen yards away. Their targets shivered and jerked, stumbling into one another, going down.

It took five seconds, more or less, to drop six men. A couple of the Cubans were alive and moving fitfully, but they were badly wounded and incapable of fighting back.

Hassan Gourad was satisfied.

He let the sudden wave of blackness carry him away.

IT WAS A CURIOSITY, Katz thought, the images that popped into someone's mind when he or she was facing death. Crouching under cover of a smoke screen, feeding a fresh magazine into his AKS, Katz thought about his daughter, Sharon, back in Tel Aviv. It was as if she stood before him for an instant, smiling, then he pushed the image out of mind and concentrated on the job at hand.

The smallest lapse could get him killed, and he preferred to let his enemies do all the dying.

Coming up, two Cubans in pursuit of a Somali warrior. The object of their attention had lost his weapon somewhere, and they were playing with him, taking their time. It was an easy thing to do, when combat boiled down to a game of one- or two-on-one, and soldiers saw a chance to work out some of their fear and frustration on a helpless target.

It was time for him to join the game.

Katz hit the unarmed runner with a 3-round burst that dropped him in his tracks. Before the Cubans could react to that, he showed himself, the AKS already swinging into target acquisition. Numbed by fighting, still uncertain of exactly what had happened, they responded slowly, taking too much time before they tried to raise their weapons.

Katz wasn't about to wait and let them draw first blood. He shot the Cuban on his left, a rising burst that rocked his target backward and dropped him in a seated posture on the ground. The guy looked dazed, but he was dead already, toppling slowly over on his side, dark eyes locked open in a sightless stare.

The second gunner got off a burst, but he squeezed the trigger prematurely, ripping up the sod between them, bullets wasted. A third burst from the big Israeli's AKS ripped flesh and fabric, lifting the gunner off his feet and slamming him against the sod wall of a nearby hut.

Between the smoke and noise, Katz felt disoriented, and he took a moment to regain his bearings. Flatbeds burned on his left, which made it south, in the direction of Somalia. To the west, or straight ahead, a mangled chopper smoldered on the outskirts of the village, adding gasoline fumes and more smoke to the noxious atmosphere.

Where were the others? Were they still alive?

Katz had faith in his men, but they weren't immortal. Anything could happen in this kind of formless, drifting battle. They were all prepared to pay the price, of course, and yet...

In twenty years of military service, Katz had seen enough friends go into the ground. Tonight, he planned to bury only enemies.

And so it was that he found five more—all Somali, this time—huddled in a group and working up the nerve to rush a hut where two of Gourad's men were pinned down. Katz came in on their flank, without a clue to what their whispered words meant, picking up the sense of it by watching them and checking out their target.

Easy.

They would take turns firing on the hut with automatic weapons—rise, fire a burst, duck back—and they were gradually working closer, trying to surround their prey by slow degrees. The cornered soldiers tried returning fire, but it was difficult, the door and window covered. Katz decided they would certainly be dead already, if Itale had supplied his men with hand grenades.

No time to hesitate. Katz had to nail them down before they scattered out of sight and out of range. Another wasted moment, and he might just be too late.

He went in firing from the hip, his first rounds chewing up the soldier who was next in line to fire upon the hut. Katz shot him in the back without compunction, dropping him where he stood.

The only standard of fair play Katz recognized in battle was the one that let him win.

His first rounds took the gunner farthest on his right, a tall man with a vintage Thompson submachine gun. Death came from the gunner's blind side, punched him over on his face, and left him squirming on the ground, while his companions tried to work out what was happening.

The recognition came too late to save them, two men swiveling to face their unknown adversary, raked by automatic fire from Katz's AKS before they had a chance to answer with their own Kalashnikovs. They fell in opposite directions, like defective bookends, and he put them out of mind before they hit the deck.

It was a closer thing with number four, the soldier cutting loose with semiauto carbine fire, but he forgot to aim, the bullets going high and wide of where Katz stood. The gruff Israeli didn't make the same mistake, a short burst from his AKS directly in the ten-ring from a range of twenty feet or so. The gunner vaulted over backward, squeezing off one last shot as he fell.

And that left number five, a slender man who had no patience with the killing game. He was in motion, running for his life, as Katz swung farther left and brought the rifle to his shoulder, sighting swiftly down the barrel. Easy pickings, even at an estimated range of twenty yards.

He stroked the trigger, milked a 5- or 6-round burst out of the AKS and watched his target stumble, going down on outflung hands. It took another moment for the runner to collapse, the last spark winking out, but there was no way for the man to save himself. Like Humpty Dumpty, he was trashed beyond repair.

Sporadic firing came from the other quarters of the village now, which told him that the action had to be slacking off. Not finished yet, by any means, but getting there.

Katz didn't want to miss the wrap-up.

Stalking past the dead, he went to find his human prey before the final curtain fell.

RAUL RODRIGUEZ HAD BEEN frightened many times throughout his life, but never quite like this. He didn't care for flying, least of all in combat situations, and the thought of actively pursuing someone who had just destroyed four other gunships turned his bowels to ice. Still, if he didn't lead the way, destroy the airborne enemy, his men were finished.

He was finished, even if he managed to survive the firefight.

"Faster!" he demanded of the pilot, crouching on the threshold of the flight deck, peering through the windscreen as they swung around Dolele from the south. Below them, vehicles were burning in the desert, several hundred yards outside the village proper.

His thoughts were focused on the helicopter that had come from nowhere, savaging his air support and thereby cutting off the chosen method of retreat to Ethiopia. If most or all vehicles in the village had been likewise damaged, he had an even greater problem on his hands.

But he would have to save his soldiers first, before the means of their evacuation was a real concern. Dead men required no transport. You could leave them where they fell, use gasoline and matches to destroy the telltale evidence of raiders on the wrong side of the borderline.

Because his helicopters had been fitted out as transports, meant primarily to carry troops from one point to another, they were light on armament. No rockets, bombs or mine dispensers. Each ship had a .50-caliber machine gun in the starboard doorway, on a pintle mount, as well as a 30 mm chain gun in the nose.

It had to be enough.

They had completed one full circuit of the village when he saw their target, felt the pilot stiffen in a flash of recognition. There were no apparent markings on the helicopter, but Rodriguez knew the outline of the Black Hawk from his combat training. It was manufactured in America and sometimes sold abroad to "friendly" groups or nations. Did the army have such aircraft in Djibouti?

No.

But there was still no way for him to readily identify the pilot, link him to a given country. It would be a futile exercise, and they had no time left to spare.

"Attack!"

The Cuban pilot glanced across his shoulder, frowned, but he didn't protest the order. Leaning into the controls, he put them on a hard collision course with the anonymous enemy, coming up behind the Black Hawk at one hundred miles per hour.

He was ready when the chain gun opened up, its thrumming audible above the engine noise, and tracers streaked away into the night. Take that! Rodriguez thought, and wished his enemy a speedy one-way trip to hell.

It was, the Cuban realized, the only way to save himself.

THE RADAR SAVED Grimaldi's bacon, warned him of a bogey coming up behind him in a rush. One glance, and there was no doubt about what had become of Cuban chopper number five. The ship was on his tail.

He took the only course available and started climbing like a madman, torturing the Black Hawk, getting everything he could out of the twin GE T700 turboshafts. It was a dangerous maneuver, with the risk of stalling out and plummeting to earth without a prayer of pulling out in time to save himself.

Grimaldi saw the tracers swarming at him, heard an armor-piercing round punch through the Black Hawk's passenger compartment. Never mind. He was alone up there, and doing fine unless they hit the engine, rotors or fuel tank.

Or the pilot.

The Stony Man flier might be quick and tough, but he was far from bulletproof. One 30 mm round would gut him like a deer, and anything beyond that would be icing on the cake for his assailants.

Dead men didn't fly, but that game went both ways.

Acceleration thrust Grimaldi back against his seat, the chopper pulling g's as he continued to climb, banking slightly to his left. He couldn't risk a loop, but he would do the next best thing and try to get behind his adversary. In the meantime, he was fighting back the best he could, the ALQ-144 infrared pulsed beacon jammer working overtime to prevent a missile locking on his ship, while the ALE-39 flare dispenser unloaded its thirty cartridges in a flurry of light and noise. He'd use anything to confuse the enemy pilot at this point, even if it didn't slow him down.

And it was working out, at least to some extent. The trailing chopper had already lost momentum, slowing as the flares began to burst across its path, a dazzling light show to assault the pilot's eyes. Grimaldi took advantage of the moment, leaning on the throttle, nervous that the rapid turn might shake the Black Hawk into pieces, worried that he wouldn't have the speed to get around behind his enemy before the automatic cannon found him, chewing him apart.

He made it, somehow, coming in behind the Cuban gunship from a hundred yards and closing fast. His sights locked on before the enemy could think to jam, his index finger tightening around the trigger, unleashing hellfire from the twin .50-caliber guns slung beneath the Black Hawk's stubby wings. His tracers lit the night like fireflies homing on a candle in the dark, prepared to immolate themselves for just a fleeting contact with the flame.

His enemy was taking hits, no doubt about it, but Grimaldi didn't know if it was good enough. He had four 70 mm rockets left, and there would never be a better time to send them on their way.

He locked on target, keyed another button, and missiles blazed toward impact. There was nothing for his enemy to do, no action he could take to pull it out in time. Perhaps, if fighting helicopters came equipped with an ejector seat, he could have beaten the flash and shrapnel, but Grimaldi doubted it.

He saw the ship disintegrate. One moment, it was hanging there, a dark shape in his sights. The next, there was a fireball, losing altitude and trailing brilliant streamers in its wake. As always, when he made an airborne kill, Grimaldi wondered what it felt like, going on that last, long ride.

He wondered, but he didn't really want to know.

It was a clean sweep on the Cuban air support, and that was something, anyway. Whatever happened on the ground, from that point forward, the invaders would be looking at a long walk home. Assuming any of them managed to survive.

All things considered, Jack Grimaldi knew it was the best that he could do.

BOLAN DODGED THE RAIN of shrapnel, taking cover in the shadow of a hut as the disintegrating chopper streaked like a comet overhead. A heavy fragment of the fuselage or engine block smashed through the hut's thatched roof and raised a cloud of dust to join the drifting smoke from nearby fires. The main bulk of the helicopter fell about eighty yards away and shattered like a giant toy on impact with the ground.

It was the end, or nearly so. Around him, gunfire had been trailing off for several minutes, slackening as shooters were eliminated and survivors found themselves without a fresh supply of targets. There were pockets of resistance, stragglers in the rubble, but the fight was definitely winding down.

The question, still unclear to Bolan from his present vantage point was, which side was winning?

All the corpses he could see were Cuban or Somali, but he knew Gourad's defenders had been taking hits, as well. How many of the native soldiers in civilian clothes were trapped in burning huts or laid out in the dusty streets right now? Before a body count was possible, they had to wrap the action up, and that was coming.

Soon . . . but not just yet.

He met a Cuban private slinking through the shadows, beat his adversary to the punch with three rounds from his AKS at something close to point-blank range. The young man staggered, then went down on one knee, a dazed expression on his face. With so much death around him, still it came as a surprise. Another moment, and the light winked out behind his eyes. The soldier toppled forward on his face.

Behind him, voices came closer through the semi-darkness, following the sounds of battle. Bolan knelt, reloaded swiftly, brought the rifle to his shoulder and aimed at the voices, waiting for their owners to appear.

Four black men in the khaki uniforms of the Somali private army came into view. Bolan let them close the gap, roughly fifty feet between him and his targets when he opened fire. He raked them first from left to right, then back the other way, his bullets slapping home with force enough to drop the gunmen in their tracks.

One of the four was stubborn, lurching toward the nearest hut and leaning up against the wall. He grappled with an Uzi submachine gun, one arm out of action, trying desperately to defend himself.

Too late.

Another burst from Bolan's AKS went in on target, knocked him sprawling. Curious, the Executioner advanced to stand over his latest kill, examining the soldier's face.

And recognized him instantly.

Mohammed el Itale had absorbed no less than seven bullets, five of which had torn his chest and abdomen. The warlord's eyes were open, staring at the smoky sky, as if all answers to the mysteries of life and death were written there.

Perhaps they were.

The automatic fire had trailed away to nothing, and Bolan took the walkie-talkie from his belt. "Striker to Phoenix," he said. "Report."

The disembodied voices came back to him, one by one, and they were music to his ears.

"All clear on Phoenix One," Katzenelenbogen replied.

"Phoenix Two, okay," McCarter added.

"Same for Phoenix Three," Manning said.

Encizo joined the list with, "Fine on number four."

"I guess that makes me the caboose," James stated, and he didn't seem to mind.

Survivors, right. They had some cleaning up to do, and logic told him that Gourad would need some help. But they still weren't finished, yet.

Not quite.

CHAPTER TWENTY-FOUR

Korahe, Ethiopia

Security had been improved since the attack the day before, but it was too late for Dmitri Kuybyshev to feel at ease. His time was up in Ethiopia. The villa had become a trap, and he was bailing out.

The late news from Djibouti was the worst imaginable—for the Cubans. All of them were dead, as far as he could tell, and the announcement of their border raid would be reported by the media from Mogadishu to New York and all points in between. More to the point, it would be heard in Moscow, where his former colleagues had good reason to suspect that Kuybyshev would be involved.

They might come hunting for him yet, those Russians of the "new breed," who were anxious to preserve their public image in the West. Right now, though, Kuybyshev was more concerned with enemies already on the scene in Africa.

Someone had taken out Rodriguez and the others. Even with the broadcast from Djibouti claiming the Somalis were involved, somehow he sensed another hand at work—the same hand that had reached out to his villa in Korahe with the skill of a professional assassin and dispatched a number of the Cuban guards.

If they could do it once, why not a second time?

"All ready," young Storenko told him, breezing through the doorway with a tight smile on his face. His aide smiled too much, but he was serious about his work, and Kuybyshev had grown to trust him in the past two years of their association—well, at least as much as any exiled member of the KGB could trust another man.

"I'm almost finished," Kuybyshev informed his aide. The packing had been easy, nothing but some clothing and personal belongings that he didn't choose to leave behind. He always traveled light, and they wouldn't be saving any of the documents that his involvement with the Ethiopians and Cubans had produced. The shredder and a match had seen to that.

"I'll have them bring the car around," Storenko said, and turned to leave.

"Yes, do."

It was a short drive to the airstrip, where a light plane would be waiting for the hop to Kenya. In Nairobi, they would board a regular commercial flight to Switzerland, relax awhile and spend their hard-earned money while Kuybyshev shopped around to find another war.

Things being what they were in international affairs, he knew the search wouldn't be long or arduous. There was no shortage in the world of people killing one another, and the would-be victors almost always craved professional advice.

The one and only true growth industry was death.

He latched his suitcase, took the folding garment bag and wandered through the spacious rooms that he would never see again. It was a grand old house, but it had served its purpose. He was moving on to better things.

The limousine was waiting when he reached the parlor, clearly visible outside, with his aide loading luggage in the trunk. Four Cubans stood by with automatic weapons, looking grim and sour, doubtless wondering what would become of them in Ethiopia without their ranking officers.

It was a problem for Havana, Kuybyshev decided. He wasn't about to let it slow him down.

He had one foot across the threshold when the rocket came from somewhere on his right and plowed into the limo's open trunk. One moment, he was looking at Storenko, waiting for the youngster to assist him with his bags, and then the vehicle was folding in upon itself like an accordion, flames spewing from the ruptured fuel tank, his aide torn apart by the explosion.

God in heaven! It was happening again!

The Russian dropped his bags and retreated toward his study, where he kept a pistol in his desk, a submachine gun in the closet. He had planned to leave the weapons, trust the Cubans with his safety on the brief drive to the airstrip, but the plan had gone to hell before his very eyes.

Dmitri Kuybyshev was running for his life, and for the first time that he could remember, he had no idea of where to go or what he ought to do.

Some of the Cubans were alive outside. He heard them firing toward the trees, for all the good it did. They had been useless in the first raid on the villa, useless to Rodriguez in Djibouti. Kuybyshev had no good reason to believe that they would help him now.

Still, any guard was better than none. If nothing else, perhaps they could distract the enemy while he slipped out the back.

Assuming that his adversaries didn't have the place surrounded.

Never mind, he had to try. The option was unthinkable.

Kuybyshev hadn't survived within the KGB, much less beyond that network's publicized disintegration, by surrendering to fate or circumstance. He made his own luck as he went along, and if he had to stab his best friend in the back, so be it.

In his life, he had been tagged with many labels—most of them derogatory, some of them obscene—but he wasn't known as a quitter.

Nor was he about to give up now, when he was fighting for his life.

McCARTER KNEW THE PLACE by heart, between the satellite surveillance photos and his own prior visit in the company of Rafael Encizo. They had used the river as their method of approach, but things had changed. The rubber boat had been discovered, as they knew it would, and now the riverside was guarded by a team of Cubans with Kalashnikovs.

No problem.

Grimaldi had dropped them to the south this time, and they had walked in, carrying their gear a half mile through the spotty forest, watching out for sentries all the way. They met one, some two hundred yards from the house, and left him there, a new grin etched beneath his jaw from ear to ear.

Ten minutes put McCarter in position, hoping that his companion found his mark in equal time. A coin toss put Encizo on the front door with an RPG, to head off any plans the Russians might have had for bailing out before the tab came due. McCarter would be closing from the opposite direction, sealing off the back door to complete the trap.

It sounded easy, but it meant that he was forced to ice another pair of lookouts, using his Beretta side arm with the special silencer attached. One shot per man, and they were out of it before they knew there was a battle going on.

McCarter was in place when it went down, the echo of a blast that had to be the RPG rocket, sending up a cloud of oily smoke beyond the villa. Moving in, McCarter crossed the lawn, met no one, thankful that the sound of the explosion would have drawn the outer guards away. He found an open door and entered through the kitchen, leading with the silenced automatic in his left hand, while his right maintained a firm grip on the AKS.

Nobody was in the kitchen, and he kept on going, smelled the reek of burning oil and gasoline before he cleared the empty dining room.

So far, so good.

A hallway branched to the left and right, expensive artwork on the walls, a deep shag carpet underfoot. The proceeds from an auction at the villa could have fed a native village for the next five years, McCarter thought. Another instance of the great disparity in classes that had always seemed more prevalent in Third World nations than at home. The revolutionaries bitched and moaned about the sins of capitalism and profiteering, but they never failed to grab the gusto for themselves when they took power from the former ruling class.

Another RPG round exploded, sending tremors through the house. McCarter waited, listening, and picked up scuffling noises from his left, a few doors down the hallway. Striking off in that direction, he passed two closed doors to find a third one standing open on a den or study. Inside, an average-size Caucasian male was standing with his back turned toward the doorway, working with some object on his desk.

McCarter stepped across the threshold and cleared his throat to make his presence known. The Russian turned to face him, not particularly startled, ready with a compact submachine gun in his hands.

The little weapon stuttered, spitting bullets, and McCarter ducked below the line of fire. This guy was good, no doubt about it, but his hands were trembling slightly, and it spoiled his aim. The slugs drilled plaster, knocking splinters from the doorjamb, but he needed to correct before he scored a kill.

McCarter didn't plan on giving him the time. His guns went off together—silenced pistol, rough and rowdy AKS—unloading with a storm of fire that drove the Russian backward, jerking, dancing like a puppet, toppling over backward on his desk. The Briton hit him with a few more rounds to make it stick, then rose and crossed the study to survey his handiwork.

The Russian was distinctly and irrevocably dead. Whatever his surviving ties to Moscow and the new regime, if any, they had just been severed with a vengeance.

It was a familiar face from yesterday, a human target cringing on the patio, but that was all behind them now. McCarter left the study, checked the other rooms in turn as he retreated toward the parlor, where the shrapnel from another RPG round had set the curtains blazing, filling up the room with acrid smoke.

Outside, the battle sounds had died away to nothing. McCarter palmed his two-way radio, pressed twice on the transmitter button, beaming spurts of static to the small receiver on Encizo's web belt. Seconds later, the response came through: two short taps, then a beat of silence, followed by a third.

All clear.

McCarter didn't speak into the radio. There was no telling who might intercept and tape their conversation, capturing a pair of English-speaking voices at the scene. Instead, he slipped out of the house and made his way back to the point where Encizo would join him, once he made his way around the killing field.

Grimaldi would be waiting for them on the far side of the woods. Another thirty minutes, more or less, would see them airborne, winging back toward Mogadishu and what passed for neutral ground. Once they were back inside the U.S. diplomatic compound, he could let himself relax.

But he would keep his guard up in the meantime.

Just in case.

El Bur, Somalia

COLONEL CHUNG'S grandfather had been a Buddhist monk. It broke his heart to learn that his beloved grandson had become a die-hard Communist, rejecting every aspect of religion. When the Red Guard came for him in 1967, following directions that his grandson had provided, it was more than Li Ziyang Peng could bear. He launched a hunger strike in prison and was dead within a month.

Sometimes, when he reflected on those grave events, Chung wondered—only for the briefest, fleeting moment—if he might have been mistaken. Was it possible, by any stretch of the imagination, that he could have sinned against creation, called a curse upon himself?

No evidence of such had been apparent in the course of his career, which showed a steady and commendable advancement through the ranks. It was his private life where things went sour: two failed marriages, his daughter's suicide, the son who shamed him and endangered Chung's career by dying with the rebels in Tiananmen Square. His family had rejected Chung, as he in turn had spurned his forebears, but it made no difference. He couldn't turn back the calendar or change the course that he had chosen for himself.

He thought about the night's events and knew Mohammed el Itale's failure in Djibouti would be reckoned as a blot on Chung's own record in Beijing. No man could reach his age without experiencing failures, but this was failure on a giant scale, a waste of eighty million yuan and countless hours, not to mention his subordinates who had been killed.

A total waste, but it could still have been much worse. Chung was going home alive, and that was something, even if it meant he wouldn't be promoted to the rank of general, as he had hoped.

Things changed.

He would be thankful to escape Somalia with his life.

Chung had dismissed the stragglers of Itale's army, tired of having them around, uncertain of their loyalty now that various subordinates were gearing up to wage a battle for control of the militia. By the time a clear-cut winner had emerged, Chung would be safe at home in China, trying to explain his failure to the army brass.

If nothing else, the prejudice his people felt toward Africans would help. He could explain Itale's failure as the logical result of dealing with inferiors. More to the point, he had those rumors of involvement by American and European agents, just the right touch of conspiracy to help divert attention from his own shortcomings as a leader. It wouldn't be simple, even so, but Chung thought he could pull it off.

He was a natural survivor, when it came to office politics.

The helicopter waited for him in a field behind the house. It was a six-year-old civilian model, more than adequate to carry Chung and his surviving aides to Mareg, where a motor launch would pick them up at midnight and convey them to a ship waiting offshore. The journey home would be a welcome respite, giving Chung a few days to rehearse his story for the court of inquiry.

There were no uniforms to pack, since he had traveled incognito in Somalia. Drab civilian clothes were all he had, in addition to the Type 51 semiautomatic pistol, his country's 7.62 mm knockoff of the Russian Tokarev. The side arm's weight was reassuring, slung beneath his left arm in a shoulder holster, covered by the tan bush jacket that he wore. Dark glasses finished the ensemble, and he called Lin Shan, the senior of his aides, to take his bags outside.

Chung was about to follow when a gunshot rang out from the general direction of the yard. He froze, uncertain what it meant, prepared to raise hell with his bodyguards if one of them had accidentally discharged a weapon. That thought vanished in a heartbeat, as a burst of automatic fire ripped through the morning stillness. Two, three weapons had been fired, maybe more.

Chung felt his stomach churning, felt the hope of going home slip through his fingers. The relentless enemy had found him somehow, and the colonel didn't even know who sent them, where they came from, why they wanted him.

He cursed and drew his pistol, wondering if he had time to reach the helicopter. Would he find the pilot waiting, or would fear put him to flight? The only way to find out was to try it. If he held his ground, made no attempt to leave, then he would surely die.

Chung cocked his pistol, left his troops to face the enemy and slipped out through the back.

THE MM-1 PROJECTILE launcher is a 40 mm weapon, with the basic outline of a vintage Tommy gun on steroids. At 21.5 inches overall, it weighs nearly one pound per inch with the cylinder loaded, twelve rounds with an effective range of 131 yards. For all its resemblance to a bloated automatic weapon, though, the MM-1 operates on the principle of a double-action revolver, advancing the rotary magazine with each squeeze of the trigger.

Bolan had loaded the piece with an alternating mix of high-explosive rounds and buckshot, wearing bandoleers of extra rounds across his chest. His backup weapons for the strike consisted of an MP-5 K submachine gun on a swivel rig, together with a Desert Eagle semiauto pistol on his hip.

He went in solo, taking full advantage of the covering terrain until he had a clear view of the house, the spacious grounds, the helicopter standing by out back.

He counted five Chinese, all dressed in civilian clothes but packing military hardware.

That left one, at least, who hadn't shown his face—Lieutenant Colonel Ziyang Tse Chung, the man Bolan had come back to kill.

A photo likeness had been beamed from Stony Man by satellite, enabling him to recognize his prey on sight. The warrior's choice of weapons was a personal concession to the fact that he was going in alone, without support from Phoenix Force or cover from the air.

The great temptation was to wait for Chung to show himself, then open up and sweep the field. It could have worked, but circumstances or fate kicked in while Bolan was scoping out the grounds. Another sentry showed up.

It came down to a fraction of a second, do or die, and Bolan drew his Desert Eagle in a single fluid motion, lining up the shot and squeezing off a .44 Magnum round from twenty feet. The young Chinese went down without a whimper, lost his weapon in the weeds, and that was it for the advantage of surprise.

It took another instant for the sentries in the yard to spot him, but the Executioner was moving now, his pistol holstered, cradling the MM-1 and breaking toward the house. He fired his first HE round as they opened up with automatic weapons, hosing the landscape without taking time to aim.

The high-explosive can landed between two gunners, detonating as it struck the ground, and sent them vaulting off in opposite directions like a pair of acrobats. One landed in a boneless sprawl, the other trying desperately to rise when Bolan hit him with a 40 mm buckshot round and flipped him over on his back.

Three left that he could see, and they were feeling out the range now, coming closer with their probing rounds. A bullet whispered past his face, immediately followed by another and another. Bolan saw one of the gunners fading back in the direction of the house, and he could hear the helicopter warming up, its rotors gathering momentum as the pilot started to make hasty preparations for his getaway.

The third round from his MM-1 was yet another high-explosive shell. He aimed directly at the nearest Chinese gunner, let it fly and watched the man disintegrate, a rag doll torn apart by a tornado.

It was too much for the others, both men running now, one toward the house, the other angling toward a nearby stand of trees where he could hope for shelter and a chance to snipe at the intruder without being so exposed. The second runner, on his left, appeared to be a greater risk, and Bolan turned to sweep him with a spray of buckshot, fifty pellets, each the rough equivalent of a .33-caliber bullet.

The runner seemed to blur, an eerie freeze-frame, as the buckshot riddled him, blood hanging in the air like mist as he went down. As Bolan turned back toward the house, he saw another man emerging, running in a crouch to reach the helicopter, glancing over toward his nemesis, a pistol in his hand.

Ziyang Tse Chung.

It could have ended then and there, but the surviving lookout found his nerve, perhaps emboldened by the glimpse of his superior in flight, and turned to make a stand. He fired a burst at Bolan from his automatic rifle, chewing up the turf a yard to Bolan's right, demanding full attention from the Executioner.

He got it, with a high-explosive round that dropped between his feet and detonated with a thunderclap. One moment he was standing there and firing from the hip; the next, he vanished like a genie in a swirling cloud of smoke.

It was too close for comfort as Chung prepared to lift off in the chopper. Bolan sprinted toward the makeshift helipad, firing as he ran. The whirlybird was rising, gaining altitude and gathering momentum.

The warrior's MM-1 had seven rounds remaining, alternating shot and high explosive. He unloaded them in rapid fire, the rising muzzle of his weapon following the helicopter as it climbed and banked away. Too late! He was losing them.

Or, maybe not.

A charge of buckshot bought some time, ripping through the pilot's legs and sending the chopper spinning as his feet slid off the rudder pedals. It was all the help Bolan needed, pouring HE rounds into the cockpit, shattering the fuselage, a giant ball of flame descending in the middle of the well-kept yard. He raised an arm to shield his face from the explosion as the chopper's fuel tank blew, a lake of fire ignited on the grass.

Endgame.

The next report Beijing received would come from someone else, and it would be bad news. Colonel Chung wouldn't be going home. His mission to Somalia was a write-off.

And a victory of sorts, for Bolan's team.

No victory was permanent, however, and the Executioner didn't delude himself into believing he had solved the country's problems in a few short days. It was a start, and nothing more. The people still had work to do.

But not Mack Bolan. For the moment, he was finished.

Turning from the flaming ruins of the helicopter, he walked back in the direction of the trees. It was a long way home, and every journey started with a single step.

EPILOGUE

Mogadishu

It was an hour, yet, before their scheduled liftoff from the U.S. diplomatic compound. They would land in Rome, pick up a military transport and be stateside by the time the sun came up the following day, safe and sound.

The word from Stony Man was brief and to the point, congratulations for a job well done. It would remain for diplomats to sift the fallout, judge reactions to the strike in Moscow and Beijing. The Russians, by appearances, weren't officially involved in what their former agent had set out to do in Ethiopia. As for the Red Chinese...

"You think they give a damn?" McCarter asked of no one in particular.

"I wouldn't think so," Grimaldi answered.

"Bloody Reds don't care what anybody thinks," McCarter groused. "They'll have another team in here next week, or somewhere else."

"We'll cope with that when it goes down," Bolan said, sipping coffee from a drab ceramic mug.

"Just so you know it's coming."

"Right."

And it was always coming, Bolan thought. The first thing he had learned in active military service was that no containment action ever wiped a problem off the books. You drew a line and held it, waited for the enemy to blink, and if your luck was fair, you got to walk away when it was over.

They had all been lucky, this time. While Hassan Gourad had lost some soldiers and sustained a wound himself, the major casualties had been among their enemies. Whatever happened next in Mogadishu, it was safe to say the endless civil war wouldn't involve Djibouti for the next few months. With any luck at all, removal of the ranking warlords might help calm things down a bit, give the UN peacekeepers time and opportunity to do their jobs.

If not, well, that was life.

There would be other missions, other adversaries waiting in the days ahead. It never failed. One dragon fell, and half a dozen others rose to take his place.

Whatever problems Bolan and Phoenix Force faced in the long days to come, he knew that unemployment wouldn't even make the list.

It would be nice to take some time, he thought, and simply watch the world go by, but he had work to do.

The savages were waiting, sharpening their knives and looking for an opening. Until the day came when he woke up in Utopia, there would be wet work waiting for Bolan and his comrades in arms.

TAKE 'EM FREE

4 action-packed novels plus a mystery bonus

NO RISK

NO OBLIGATION TO BUY

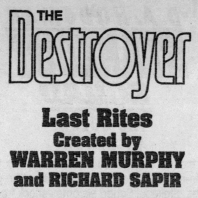

In September, don't miss
the exciting conclusion to

D.A. HODGMAN

STAKEOUT
SQUAD

THE COLOR
OF BLOOD

The law is the first target in a tide of killings engulfing Miami
in the not-to-be-missed conclusion of this urban police
action series. Stakeout Squad becomes shock troops in a
desperate attempt to pull Miami back from hell, but here
even force of arms may not be enough to halt the hate and
bloodshed....

Don't miss THE COLOR OF BLOOD, the final installment of
STAKEOUT SQUAD!

Look for it in September, wherever Gold Eagle books are sold.

**Don't miss out on the action in these titles featuring
THE EXECUTIONER®, ABLE TEAM® and PHOENIX FORCE®!**